THE
WAYWARD
SPY

★ ★ ★ ★ ★

THE
WAYWARD
SPY

· A NOVEL ·

SUSAN OUELLETTE

CamCat
Books

CamCat Publishing, LLC
Brentwood, Tennessee 37027
camcatpublishing.com

Hardcover ISBN 9780744300536
Paperback ISBN 9780744304442
Large-Print Paperback ISBN 9780744300550
eBook ISBN 9780744300567
Audiobook ISBN 9780744300574

Library of Congress Control Number: 2020949413

Cover design/book design by Maryann Appel
Map illustration by PeterHermesFurian

5 3 1 2 4

For Elaine Ash,
a superb freelance editor and friend.

Had you not persuaded me to dust off this manuscript,
I wouldn't be a published author today.
Your vision and persistence brought this story to life.

For that, I'm eternally grateful.

Tbilisi is the capital of the country of Georgia.

To the north lies Russia.

To the south lie Turkey, Armenia and Azerbaijan.

This birthplace of Joseph Stalin has suffered periodic eruptions of unrest, corruption and Russian meddling since gaining independence from the Soviet Union in 1991.

★ ★ ★ ★ ★ ★ ★ ★ ★ ★ ★ ★ ★ ★ ★ ★ ★ ★ ★
★ ★ ★ ★ ★ ★ ★ ★ ★ ★ ★ ★ ★ ★ ★ ★ ★ ★ ★ ★
★ ★ ★ ★ ★ ★ ★ ★ ★ ★ ★ ★ ★ ★ ★ ★ ★ ★ ★
★ ★ ★ ★ ★ ★ ★ ★ ★ ★ ★ ★ ★ ★ ★ ★ ★ ★ ★ ★
★ ★ ★ ★ ★ ★ ★ ★ ★ ★ ★ ★ ★ ★ ★ ★ ★ ★ ★

PROLOGUE

Tbilisi, Georgia

The assassin slid the gray canvas bag onto an empty chair to the right. With a final glance at the men seated at the adjacent table, their backs to her, she exited the café's sun-drenched atrium. Her client had wanted something more dramatic, like a car bomb. But with such short notice, she'd been forced to improvise with the materials on hand. The client wouldn't care. Dead was dead.

After crossing the busy street, she looked over her shoulder. The targets were standing, shaking hands. She was supposed to be further away before dialing the pre-programmed number, but she had to act before they separated.

Slipping a hand into her purse, she pulled out the cell phone and hit the number three. The atrium, a glass-enclosed outdoor dining area at the popular café, exploded into a million tiny shards. A chair flew through the air, landing on the sidewalk in front of the building. Car alarms wailed. Then people.

The American, partially pinned under a mangled metal table, lay still, bleeding profusely from what remained of his right thigh. The other man was motionless, face down on the sidewalk. Crowds gathered on the street as the acrid smoke from the bomb began to dissipate.

When sirens sounded in the distance, the assassin slipped away from the panicked crowd. Under ordinary circumstances, heads turned at the sight of her lithe body, high cheekbones, and striking, olive-colored eyes. Today, she was shrouded in a shabby overcoat, oversized wool hat, and dark sunglasses. The get-up made her feel detached from herself, as if someone else had executed the attack.

The woman turned into the alley where she'd parked hours before. She removed the sunglasses and pulled the cap from her head, unleashing a thick mane of lush, black hair. With a final glance behind her, she smiled. By all measures, it had been a successful morning.

CHAPTER ONE

House Permanent Select Committee
on Intelligence, U.S. Capitol Building
November 2003

Maggie Jenkins hurried across the stone pavers outside the east front of the U.S. Capitol Building. The autumn wind was especially biting before sunrise. She ducked into an arched entryway to the left of towering marble stairs, tugged open the heavy wooden door, and slipped inside just before a sudden gust slammed it shut behind her. She glanced left at a plaque honoring two Capitol Hill police officers who'd been gunned down by a madman in that very spot five years earlier. Until the chaos of September 11, 2001, she couldn't have imagined a more horrific day on the Hill.

"Morning, miss."

The officer's greeting pulled her back to the present.

"Morning."

She plopped her Kate Spade satchel on the x-ray machine's conveyer belt and passed through the metal detector.

The officer's attention turned to the machine's video screen. "ID, please."

Maggie fished her badge from the pocket of her black trench coat. Getting to work so early meant that it was going to be a long day, but working regular nine-to-five hours hadn't been an option for months. There'd been one major national security episode after another this year—from the U.S. invasion of Iraq to the ongoing manhunt for Saddam Hussein. And besides, the longer she stayed at work, the less time she spent at home. Alone and missing Steve. Three months left on his overseas tour. It felt more like three years.

The officer nodded as Maggie snatched her purse and headed for the Crypt. She paused, savoring the silence in the dimly-lit cavernous room. Soon enough, ringing phones, humming computers, and whirring copy machines would replace the hush.

Her heels clicked across the smooth stone floor as she made her way to the elevator on the far left. Every now and then, wandering tourists would mistake this elevator for a public one. They'd soon discover that it had a sole destination—a rather unremarkable hallway in the attic of the Capitol Building.

Inside the car, Maggie repeatedly punched the up button. A minute later, the old doors groaned open, depositing her forty feet from the entrance to the House Intelligence Committee office. She mumbled a greeting to the night guard, who buzzed her through the main door.

The hearing room directly ahead was dark; she opted for the lit corridor that wound its way around the backside of the windowless space. Uninspiring framed prints of the nation's capital dotted the tan, soundproof, textured walls.

A little further up the hall, her boss Frank Reynolds ducked into his office, shutting the door behind him. *Odd.* He usually wasn't in before 8 a.m. She shrugged and turned into the second office on the left, a small space with worn, government-issue gray carpeting and walls painted to match.

Maggie hung her coat and purse on the coat rack in the corner, slid into her chair, and fired up the Compaq desktop computer. She grabbed a pad of paper and wrote out her to-do list.

- *Finish chairman's briefing book for today's hearing*
- *Ask Agency for latest intel on Putin*
- *Call mom—wedding dress fitting moved to Dec. 4th*

The computer screen brightened from black to green. She logged in, opened the briefing document, and picked up where she'd left off last Friday.

"Could I speak with you a minute?"

She glanced up, then returned her gaze to the monitor. "You're here early, Frank. What's up?"

"Maggie . . ."

She was racing against a deadline. "Can it wait a bit? Have to finish this." The Committee's chairman needed the briefing book ASAP.

"Maggie," repeated Frank. She saved the document and swiveled in her chair. "Sorry—" She paused, startled by the sudden appearance of another man next to him. The CIA's Deputy Director of Operations.

"Warner?" She glanced at the day planner on her desk. Had she forgotten an important meeting?

"Can we talk?" Warner Thompson approached her desk.

He was the CIA's spymaster, a powerful man whose calendar was filled with urgent matters of national security. "What are you doing here? Shouldn't you be in Langley?"

"We need to talk."

She stood, her thighs pressed against the edge of the desk. Warner looked like he hadn't slept. She stared back at him, suddenly aware how odd it was that her fiancé's boss was in her office. "Is everything okay?" A sudden weakness swept over her.

Warner closed his eyes for a moment, as if to collect himself. "I don't know how to say this."

"Say what?" she said as she backed against the chair and sank into it.

Maggie's thoughts occupied two opposing camps engaged in battle. The side that fought hardest was the one insisting Steve was fine. Of course he was. He wasn't in Iraq. Or Afghanistan. He wasn't dodging mortar attacks and suicide bombers. Steve was a spy, a silent soldier, fighting the country's enemies in the shadows, where it was safer. But then there was the other side. The one that knew. She just knew.

Warner knelt beside her. "I'm so, so sorry." His voice cracked. "I came right over as soon as I got the call."

Maggie closed her eyes.

A supersonic slideshow of images flashed through her mind. Steve on his motorcycle. His lopsided grin. The day he proposed. Her wedding dress. News footage of soldiers' flag-draped caskets. The Memorial Wall at CIA Headquarters. All those stars for the CIA's dead.

Not Steve. No star. Not dead. "It's a mistake." She shook her head. "Maybe he's out with an asset and can't report in." Words tumbled from her mouth. "You know how Steve gets when he's in the middle of something big."

"No, Maggie, it's not . . . I'm so sorry."

She looked at Frank. He glanced away.

She fixed her eyes on Warner's. "What are you saying?"

He cleared his throat. "There was an explosion at a café in Tbilisi. We don't know if Steve was the intended target. It could've been mistaken identity or simply being in the wrong place at the wrong time." He took Maggie's hands in his. "Do you understand what I'm saying?"

"Who's we?"

"What?"

She freed her hands and clasped them together. "You said, 'We don't know if Steve was the intended target.' Who's we?"

"The Tbilisi station chief and I."

Her insides constricted, as if a seizure and a heart attack had joined forces against her. "So, the station chief thinks someone killed Steve?" The question sounded absurd. These kinds of things happened to *other* people.

Warner nodded and rubbed his face with trembling hands. "They have his body at the embassy. There was nothing they could do. It was too late."

Maggie heard a moan. When the moan turned into a wail, she realized it was coming from inside of her.

CHAPTER TWO

The ringing telephone startled Maggie from a fitful nap. Her gaze flitted around, taking in the bedside clock. For a second, she thought she'd slept through the wake. She ignored the phone, rolled onto her side, and stared at the empty half of the bed. Steve's side. Her fingers traced the outline of his pillow, the spot where he'd last kissed her before leaving for his 4 a.m. flight to Tbilisi. "I'll be back. I promise, Maggie," he'd whispered.

For the last eight months, it had been just her in the house, yet she'd never felt truly alone. There'd been calls from Steve. She'd occupied herself working long hours and taking marathon runs on the trail. All helped fill the temporary emptiness until his return.

Now, the emptiness was endless. There was no one, nothing to look forward to, nothing to fill the void.

Kate, her friend from their CIA days together, had offered to stay over for a couple of nights, but then something came up with her husband. Her best friend from college couldn't make the trip from Boston—she was overdue with her second baby. Old high school friends left sympathetic voicemails, but never called back. Everyone was busy. They were married, having babies, leading normal lives. And when you couldn't tell your girlfriends anything true about your future husband, it was much easier to withdraw, to protect Steve, to keep his secrets secret. Other than Kate, none of her friends had a clue what he actually did for a living.

Her head was pounding. She didn't need a mirror to tell her what days of sobbing had done to her face. Her right hand found the damp facecloth on the floor beside the bed. Five minutes of cool moisture probably wouldn't help much, but it was better than nothing. And she had to pull herself together before her parents flew into town.

Her stomach was in turmoil at the thought of seeing Steve's body. The funeral home had assured her that his face was in good condition, and that no one would be able to see the destruction the bomb had wrought on the rest of his body. Maggie let out a guttural scream and threw the facecloth across the room. It landed with an unsatisfying splat against the wall.

Downstairs, the doorbell chimed.

Maggie groaned and dragged herself from the bed. She tugged the black dress from the hanger and slid it over a silk slip and a pair of black stockings.

"Shoes . . . where are my shoes?" The doorbell chimed again as she rifled through a jumble of high heels on the closet floor.

"Just a second," she muttered, abandoning the shoes and scampering downstairs.

When she opened the front door, bitter wind greeted her with a slap. Maggie squinted up at her visitor. "You look exhausted, Warner."

Warner shook sleet from an umbrella and wiped his polished wingtips on the sodden welcome mat. "And I feel like hell." His gray-flecked eyes searched her face. "How are you?"

She shivered against the cold. "Hell pretty much sums it up."

"Look, I . . . can we talk for a few minutes?"

Her throat tightened. "Of course. Come in." She was due at the funeral home in an hour. "I have a few minutes." Maggie ushered him into the living room. The soft sage-colored walls felt naked, cold. Assorted frames stood stacked in the corner waiting to be rehung. Their formal engagement photo lay atop the pile. A light film of dust muted her fiery hair and his bright eyes. Steve was supposed to hang the pictures. That was the deal—if she painted the walls, he'd put it all back together when he came home.

In the kitchen, she swallowed the lump in her throat and turned to Warner. "Coffee?" she offered. "We have time. I was going to pick my parents up at Dulles, but their flight was delayed. Snow. So, they'll take a cab directly to the funeral home," she rambled, certain if she stopped talking, she'd collapse in a heap. "They'll be landing soon."

"I'll send a car."

"I should be the one—"

Warner raised his hand. "No. Consider it done."

"Okay." She turned toward the stove. "How about that coffee? Or tea? Herbal? Decaf?" The burner clicked and hissed under the copper kettle.

"Save yourself the trouble. I'm fine." He stared out the window into the darkness. "I have some new information about Steve. It's . . ."

"It's what?"

Warner shook his head. "It can wait."

"What can wait? You obviously came over here to tell me . . . something."

She fought to keep from shouting.

"This isn't the best time to talk about it, but I don't want you to hear it from someone else first."

"Hear what?" She hugged her arms around her waist. The fern nestled in the bay window reached out to her, still clinging to life. It was Steve's. All the plants were. Whenever he was overseas, they suffered greatly from her benign neglect.

"Well," he cleared his throat, turning toward her, the pain in his face hardening. "Our people on the ground in Georgia say that Steve was meeting an asset at the café when the bomb went off."

"And?" Maggie snatched pearl earrings off the counter, fumbling to put them on. "That's exactly what you told me three days ago."

"I know," Warner conceded. "But now we have another source confirming the original report."

"Who?"

"I can't tell you that."

She rubbed her forehead and stared at him.

"I don't know, Maggie. None of this makes sense. Steve's tradecraft was exemplary. Normally, he'd never meet an asset in a public place, especially not a Chechen."

A Chechen? She knew Chechnya well from her time as a CIA analyst. A Russian province that bordered Georgia to the northeast, it was home to both radical Muslim terrorists and innocent civilians decimated by two recent wars with Russia.

As far as Maggie knew, Steve's mission was to cultivate ties with Georgia's intelligence agencies and recruit Russian spies who strutted around Georgia as if they owned the place. "Since when has he recruited Chechens?"

Warner pulled a stool up to the granite island. He sat, smoothing the pleat in his crisp, black pants. "That's not really important. It's this new information that has me worried." He folded and unfolded his hands, finally placing them on the counter. "It may be a very serious matter."

Maggie flinched. "What?"

"Steve may have been selling information to Russia . . ."

She stared. Steve was an Eagle Scout, honest to a fault. And he was the most loyal man she'd ever met.

"At this point, it's still just a rumor from this new, unvetted source." Warner shook his head. "But this is Steve we're talking about. He wouldn't get involved with the Russians, not without authorization. I don't know why—"

"Is it true?" she interrupted, her voice barely a whisper.

Warner's brow creased. "I'm not sure."

Maggie's skin burned as if she'd been shocked. "Why won't you tell me who your source is?"

"I told you I can't reveal that. Not even to you." He straightened himself on the stool. "There will be a thorough investigation, and, of course, I will keep you informed of any developments."

His suddenly impersonal tone startled her. "What exactly are you saying, Warner? That I'm supposed to wait for some bureaucrats to decide whether my fiancé was a traitor or not?" She shook her head. "No. You will not shut me out of this process. Clear me into whatever classified programs you have to. I want . . . no, I need to be part of the investigation."

"Even if I could, you're too emotionally involved to handle—"

"Emotionally involved? Really?" Her voice rose over the screech of the kettle. "We were supposed to get married! In April, in case you forgot." She choked on a sob. "There has to be something else going on here. There has to be!"

Warner stood and reached around her to shut off the burner. "I'm in this with you, Maggie. Whatever it takes. We'll find the truth. We will find who killed Steve."

The kettle's whistle gave a final, dying gasp, and the house fell silent for a moment.

Warner checked his watch. "I'm headed to the funeral home. Let me drive you."

"No, I'm okay." She felt gutted, as if her core had been ripped out.

"You shouldn't have to do this alone." He touched her lightly on the arm.

She placed her hand over his and lingered for a moment before pulling away. He was right, she shouldn't be alone, but she was. Because Steve was dead. "I'm . . . no, it'll be fine. I promise not to do anything stupid. No motorcycle."

They smiled.

"That was crazy, Maggie."

"Yeah, Steve was pretty freaked out." He and Warner had been working late one Friday night when she decided to bring them Chinese takeout.

"The look on his face when you pulled up on his precious motorcycle . . ." Warner laughed.

"I know. He . . ." She shook her head. "I wish I'd had a camera." Fresh tears sprang to her eyes.

"I'm sorry, I didn't mean to . . . please let me drive you to the wake."

She waved a hand at him. "No, really, it's okay. I promise."

Warner nodded. "I'll show myself out then." He locked eyes with her. "See you in a bit." He smiled weakly, then left her alone in the middle of the kitchen.

Forcing herself to move, she shuffled into the powder room. The mirror above the sink painted an unflattering picture. Mascara trails lined the puffy skin under her eyes, and angry blotches jostled for space between the freckles on her cheeks. Her hand trembling, she smoothed on more makeup, a mask to cover the pain. Her hair was frizzing from the incessant drizzle and accompanying cold fog outside. She didn't care. "I don't think I can do this," she said to her grim reflection.

Back in the kitchen, it took only a minute to down three healthy shots of vodka. It was Steve's vodka, from Russia. He would understand.

Warmth flowed through her. *That's better.* Maybe she could do it after all. She could stand up and tell the world that Steve was no traitor. That he hadn't betrayed her. She straightened her dress, ready, she thought, for the worst night of her life. As she reached for her purse, the phone rang again. There was no one she wanted to talk to, but what if her mom had been trying to reach her? She was the only one who regularly called her home phone.

"Miss Jenkins?" His accent was thick.

"Yes?"

"I'm a friend, from overseas. I want to extend my condolences about your fiancé. We never meant for it to end up this way."

The pounding in her ears made it impossible not to shout. "Who is this?"

"Steve was of great assistance to us. We want to repay him for his efforts in whatever way we can."

Maggie steadied herself against the refrigerator door. "Who is this?" she repeated

"There will be rumors. We will deny every one of them, help you keep his memory clean. He was a good man." The caller paused. "And Miss Jenkins, you may call me Ivan Nik—" The name garbled into a word salad.

"Who? What name did you—"

Too late, the line went dead.

CHAPTER THREE

At 6:45 p.m., Maggie slipped through the door into the Hutchinson Funeral Home. The scent and sight of flowers assaulted her from every angle, from rose-filled vases lining the entryway tables to floral balloon drapes that appeared to blossom from the verdant green walls.

A funeral home employee smiled from behind the reception desk, offering to take her coat and umbrella.

"Thanks." She handed him her things and twisted her engagement ring.

He peered over his glasses.

"Which service are you here for?"

"Steve Ryder's." Her breath caught. "I'm his widow, well, not quite, but, um, he was my fiancé." *And a traitor?* Where was Warner? She glanced around. Maybe he knew someone named Ivan Nik-something-or-other—whatever the name was.

"I'm very sorry for your loss," the man said, interrupting her thoughts. "Right this way."

He ushered her down a corridor along a thickly padded, cream-colored carpet to the visitation room on the left. The open casket lay straight ahead, solitary before a row of empty wooden chairs. Splendid flowers fanned around the mahogany coffin bearing the body. Steve's body.

"Maggie." A hand touched her shoulder.

"Mom!" She whirled around and clung to her mother.

"Oh, honey, I'm sorry." Colleen Jenkins pulled away and wiped tears from her daughter's cheeks. "He loved you so, so much."

"Mom," Maggie whispered. "What am I supposed to do now?"

"I don't know. But I'm here. I'll help you."

Nobody could help her. Nobody could make this right again, not even her mother. She glanced toward the casket then looked back over her mother's shoulder. "Where's Dad?" Maggie hadn't expected him to show up, but some small part of her always held out hope that he'd do the right thing. It was an absurd hope, really. He always disappointed.

Whiskey had become his priority when she was in junior high. Then women. Over the years, he'd walked out on them several times, but her mother always let him come crawling back. Each time, Maggie hoped that things would be different. Each time, it was worse.

"Oh, honey, he wasn't feeling well. He wanted to be here, but . . ."

"Whatever, Mom." She was glad he hadn't shown. Steve would be, too. He'd always said that the more energy she devoted to trying to understand her derelict father, the more miserable she became. *Let him go, Maggie. He'll never be the father you deserve.* How right he was.

"You ready?" Colleen Jenkins asked.

"No."

"We should go in. You need to see Steve. To say goodbye. Before people get here." Her mother clutched her hand and led her into the reception room. Maggie placed her purse next to a guest book on a table just inside the entrance. Her heart thrummed so strongly she felt the vibration in her throat. A dark haze clouded her peripheral vision.

"Take a deep breath. I'm right here." It was exactly what her mom used to say when Maggie woke up gasping for air after a vivid nightmare. If only she could be that child again, the horrible dreams forgotten by morning.

She exhaled through pursed lips. The fifteen feet to the coffin might as well have been twenty miles. Each step took tremendous physical effort, as if her feet were encased in concrete. A tiny voice in her head whispered, *Maybe it's not him. Maybe they're wrong.*

Her mother released her hand and looped her arm through Maggie's, gently tugging her forward the final few feet.

"He's so pale, Mom."

Maggie lowered herself onto the cushioned kneeler set in front of the coffin, eyes squeezed shut. Next to her, she could sense her mother making the sign of the cross. After a brief prayer, her mother placed a soft kiss on her cheek, and slipped away, giving Maggie final moments alone with the love of her life.

Maggie forced her eyes open. He looked like a reproduction, a mannequin, not the real Steve. His dark wavy hair appeared immobile, weighed down by too much hairspray. Those dimples, the ones that were always there, even when he smiled in his sleep, were gone. There'd never be that hint of mischief in his eyes again. He looked fake, not dead. His face and hands showed no sign of the trauma he'd been through, but she knew that underneath the dark suit lay his annihilated body. As much as she wanted to, Maggie couldn't touch him, afraid he'd be too cold. She swayed on the kneeler. *Please, God, no.* The words from old, familiar prayers refused to come and comfort her. She ached for another drink as she heard mourners filtering into the hall outside the visitation room, their conversations muffled by soft music and dim lights.

"I love you," she said, her trembling hand hovering over Steve's cheek. This was it, the final time she'd be alone with him. Only he was already gone. Her chest heaved as she silently wept.

Maggie roamed, dazed, from one group of friends and strangers to the next. Their words of condolence tumbled inside her head like grains of sand tossed by ocean waves. She recognized people, but their names eluded her. Every breath was an effort, every exhale a fight against the crushing pressure on her chest. When she closed her eyes, Steve was right there, smiling, head tilted just so.

"Maggie!" At the sound of her name, she extracted herself from the awkward embrace of yet another of Steve's relatives. New York Congressman Richard Carvelli had just made his grand entrance. What the hell was *he* doing here? He shook off his entourage and approached her.

"Maggie, Maggie, I'm so terribly sorry," he said without a hint of sincerity. "If there's anything I can do, please let me know."

He glanced around and spoke louder. "I fully intend to press the government for the truth. You, and indeed all Steve's loved ones, deserve to know exactly what happened to this brave young American."

"If you'll excuse me, Congressman." She turned her back, not caring how rude she appeared. Richard Carvelli had earned her contempt. It was beyond her how a man like him, with his primal lust for the camera and serial womanizing, had wormed his way onto the Intelligence Committee.

"I've been looking for you, dear," a voice said, pulling Maggie from her thoughts. Her once future mother-in-law, resplendent in a tailored black suit and expertly coiffed hair, dabbed at swollen eyes.

"Mrs. Ryder . . ." She hugged her, this woman she hardly knew. Steve's parents had been disappointed, to say the least, about his career choice. Ryders were not spies; they were law firm partners, CEOs, Wall Street barons.

"I always knew it would come to no good. This crazy job, spies, and terrorists, and such," she choked.

Maggie made small talk, then excused herself and fled into the hall, collapsing in a paisley wing chair. She closed her eyes and saw Steve's face, the broad smile. Everything ached.

"Maggie?" The voice sounded familiar.

She peered through her lashes. "Yes?"

"It's me, Peter."

It took a moment to place the tall blond with ice-blue eyes. It'd been over three years since their one and only date. "Of course, Peter." She stood, tugging the dress back in place over her slim hips. "I'm sorry. It's been a rough week," she explained. *The understatement of my life.* Her date with Peter had been at a party, the same party where she'd met Steve.

"I was the first one at the scene."

Maggie's pulse quickened. "You were in Georgia? With Steve?" Steve and Peter Belekov had been in the same cohort at The Farm, the CIA's not-so-secret training facility located a few hours southeast of Washington, D.C.

"Yeah," he nodded, "we were the only two case officers in the Tbilisi station." His gaze swept the length of her body. "He couldn't wait to get home to see you."

Her face grew hot.

Peter hesitated only a moment before pulling her into an awkward hug. "I flew back with him so he wouldn't be alone."

"Thank you," she whispered into his broad chest.

"I'm so sorry."

Maggie pulled away. "What happened, Peter?"

"I don't know, exactly. I identified the bod . . . I mean, Steve."

Peter's face went blurry before her. She blinked furiously.

He glanced around and lowered his voice. "I asked the Georgian security service to let me see his asset, but they told me there were so many body parts from so many people, that they were still trying to sort everything out."

A swell of nausea rippled through Maggie's midsection.

"You okay?"

She focused on a spot on the rug and silently counted to ten.

"I'm sorry, Maggie. I shouldn't be telling you all this."

"Why did he meet this asset at a café?" she asked, raising her head to look at Peter, her eyes challenging him. "I thought those sorts of things happened in less public locations."

Peter shrugged. "I wish I knew. He was acting so—"

"I see you've met Peter," Warner's voice boomed.

"Mr. Thompson," Peter nodded. "I was just telling Maggie about how much Steve was looking forward to coming home."

Warner ignored him. "You okay?" He rubbed her shoulder.

Her adrenaline surged with the desire to get more information from Peter. "Yeah, I'm fine."

"You should be in there, Maggie." Warner nodded toward the casket. "With Steve."

Several people stood in the visitation room, shifting their feet as if uncertain how long they should stand before the body. "Come on, I'll go with you." He led her away without a glance back at Peter.

She leaned in, whispering. "I need to talk to you."

"About?"

"I got a phone call from some . . ." She clutched his suit jacket.

"Warner!" someone called from down the hall.

"Congressman Nelson, good evening," Warner replied, then lowered his voice to Maggie. "He left me a message earlier, wanting to know what happened to Steve."

"But, Warner—"

"I'll see you tomorrow." He planted a kiss on her forehead.

She watched him stride away to shake the Intelligence Committee chairman's hand. Her ultimate boss, Congressman Nelson seemed to be a decent man. But his presence felt intrusive. Before this week, had he even known that she was engaged to a CIA officer? She should probably thank him for coming, but the effort seemed too much. Maggie scanned the funeral home's large central room, where dozens of people sipped bottled water and nibbled on cheese and crackers. At the far side of the room, just beyond a gaggle of dark-suited men, Peter and Richard Carvelli were engaged in what looked like a heated discussion. Peter towered over the congressman, but Carvelli was right in the younger man's face. In response, Peter jabbed a finger into the congressman's chest.

"Maggie, there you are." Her mother nodded toward the visitation room. "Some more people just arrived. You should be in there to greet them."

Maggie swayed, fatigue permeating every inch of her body, but she dutifully followed her mother.

"Honey, your purse." A black clutch purse dangled from her mother's fingers. "You left it next to the guest book. Better check that everything is intact."

She nodded, but her mother had moved ahead to thank people for coming. Maggie slipped the purse strap around her wrist and steeled herself for more condolences from people she hardly knew.

When, finally, the flow of well-wishers slowed, Maggie slid into an empty chair in the visitation room. She stared, unblinking, at Steve's face. There was no way forward without him. With trembling fingers, she tugged at the clasp on her purse. She needed to hear his voice. The last message he'd left her was still on her voicemail. As she pulled out her phone, a sheet of paper embossed with the funeral home's insignia fluttered onto her lap. The words leapt from the page.

They're not telling you the whole story. Peter.

CHAPTER FOUR

Maggie shuffled over to the kitchen table Friday morning, a tattered pink terrycloth robe hanging limply on her shoulders. She'd slept fitfully, dreaming of Steve, explosions, and blood.

"I'm going to find out what happened to Steve. The truth, Mom."

Her mother raised an eyebrow from the other side of the counter. "You already know what happened." She flipped an egg, keeping her concerned gaze trained on her daughter.

"I don't know the whole story. I need to talk to Warner before the funeral."

"That reminds me. He called a little while ago to see how you were doing." She slipped a dish onto the table. "Toast and eggs. Over easy, your favorite."

Maggie nodded at the food. "You didn't have to do this." She forced down a bite.

"Coffee?"

She nodded.

"You need your strength, honey." Colleen Jenkins was already showered and dressed in a smart black skirt and blazer. Her auburn hair was pulled into a bun, secured with the vintage chignon cap she'd worn to every wedding and funeral Maggie could remember. "I meant to ask if you looked into having a priest at the funeral."

Maggie lowered the fork. "Mom, you know Steve's family is Episcopalian."

"Well, that hasn't stopped me from praying the Rosary for him."

"Fabulous." Steve's mother had balked at their plans for a Catholic wedding; pushing for a priest to help officiate her son's funeral wasn't a battle worth waging. Maggie stared out the window. Wispy clouds streaked across a crisp blue sky. No doubt she and Steve would've gone for a run before breakfast. She sipped the coffee, its warmth softening the lump that was crowding her throat. "So . . . Dad . . . why didn't he come?"

Her mother feigned confusion. "What?"

Maggie wrapped her fingers around the mug. The sun through the window glinted off her engagement diamond.

"Oh." Her mother smiled tentatively. She sat across from Maggie. "I told you. He wasn't feeling well."

Maggie pulled her hair back, twisting it into a loose, makeshift knot. It held briefly before the curls broke free.

"He couldn't pull it together for me?"

"Your father is a complicated man."

Maggie ignored her and set to work on the breakfast dishes. She scrubbed a plate that needed only a light rinse, banged the silverware drawer shut, and absentmindedly rooted around in the refrigerator.

"I'll finish cleaning." Her mother took Maggie's hand from the fridge handle and closed the door. "You have to get ready."

"Mom?" Her voice cracked. "What am I going to do?"

Colleen Jenkins put both hands on her daughter's arms. "Come home."

"I'm twenty-eight years old," she protested, even though the idea of letting her mom take care of her was appealing.

"You'll always be my little girl."

Maggie offered a half-hearted smile. "I know." Maybe she could go home. Just for a while, until she figured out what to do . . .

"Your father and I would be so happy to have you back."

That was all it took to snap the spell. Move home? Hell, no. She loved working in the intelligence world, making sense out of obscure information, advising policymakers on threats to national security. What she did actually mattered. And more importantly, there was Steve. He would've been horrified at the thought of her moving back to Boston. *Your Dad's toxic, Maggie. Stay away.*

"You know I'd do anything for you, Mom. But my life is here, and even though I have no—" her throat ran out of air so she took a breath—"no idea how I'll survive without Steve, I can't run away from everything that's happened."

"How can being alone be better than being home?"

Maggie inhaled deeply. She was so tired. So empty.

"I need to start fresh. On my own."

"But Steve is gone. You're going to need a support system. Your aunt works at that big financial firm in Boston, remember?

She could find you a steady position of some kind. Your bedroom is there just the way you left it. And you'd have your high school and college friends. Maybe you could meet a man and settle down."

"Settle down?" With Steve's body still above ground, her mother was talking like this? "That's precisely what Steve and I were planning to do, Mom!" She waved her engagement ring before her mother's eyes, ready to pounce should she utter another insensitive word.

Her mother blanched. "Look, I—"

The doorbell rang. Her mother jumped at the chance to change the subject. "Maybe it's the florist, again." The townhouse was becoming overrun with flowers, intermingling scents saturating every room. She scurried off to answer the door.

More flowers? As if they could fix anything.

CHAPTER FIVE

"As we lay Steven, our beloved son and friend, to rest," the minister intoned, his voice as dull as the wispy, gray morning clouds hovering over the cemetery.

Maggie bit down on the inside of her cheek to keep her lips from trembling. To her right, Warner stood erect, not moving a muscle, eyes transfixed on Steve's casket. He looked suddenly older, weary. She wanted to tell him it was okay, that Steve had died doing a job he loved. But it wasn't okay, and she didn't have the strength to hold up anyone else when she was so close to collapse herself.

She tried to focus on the minister. As he praised Steve's devotion to country and dedication to the war on terror, her every nerve screamed. He was so much more than a hero, a label thrown around too loosely these days. Steve was patience. And love. Every time she pushed him away, not trusting his love, he waited, reassured her, and he stayed. He stayed when it would've been so easy for him to go. *I don't deserve you*, she'd said after the last fight. She had started it. She usually did.

He'd wanted to go for a solo motorcycle ride the weekend before his latest overseas deployment. Maggie had assumed he wanted to get away from her. No, he'd explained, what he needed was time to prepare for their goodbye. He loved his job, but he didn't want to leave her. This deployment would be the last, he promised that night as they lay curled together under a soft blanket. And it was his last, just not the way they'd imagined.

Several dozen mourners stood as one, huddled together against the cold November wind. They formed a grim semicircle around the gaping hole in the ground that enveloped Steve's casket. Clumps of damp soil slid in, landing on the gleaming wood as if they, too, were ready for their ultimate resting place.

As the minister spoke, Colleen Jenkins tugged on her daughter's coat. "Who's that girl?" she whispered.

"Who?" Maggie strained her neck to look past her.

"I saw someone behind the tree over there."

There was no one. She returned her attention to the ceremony. It was time to place her rose on Steve's casket. She approached and dropped the perfect red bloom. It landed with an almost imperceptible *poof*. The minister said a closing prayer and it was all over with a final "amen."

A few stray pebbles plinked off the top of the gleaming casket. Maggie stared into the hole, oblivious to the gust of wind that swirled her hair into a mad dance. She knelt. The damp ground penetrated her black stockings. It would be so easy to lie down next to him. Right here, in the cemetery. Just lie down and die.

"Honey," her mom called.

Maggie took in the gravestones all around her. This was it. Really the end. She whispered a final "I love you," stood, and joined her mother.

They walked together in silence until Maggie spotted Priscilla, Warner's secretary. "Be right back, Mom."

She hurried over to the petite, older woman.

"Maggie, dear, I'm so sorry. Steve was such a nice young man."

"Thank you." The words seemed so inadequate, but what else could she say?

"Warner is just crushed."

"I shouldn't leave my mother waiting—"

"Of course, dear. I won't keep you, but there was something . . . what was it? Oh, yes, Peter Belekov asked me to send his regrets. He was ordered back to Tbilisi late last night."

"By who?"

"Well, Warner, of course."

Of course. "Thanks, Priscilla." She gave a weak smile.

"You take care of yourself, Maggie. Let me know if there's anything you need."

She nodded, already tiring of all the vague offers of help and support. There was nothing anyone could do for her, short of bringing Steve back to life.

The wind grew steadier as mourners filed toward the parking lot. Maggie's heels, sensible though they were, sank into the grass with every step.

Ahead, she noticed Warner and Congressman Carvelli engaged in conversation. They'd been classmates at Yale. She got the impression that Warner merely tolerated Carvelli on a professional level and hardly at all on a personal one.

"Maggie!" A slight blonde was scurrying across the cemetery parking lot, waving her hand.

"Kate!" Maggie hadn't noticed her at the church.

"I'm so sorry about Steve." Kate Johnson's enormous, brown eyes filled with tears. "You were so perfect together. I always knew he was the one for you."

It was true. Kate had seen the way Steve looked at Maggie. After they'd been dating for only a month, Kate had predicted a wedding.

"I miss him so much already. I don't know what I'm supposed to do next."

Kate wrapped her arms around her. "Just *be*. One breath at a time."

Maggie sniffed. "I'll try." She pulled away. "Can you come by the house for a bite to eat?"

"All these people going?" Kate's gaze flitted around the parking lot.

"Yeah, some of them."

Kate glanced around again. "Actually, I was hoping we could have lunch, maybe tomorrow?"

"My mother has a morning flight to Boston . . ."

Kate shoved her hands into her coat pockets and whispered at the ground. "I really have to talk to you."

"I . . . guess . . . after the airport, I could meet you somewhere close to your place," Maggie offered.

"Let's stick with Tyson's Corner. Shopping malls are safe."

"Safe?"

Kate turned and called over her shoulder. "Meet me outside Macy's. Eleven o'clock."

Maggie watched her friend rush away. *Odd.* Just like the note that Peter had left in her purse. *Why all this secrecy?* Her head pounded. Trying to make sense of anything was impossible. Maybe in a few days she'd be able to think straight.

Across the parking lot, her mother stood next to the black funeral home sedan that had picked them up this morning. She motioned for Maggie to rejoin her.

"That's the young lady I saw over by the tree. Who is she?" her mother asked as the driver opened the rear passenger door.

"Remember my old roommate, Kate?" She slid into the backseat. Eight years ago, she and Kate Johnson had met as CIA college interns. Instant friends, they'd shared an apartment until three years ago when they both left the CIA, Kate for the National Security Agency and Maggie for Capitol Hill.

"Kate?" her mother searched her memory. "I can't seem to remember her. Is she always such a nervous type?"

CHAPTER SIX

S aturday was gloomy, the kind of day where the sun surrenders to the clouds at dawn. At 11:00 a.m. sharp, Maggie stood outside the lower-level entrance to Macy's. The last time she'd been here was with Steve. To finalize their wedding registry. It had taken nearly an hour to convince him that they would, in fact, need a bread maker. And a waffle iron. He'd conceded, knowing full well that given Maggie's lack of domesticity, he'd be the only one to use them.

She swallowed and stared up at the red star in the store's logo. Everything felt so difficult, even lunch with an old friend. There was no sign of Kate yet.

Maggie tugged on the heavy glass doors and slipped inside. As she turned to head for the shoe department, a woman stepped into the aisle in front of her, holding an armful of clothes. It was Kate. "Meet me in that dressing room over there," she said, nodding to the right.

Maggie grabbed a half-dozen denim ruffle miniskirts from the rack. "I thought we would get some lunch? Didn't know we were going to shop," she called out, following her friend.

Kate tugged her down to the dressing stall in the corner. "I need to talk to you. It's really important." Several blouses escaped her grip. With a shaking hand, she snatched them from the floor.

Maggie followed Kate into the cramped, mirrored room, and held up a skirt with *Sassy* bedazzled across the back. "Am I supposed to wear this get-up to work?"

Kate shrugged without even glancing at the skirt. "Sure." She stuck her head outside the dressing room again.

"Are you in some kind of trouble, Kate?"

"Not yet."

The fluorescent lights made Maggie's hair look brassy, her skin sallow. "What's going on?"

Kate sat on a narrow bench, clutching the clothes in her arms. "This is probably the last thing you need to hear, and I'm not sure if it's relevant or not, but here goes." She exhaled sharply. "I saw a cable that I think, maybe, might have something to do with Steve."

She could muster only one word in reply. "What?"

"The cable crossed my desk on Tuesday. It references a terrorist attack in Tbilisi."

Maggie's pulse quickened. "The one that killed Steve?"

"Yes, but it's more than that."

"More than what, Kate?"

Maggie's friend stiffened and looked up at the ceiling. "Oh no, they have cameras in here, don't they?"

"Probably, but I'm not planning on stealing anything. Are you?"

Kate was acting crazy. She snatched her purse and bolted to a stand. The dresses she held fell into a clattering pile of hangers and wool. "Let's go. We've been here too long."

"Kate?"

"We should keep moving. The Rain Forest Café. It's loud in there." She peered out the door. "Come on!"

Maggie struggled to keep up with her diminutive friend as she wove a furious path through a maze of clothing racks. When she ducked to avoid a sales clerk's pungent perfume attack, she lost sight of Kate. But moments later, she spied her blond hair bobbing through belts, purses, and hosiery. *This is absurd.*

Kate was waiting for her near Macy's entrance to the mall. "Meet me in five minutes. I'll be sitting behind the giant elephant."

"What? What elephant?"

Kate shot her a look. "Trust me. You can't miss it."

She waited until Kate disappeared from view, then walked slowly toward the restaurant. Lunchtime on a Saturday. The place would be teeming with squealing children and pulsating with jungle sounds. A headache would surely follow.

Maggie found Kate at a table partially hidden by a giant elephant statue.

She waited for Maggie to sit, then plunged in, picking up where she'd left off in the dressing room. "On Wednesday, my supervisor told me to destroy all copies of the cable."

"Why?"

Kate shrugged.

"What, exactly, does the cable say?"

"Maggie—"

"Kate, look, I'm exhausted. Please, just tell me. Is Steve's name in it? Does it say who did it?" Questions tumbled from her mouth.

"Steve's name isn't in it, but I did some research and found no other bombings in Tbilisi last week. It has to be about him."

Maggie frowned. "So what? I'm not surprised that the NSA would pick up chatter about the death of an American overseas. Are you?"

"No," Kate conceded. "But my boss said it's a criminal matter."

"A terrorist attack *is* a criminal matter." Her friend seemed to be overreacting.

"Maggie, this is different." She leaned across the table and lowered her voice. "He said it was a criminal matter that would be handled exclusively by the FBI."

"Meaning?"

"They only give the FBI exclusive jurisdiction if they suspect American involvement in a crime." Her eyes darted around to the surrounding tables. "And there might be."

A sudden buzzing in Maggie's ears drowned out the ambient clatter of noise. She sank against the black booth cushion. "Wait . . . are you trying to say that an American was behind the bombing?"

Kate shook her head.

Maggie realized she'd been holding her breath. "Then what does it say?"

"It implies that a U.S. official might be selling intelligence to Russians."

A lump formed in her throat. First, Warner's source had suggested that Steve was selling intelligence. Then there was the mysterious phone call from Ivan who'd implied that Steve was a Russian asset.

And now there was an NSA report implicating an unnamed U.S. official. It was suddenly difficult to breathe.

"Maggie?" Kate reached across the table and clasped her friend's hands. "Are you okay? You're so pale." She waved down a waiter. "Could we get some water?"

"I don't know what's real and what's not anymore," Maggie whispered.

Kate accepted two tumblers of ice water and handed one to Maggie.

She sipped and inhaled deeply. If an American was selling intelligence to Russia, she'd find out who it was. It couldn't be Steve. There was no way. She'd prove it. "Do you think the FBI will lock the CIA out of the investigation?" If that happened, Warner would never get to the unfiltered truth. The most he'd get would be a high-level FBI summary of what had transpired in Tbilisi.

Kate studied her for a moment. Apparently satisfied that Maggie wasn't going to pass out, she replied, "Basically, yes. No CIA or NSA involvement, unless these agencies come across intelligence relevant to the investigation. In that case, these agencies will share whatever they learn about the attack at the deputies' meetings."

The deputies? Deputy director-level officials from various intelligence agencies, including the CIA, met monthly to discuss the most pressing intelligence issues. Warner Thompson was a regular meeting participant. "Have the deputies met to talk about the attack yet?"

"They met Thursday afternoon in Langley." She paused for a beat. "And it wasn't a regularly scheduled meeting."

Maggie's pulse quickened. Steve was murdered on Monday, and on Thursday senior intelligence officials met to discuss a cable about a bombing in Tbilisi. Obviously, the NSA cable and the meeting were about Steve. "Why would they hold an emergency meeting about Steve's murder? Is this something they do every time a CIA operative is killed?"

"I can't go into it. Not here." She glanced around nervously. "I kept a copy of the cable for you even though my boss told me to destroy all of them."

"Kate . . ."

"I'll slip it to you when we leave. I hate to sound like a bad cliché, but you probably should destroy it after you read it. If anyone ever found out I did this . . ."

Maggie understood. Kate had directly disobeyed her boss, mishandled classified material, and provided information to someone without a "need to know." She hesitated. This was a rule-breaker.

Kate leaned toward her. "I think I'm the only one in my office who read the cable. Well, the only one if you don't count my supervisor, probably his boss, and the translator and his boss. Whatever. The point is, if this cable turns up somewhere, I'm screwed." She sighed. "I debated whether I should drag you into this, but when they ordered the cable yanked, alarms went off in my head."

Maggie absorbed the shock waves, too stunned to speak. She finally cleared her throat. "Why did the NSA recall all the copies of the cable? Intelligence agencies share sensitive information all the time."

"I have no idea."

Warner would know. And he wouldn't allow the FBI to lock him out of the investigation.

Her friend glanced around the restaurant. "I should go."

"Just one more thing, Kate. Have you ever heard of a Russian named Ivan Nik-something?"

"Nik is the first syllable? You don't know the rest?"

"No. He called me the night of the wake. Implied that he knew Steve."

Kate lowered her head and whispered. "Ivan Nikolayevich?"

"Could be."

"Oh," Kate looked distressed.

"What is it?"

"I've seen that name—"

A teenaged waiter appeared to take their order. He ogled Maggie. She ignored him. "You hungry, Kate?"

"Not really."

"Let's go." Maggie slapped five dollars on the table. "Sorry, no lunch today. There's your tip."

Kate grabbed Maggie's leather bomber jacket from the chair. "Here." She walked away without another word.

"But—" Maggie slipped on the jacket. When she reached inside the right pocket, she felt an envelope.

The line had just been crossed.

CHAPTER SEVEN

Inside the Jeep, Maggie pulled the envelope from her jacket, gently, as if it contained sacred text. She could let Warner run the official investigation, or the FBI, or whoever was in charge, or she could open the envelope and pursue the truth, no matter the consequences.

The moment of indecision was brief. She tore at the envelope, frantic to bring its words to light.

**TOP SECRET/SENSITIVE COMPARTMENTALIZED
INFORMATION (TS/SCI)**
NSA02-7463GG
ORIGINATING AGENCY: National Security Agency,
Ft. Meade, MD
DOI: 3 November 2003 1755Z
DIST: 4 November 2003
COUNTRY: Georgia (GG)
DIST: NSA/Ft. Meade, MD; FM Joint Staff/
Washington D.C.; DIA/Bolling AFB/Washington D.C.;
CIA/DDO DDI NPC CTC/Langley, VA

SUBJ: Suspected Terrorist Attack (TS/SCI)

TEXT: Four people were killed in a bombing in
Tbilisi yesterday. Among those killed were two
unidentified local women, a man named (First Name
Unknown) Takayev, and a U.S. official. (TS/SCI)

COMMENT: We are awaiting additional details about
this apparent terrorist attack. Previous reporting
indicates that (FNU) Takayev believed a U.S.
official was selling intelligence to unidentified
Russians and that Takayev himself was involved
with Chechen terrorists who are trying to buy
nuclear materials from the Russian mafia. The same
terrorists have close ties to al-Qaeda operatives
in Pakistan and Afghanistan. (TS/SCI)

She squeezed her eyes tight, willing Steve to enlighten her from beyond. "Who's Takayev?" she whispered. Had Steve been Takayev's handler? There was only one way to find out. She dumped the insides of her purse on the passenger seat. Lipstick, coins, an MP-3 player, and assorted receipts scattered. She plucked her cell phone from the mess and punched in the number.

"Hello?"

"Warner, I need to see you. I'll be over in ten minutes."

"What's wrong, Maggie?" He sounded tired.

"Everything." She hung up. How could he have kept this from her? He had to have seen this cable at the last deputies' meeting. Peter Belekov's words rang in her head. *They're not telling you the whole story.*

She navigated recklessly through new developments of McMansions that had sprung up during the now defunct dot-com boom. Many residents of McLean, Virginia, were transients, coming and going with the fortunes of the stock market and changes in the political winds. This formerly sleepy bedroom community was now home to wealthy lobbyists, politicians, and media moguls. Here, old brick ramblers from the 1960s stood quietly in the shadows cast by monstrous villas squeezed onto neighboring lots.

She cornered into a winding driveway. Beyond a grove of firs stood a Georgian-style colonial. A large dwelling, even by McLean standards, it was too much of a house for one person, but just enough for a man of Warner's stature. He was waiting, leaning casually against the ornately carved maple front door. From afar, with his faded jeans and Yale sweatshirt, he could have passed for a coed.

"I was just about to go into the office when you called," he said.

"This won't take long," she replied crisply.

He waved her into the foyer, a sparsely appointed but sunlit space. He'd moved in six months ago, after his wife served him with divorce papers. To Maggie, his old house felt much more lived-in, if only because of the twins, whose toys never seemed to remain in their proper places.

"If this is about the wake and the funeral, I'm sorry. I got busy, distracted . . . I didn't spend enough time with you." His eyes were moist. "I should have."

Maggie waved off his apology. It was impossible to measure sincerity in a person whose profession is based on deception.

"Why didn't you tell me about the cable?

"About what?"

"The cable. Takayev." Her face grew hot as she fought for control of her voice. "The man killed along with Steve?"

"It seems like you know a hell of a lot more than I do." Warner crossed his arms. "Where are you getting this information?"

"You know exactly where. The NSA cable."

He looked genuinely perplexed.

"Seriously, Warner? You're playing innocent with me?"

"What the hell is that supposed to mean?" His eyes grew steely, his tone cool.

Maggie retreated, a tactical move only. "I know you saw the NSA cable at the deputies' meeting."

No flicker of recognition. "There hasn't been a deputies' meeting since last month."

"That's a lie. The deputies met two days ago. An emergency meeting."

Relief washed over his face, smoothing the creases in his tanned forehead. "I wasn't there. I took Thursday off."

"You did?" It was her turn for confusion.

Warner put a hand on her shoulder. "Come into the den. I shouldn't keep you standing here."

She followed him across the foyer's bluestone floor. His den wasn't the kind of place where she pictured herself curling up with a good book. Two stiff, cube-shaped chairs that looked as if they'd been forged from concrete slabs sat opposite a massive wooden desk.

The walls consisted of mahogany panels that made the room feel much smaller than it was. Against the back wall was a straight-edged gray sofa with no signs of use, never mind wear. There were no pictures on the walls, but a framed photo of the twins in matching dresses stood on the corner of his desk. This house was not yet a home, but perhaps Warner didn't care. Most of his life was spent at the Agency anyway.

"I haven't seen any NSA cable." Warner sat in one of the chairs and crossed his legs. "How did you get it?"

Maggie remained standing and drew a breath. She had to protect Kate.

"Wait." Warner raised his hands. "Don't tell me. The less I know about that, the better off we'll all be."

She shifted on her feet. "You can get the cable at work, right? I bet it's sitting in your inbox."

"What does it say?"

"It references a bombing in Tbilisi, so it's obviously about Steve. And it mentions a man named Takayev. I'm assuming Steve was his handler? I'm right, aren't I?"

He waved his arms in exasperation. "I don't know off the top of my head, Maggie. I'll look into it as soon as I go to Headquarters."

"And you'll let me know?"

Warner frowned. "If I can. You know how this works. I can't disclose—"

Maggie raised a hand to stop him. "Yeah, yeah, I know. 'Need to know' trumps everything, even though I, of all people, have a need and a right to know what happened."

"I get it. I do, and I will tell you everything I can."

She crossed her arms.

"What else does this cable say?" Warner demanded.

"It claims that this Takayev guy might be involved with Chechen terrorists who are trying to buy nuclear materials from the Russian mafia." She shook her head. "If Steve had known anything about that, he would have reported it. Right?"

"Yeah. But I don't remember seeing—" Warner closed his eyes. "A report like that would've caught my attention. Maybe . . . there is that Finding."

"Finding? A Presidential Finding?" She straightened. "Was Steve working on a covert operation?"

Warner frowned. "I can't go into that."

Maggie's mind clicked into full analytic mode. "Takayev supposedly knew that a U.S. official was selling intelligence. But that doesn't mean Steve was the one selling secrets. It could be anyone with a security clearance."

The ticking of an antique grandfather clock filled the silence.

Warner's voice was soft. "I'm not making any assumptions about Steve yet. One way or the other."

"He wouldn't betray his country. Not the Steve I knew."

He nodded, eyes downcast.

Maggie's shoulders sagged. If Warner needed proof of Steve's innocence, she'd find it. "One other thing. Who is Ivan Nikolayevich?"

"Why are you asking?"

"A man with a Russian accent called me the night of the wake. He said that Steve had done a lot for them and that he wanted to repay me."

Warner burst out laughing, then sobered immediately. "This has to be some sort of twisted prank."

"A prank? What?"

He leaned back in his chair. "Ivan Nikolayevich Bukovsky is the head of Russian intelligence. I assure you, it wasn't him calling."

"Why would someone—" Maggie bit down on the inside of her cheek.

An unspoken question hung in the air between them. *Who would do such a thing?*

The telephone on the desk trilled. "Dammit," he muttered. "Could you excuse me for a minute?"

"Sure." She slipped out into the foyer.

Warner's voice echoed into the hall. "Wednesday is my night with the girls." He paused a moment. "Let me take them to dance class, then . . . Fine, I'll just show up . . . What are you going to do about it?"

Maggie crept closer. She knew his marriage had fallen apart, but it sounded worse than she'd imagined.

He slammed down the phone.

She slid back to the far side of the foyer and pretended to study the prints hung on the wall.

Warner joined her a moment later. He pointed to a nightscape of the Eiffel Tower. "Got that one when I was stationed in Paris. 1987, I think." He sighed, cleared his throat. "I'll see what I can find out about the NSA cable and this Takayev character. In the meantime, please don't go poking around where you have no business—"

"No business!" Maggie cut him off. "Steve isn't my business?"

Warner threw up his arms in frustration. "That's not what I meant. I just don't want you getting yourself in trouble nosing around into things you're not cleared for. Just . . . just let me handle that side of it. Okay?" He closed his eyes. "I need the truth, myself."

Warner had been more than Steve's boss. He'd been his mentor, the one who'd helped him process the death of his father on 9/11, the one Steve had asked to be his best man at their wedding.

"I know you do," she conceded weakly. It felt like she was bleeding to death by a thousand little cuts. Every day was worse than the previous one. Not having Warner by her side would make everything that much more painful. "Are you okay?"

"I'm . . . I'm hanging in there."

"How are the girls?"

He flushed. "I haven't seen them in weeks." He ran a hand through his hair. "Shannon is making this divorce as nasty and difficult as possible. I get a phone call a day with them if I'm lucky."

"You need a better lawyer."

Warner nodded and glanced at his watch. "I have to go into the office. With everything that's happened, I have a lot to catch up on."

"I should be going, too. There are thank you notes, and other things I need to do."

"That can all wait. People will understand." His voice was subdued. "But please, Maggie. I mean it—please don't accept any more classified documents from anyone. The last thing I want to see is you in legal trouble."

"I won't. I promise."

"I'll hold you to that." He pasted on a kind smile. "C'mon, I'll walk you outside."

Out in the driveway, she turned to wave, but Warner had already slammed the front door and was hurrying to his BMW. Promises or no promises, if Kate, or anyone else for that matter, found information on Steve, she'd be all over it.

★ ★ ★ ★ ★ ★ ★ ★ ★ ★ ★ ★ ★ ★ ★ ★ ★ ★ ★ ★
★ ★
★ ★ ★ ★ ★ ★ ★ ★ ★ ★ ★ ★ ★ ★ ★ ★ ★ ★ ★ ★
★ ★ ★ ★ ★ ★ ★ ★ ★ ★ ★ ★ ★ ★ ★ ★ ★ ★ ★ ★
★ ★ ★ ★ ★ ★ ★ ★ ★ ★ ★ ★ ★ ★ ★ ★ ★ ★ ★

CHAPTER EIGHT

June 2000

Maggie *offered a half-hearted laugh at her date's inane joke about the remote odds of Governor Bush winning the upcoming presidential election. "Be right back, Peter." She slipped inside the third-floor apartment, leaving him on the balcony with two of his Agency colleagues, who inexplicably found him funny. Dozens of CIA employees crowded into the two-bedroom apartment's small living room and kitchen. She maneuvered around an oversized faux suede sofa and several clusters of people whose voices rose over Eminem's most recent swaggy, staccato-beat hit song.*

She caught sight of a tall man with dark, wavy hair watching her, a bemused smile revealing deep dimples. Flustered, she turned into the galley kitchen in search of a much-needed drink.

"Red or white?"

She whirled around. Up close, he was even more attractive. Cobalt blue eyes and strong features completed the face she'd glimpsed across the room. "What?" She flushed.

"Do you prefer red or white wine?" He reached behind her for an empty glass and placed it on the island separating the kitchen and the living room.

"White, I guess. When it's this warm outside . . ."

He smiled. Those dimples again. "Perfect. I brought this bottle. You like sauvignon blanc?"

"I don't really know much about wine. My favorite kind is whatever is in my glass."

His laugh was robust. And genuine.

"Are you one of them?" She nodded toward the crowd in the living room.

"If I told you, I'd have to kill you."

"The way this party's going, you'd be doing me a favor."

He laughed again and extended his right hand. "Steve Ryder."

The warmth from his touch spread up her arm and across her chest and face. In the presence of this real-life American James Bond, she suddenly forgot how to speak. Good Lord, he was gorgeous.

"This is the part where you tell me your name."

She blushed furiously. "Maggie Jenkins."

He continued to hold her hand. "You're not one of them, are you?" He tilted his head toward the crowd.

"Me? Ha! No. I'm just a lowly intelligence analyst."

"Why have I never seen you at Headquarters?"

She'd never seen him at Langley, either. Of that she was certain. "Actually, I left the Agency a year and a half ago to work for the House Intelligence Committee."

"Well, then, I suppose I should behave myself so I don't get hauled up to the Hill the next time an operation goes bad?"

Someone jacked up the volume for a Coldplay song. He pointed to his ears and motioned for her to follow.

Maggie hesitated, looked around for Peter. She didn't want him to think she was abandoning him. Steve had his hand on the front door and gave a little nod. Their eyes locked.

All the noise faded away. She smiled and joined him.

"Let's get some air," he suggested.

Together, they stepped into the outdoors hallway that ran between apartments.

"I think you're the most unpretentious person I've met in D.C."

She shrugged. "Sophistication is highly overrated."

The conversation stalled. Every time he looked into her eyes, she lost her train of thought. A loud crash followed by raucous laughter emanated from inside the apartment.

"It's only going to get crazier in there. Trust me, I know these guys."

Maggie glanced at her watch. It was only 9:15.

"I want to show you something."

"What?"

"Don't worry, we'll be right back. Nobody will miss us." He took her hand and led her down the nearby stairway to the ground level.

The June evening air was still, heavy with humidity. Maggie felt herself growing warmer.

Steve led her to a sleek black and silver motorcycle that gleamed under the full moon's light. "Ever ride one?"

She shook her head.

"Would you like to?"

Racing around on the back of a motorcycle with a man she didn't know? "Um, I—"

"I bet the monuments look spectacular tonight."

This was crazy. "Sure, why not." She could think of a thousand reasons why not.

"Here." He handed her a silver helmet with a black-tinted visor. "I only have one helmet. Usually ride solo."

"Are you sure?"

"Yep."

She tugged it down over her head, flattening her curls.

He leaned in close, fastened the strap for her, and mounted the bike. "Hop on the back."

Maggie swung her leg over the seat, her body resting against his.

"Hands around my waist, and hold on tight."

She hesitated, then reached around him.

When he twisted back, his abdomen muscles shifted under her fingertips. "Ready?"

Nodding, breathless, Maggie held on tighter.

The engine roared to life under them, then settled into a satisfying hum. He drove slowly out of the apartment complex but sped up along Arlington Boulevard.

As the motorcycle leaned into a curve, Maggie squeezed her legs against his. On the straightaway, he rested his left hand on her knee. Steve sped up to make it through a yellow light. She laughed, exhilarated.

The moon hung low over the Memorial Bridge. Below, the Potomac River shimmered as if topped with a million diamonds. Ahead was the Lincoln Memorial, spotlights directed at its gleaming, white marble edifice. They veered off to the left, where Steve slowed to find a parking spot along Constitution Avenue. He slipped the bike between a car and a shuttered food truck and killed the engine.

"Let's go see Mr. Lincoln."

Maggie pulled off the helmet and fluffed her hair the best she could.

Steve took her hand in his. Their fingers fit together perfectly, as if they'd been created precisely for this moment. The smooth skin and neatly trimmed nails on the top of his hand belied the calluses scattered across his palms. A rugged man who cleans up well, Maggie thought.

He led her toward the Vietnam Veterans Memorial. To the left, an old man placed a folded-up piece of paper at the base of the memorial, ran his fingertips across a name, and bowed his head. They paused for a moment and took in the expanse of the wall. All those names. Young men gone far too soon.

They set off for the Lincoln Memorial where more people congregated, some sitting by the reflecting pool, others snapping photos, and still others gazing off toward the Washington Monument and the Capitol Building beyond. Maggie had taken many visiting friends and family into D.C. to see the National Mall, but being here tonight, with Steve, was another experience entirely. She felt buoyant, as if everything was new, and she was seeing the world through his eyes. Even as they strolled in silence, there was a connection. They smiled simultaneously as a small child, up past his bedtime, spun in circles and fell in a dizzy heap. Steve copied the little boy, spinning and falling, which sent the child into peals of laughter.

"Your turn," he called to Maggie.

She offered up a pirouette. "Ta da!"

The boy's parents, seated on a plaid blanket on the grass, applauded and smiled.

"Lovely," Steve added. He bid goodnight to the boy and bounded back to her side. "So, tell me, why did you join the Agency, Maggie?"

She thought a moment. "When I was a kid, I was fascinated with the Soviet Union. The whole Evil Empire thing, you know?"

He nodded.

"And as cliché as it sounds, I wanted to be on the side of freedom. Truth, justice, all that stuff."

"A girl after my own heart."

Maggie thought her own heart might stop. She lowered her voice. "Are you one of those idealistic patriots, too?"

Steve nodded gravely. "I am. But don't tell anyone."

"Or you'll have to kill me?"

They laughed, a comfortable intimacy blossoming between them.

Together, they climbed the 145 stairs from the reflecting pool to the base of Lincoln's statue. Catching their breath at the top, they looked out across the Mall, down to the Washington Monument, and over to the Capitol Building in the distance.

"It's beautiful," Maggie breathed.

Steve touched her face and turned her towards him. "So beautiful." He leaned in closer, and they kissed, tenderly and slowly.

CHAPTER NINE

"Hello, anyone here?" Warner called out to the empty office. Just as he'd expected. *Good.* The 24-hour Operations Center down the hall would be buzzing, but few, if any, of his seventh-floor colleagues would be in this late on a Saturday. Barring a major catastrophe, he had the entire evening to himself to sort through the whole mess.

There were days' worth of unread classified messages on his desktop computer, 362 in all, most from the field. What was really on Warner's mind was finding out if the NSA cable was authentic. Because there was a chance it was as phony as that Russian phone call to Maggie.

If that were the case, she was being played. And if Maggie was being played, whoever was doing it would feel the full weight of the CIA's power. He'd make sure of it.

He searched through the stack of paper in his inbox. Not there. He checked his phone messages. Nothing again. Maybe the entire NSA matter had been dismissed at the deputies' meeting. He dialed the home number of Barbara Ferguson, the director of the Counterintelligence Center.

The Center was an amalgamation of personnel from the Agency's Directorates of Operations and Intelligence, the FBI, and assorted other acronym-heavy organizations. Barbara's answering machine picked up.

"Damn!" He hung up and flipped through his Rolodex. DIRNSA, the Director of the NSA, wouldn't be happy to hear from him on the weekend, but this was important. His wife answered— he'd just left for a trip overseas. Next? The FBI counterintelligence chief, *that S.O.B.* "Forget him," Warner muttered. He'd be about as helpful as an umbrella in a hurricane. He finally left a message on his secretary's answering machine. The rest of the world, it seemed, had a life outside of work.

Warner began scrolling through his unopened e-mail messages. Most were inconsequential administrative notices. He paused only to read operations reports from the field. A promising new asset in China, an urgent report from an asset in Indonesia, the murder of a Mexican drug cartel informant. His finger froze on message 361. It was a special channel, "eyes only" message from Peter Belekov. He hadn't expected to hear from him so soon after sending him back to Georgia just 48 hours ago.

To: DDO Thompson
From: Peter Belekov
Subject: Steve Ryder's notes

Per your instructions, I went through Steve's paper files.
Below are notes he wrote a few days before his last meeting
with his asset, GG-AVENGER.

"Last week, AVENGER told me he believes that a U.S. official
has been providing intelligence to the Russian military or the
Russian mafia. (I've found there's little difference between the
two organizations—corrupt military officers make a good living
working with the mafia.) I tasked AVENGER to find out more."

Per your instructions, Tbilisi Chief of Station, has not been
advised of my "research." Given what I've heard from my
source about Steve being the one selling intelligence, could
it be that he wrote these notes to deflect suspicion from
himself?

Peter

Warner drummed his fingers on the desk. "I'll be damned,"
he muttered. Why hadn't Steve mentioned his suspicion about a
U.S. official? Failure to report this to him raised questions. Very
uncomfortable questions about Steve's loyalty. To him. And to the
country. What did Steve know and whom did he tell?

But first things first. He needed to figure out who GG-
AVENGER really was. GG was the Agency's country code for
Georgia, so clearly, the guy was a local in Tbilisi. Maggie speculated

that the Takayev mentioned in the NSA cable might be the name of Steve's asset. If so, then AVENGER would be Takayev's code name.

Warner rifled around in his file drawer. Where the hell was his password for the Asset Identity Database? He tried every single one he could recall, but none worked. Priscilla knew them all, but she wasn't home. And just his luck, the stubborn woman refused to use a cell phone.

At this hour, the chances of anyone being in the CIA station in Georgia were slim. Warner decided the matter couldn't wait. He'd have to breach security protocol.

Peter's gruff voice answered the phone thousands of miles away. "Yeah?"

"Thompson here. You need to go in and call me back secure. Now." Warner hung up. It would take Belekov five minutes to get his bearings, ten to get to the station, and then another five to disarm the alarms and get himself situated. They'd have to figure out a cover story for Peter coming to the station in the middle of the night. Insomnia? Work overload? It wasn't that the Tbilisi Chief of Station couldn't be trusted, necessarily. It was just that Warner wanted to keep things as quiet as possible until he figured out what the hell was going on.

Now that the business of getting Steve's body home, consoling family and friends, and putting him to rest was over, Warner felt heavy with fatigue. How long ago had he been Steve's instructor down at The Farm? *Eight years already?*

It was hard to believe. He'd seen in Steve an instinctual talent, the same drive for adventure that had brought Warner from a life of privilege to the world of espionage. He'd encouraged the young case officer to pursue his passion despite his family's disappointment in his career choice. He knew what that was like firsthand. He'd nurtured Steve, helped him win plum assignments, and looked on with pride as he recruited top-notch assets and engineered several impressive intelligence coups. In many respects, he'd been the kid brother Warner never had. And now that Steve was gone, it hurt like hell.

His secure line lit up. "Peter?"

"Yes, sir." His voice sounded less groggy, but more muffled from the scrambling technology that protected their conversation from prying foreign ears.

"Thanks for making it in so fast. And for the memo. The Chief of Station still doesn't know, right?"

"That's right."

"Good. Let's keep it that way for now. Steve had an asset code-named AVENGER. Do you know if his real name was Takayev?"

"I have no idea. I didn't have access to all of Steve's asset files and vice ver—"

"I know," Warner interrupted. "Operational security. The rules. Yup. But Steve's gone and," he lied, "the system's down for maintenance over here."

"Are you directing me to go into his computer files?" Peter sounded reluctant.

"Yes, directing you, ordering you. You're covered. I'm the boss, remember?"

"Right."

Warner pictured sweat beading on the young case officer's forehead. "I'll hang on the line."

"Great. It'll be just a minute, booting up now." The sound of a clicking keyboard carried across the line. "Here we go. I'm in."

Warner's gut tightened.

"Okay, I found AVENGER. Hang on . . . Takayev, yes, that's his real name. Josef Takayev."

Warner squeezed the phone. He'd hoped that the Takayev Maggie had read about in the NSA cable would turn out to be someone Steve didn't know. But now it was clear that not only did Steve know Takayev, he'd recruited him to spy for the United States. And now they were both dead.

He cleared his throat. "Nice work, Peter. We still have to keep this quiet. I have a small team working on the investigation here," he lied again. "It's standard operating procedure to bring in an outside team to look into such matters. Can't have people with personal stakes leading the investigation." In truth, outside of whatever the FBI planned to do, the investigation team consisted of one person—himself. "Oh, and Peter? One more question. Did any of the articles in the local papers mention Takayev?"

"Not that I've seen, sir. I mean, I never heard of the guy until now. I'll double check, but as far as I recall, all the reporting has focused on Steve. The killing of an American official is a big deal over here."

"Has the media identified Steve as CIA?"

"Not yet."

It was only a matter of time until that information leaked. The situation was getting more complicated by the moment. If it was true that Steve, a CIA operative, was selling intelligence, and the media found out, the Agency would take yet another public relations hit. He'd be dragged before Congress to explain how he didn't know that one of his own employees was a traitor. Warner groaned. What he wouldn't give for the good, bad old days, when the enemy was known, and the mission was clear. Back then, the enemy was the Soviet Union. And the mission was to stop the spread of communism. There were rules, rules that both sides obeyed, more or less. Each side spied on the other's government and tried to recruit spies from within the enemy camp. Those rules no longer applied. These days, the espionage business was a free-for-all. Multiple actors with multiple interests, willing to do whatever it took to advance their agendas, switching sides on a dime, and perfecting the strategy of asymmetric warfare.

"Peter, about that cable you sent me last night. The one about AVENGER telling Steve he believed that a U.S. official has been providing intelligence to the Russians? Do you think this might tie in with your source? The one claiming that Steve was dirty?"

"Not sure. I'll contact him tomorrow. He seemed credible, but he was a walk-in, so I'm not sure what to make of him yet."

"A walk-in?" In the Cold War days, informants offering to tell the CIA everything they knew about their country's secrets set off immediate alarms. Sometimes, walk-ins were sent for disinformation purposes or to distract the CIA from something else. But then again, as much as the Agency was loath to admit it, some of the best spies they ever had were walk-ins. Regardless, until they could verify who this person really was, Peter was right to be suspicious.

"Thanks, Peter. Don't hesitate to go special channel again if you come across any new information. This is important."

Dread thrummed through Warner's body. What if it turned out that Steve was the U.S. official Takayev claimed was selling intel to the Russians? Had Steve's own asset unwittingly revealed his handler's treason? If any of this were true, the personal betrayal would be agonizing. Professionally, it would be a disaster. Steve, his golden boy, the one he'd mentored since day one, a traitor? Warner's career would be as good as over.

CHAPTER TEN

On Sunday morning, Maggie grabbed a Phillips head screwdriver from the junk drawer. She thumped the orange handle against her palm as she compiled a daunting mental to-do list: commit the cable to memory because carrying it is too risky; go in to work and snoop for whatever could be found; and figure out what really happened to Steve. Warner had asked her not to accept any more classified documents. He never said not to look at the ones she already had.

Upstairs in the guest bathroom, she unscrewed the shower nozzle's plastic cover. "You're a clever one," she murmured. Gently, she grasped a corner of the tightly folded plastic bag and tugged it out. Not even the FBI would think to look there for classified documents. Credit for her tradecraft went not to CIA training but to her childhood propensity for hiding diaries and notes, trying to keep her personal life from prying eyes. When she was nine, she'd caught her mother leafing through her diary, and even though she had few secrets at that age, it was a betrayal she'd never forgotten. Earlier this year, when Steve was fixing the shower, it struck her that she could hide something small inside the nozzle. At the time, she had no particular object in mind. But everything changed yesterday when Kate slipped her the envelope.

Maggie unzipped the bag and pulled out the paper, smoothing open the accordion folds. She read the cable several times, closed her eyes, and whispered it aloud. No way she could carry it around; with her luck, it would fall out of her purse at work. She re-folded the paper, tucked it in the bag and curled it into the nozzle housing. She fastened the cover in place and took a final glance to be sure everything looked normal.

She turned to the sink, splashed cold water on her face, and stared into the mirror. A disheveled mess stared back—a tangle of red curls, day-old makeup, and a baby blue velour tracksuit that had seen better days. *Way too much wine last night.* It had helped her sleep but . . . A shower would help, but there was no time to waste. Steve's aviator sunglasses were the last best option to camouflage her overall state of distress.

Thirty minutes later, she flashed her staff badge at the police officer guarding the Document Door on the Capitol Building's east side. He searched her purse thoroughly, standard operating procedure for the past couple of years. Apparently satisfied that her lipstick case did not contain a weapon of mass destruction, he let her through with a "Have a nice day, ma'am."

Maggie entered the Crypt, her tennis shoes padding faintly on the stone floor smoothed by centuries of wear. The weight of the building's elegant Rotunda and massive dome bore down on Doric columns and sandstone arches positioned strategically throughout the room. Chandeliers around the Crypt's perimeter failed to brighten it, instead casting hushed shadows on people and objects below. But the lighting was appropriate, she thought, for a room originally intended as a memorial sanctuary over George Washington's tomb, which stood empty one floor below.

Maggie treasured this building for all its architectural and historical magnificence, even more so since its brush with destruction at the hands of malevolent fanatics who never fathomed the fundamental courage of ordinary citizens. She paused, thanking God for the passengers on Flight 93, whose sacrifice ensured that the Capitol Building wouldn't be destroyed on that fateful September 11th.

She swallowed the lump in her throat as the elevator door rattled open. Crying was not on her to-do list. Officer Jim, as everyone called him, was guarding the entrance to the Intelligence Committee. She'd hoped there'd be some random weekend guard who didn't know her or anything about Steve. No such luck.

"Hey there, officer, what are you doing here?"

Jim glanced up from a newspaper. "I should ask the same of you." His eyebrows drew together. "How are you, Maggie?"

"I'm doing all right, Jim, I guess. Thought I'd come in and catch up on emails and stuff," she rambled. "I have another week off, but I was driving myself nuts at home."

"You shouldn't rush back to work. You'll need time, you know."

"Oh, I know. But . . ." She ran out of words.

"You going to be here long?"

Maggie shrugged, afraid her voice would betray the emotion below.

"Just wondering. One of the Members called a while ago to see if anyone would be here today. Guess he's coming in to do some work. Said he doesn't have the combination . . ."

She didn't hear the rest of his sentence. She didn't want to see anyone, especially a congressman. But if she hurried, she could get her work done before he showed up.

"I'll be here for a while, Jim."

"Great. I'll call and let him know the office is open." He nodded to the solid oak door to his left. "I'll buzz you in."

Maggie dialed the combination lock—36 right, 14 left, 27 right, *click*—then keyed in her pin on the number pad on the wall. The alarm light flashed from red to green. With the lock and alarm disabled, anyone could enter the committee space once the guard pressed a concealed button that released the final locking mechanism.

Jim reached under the desk and hit the button. A loud buzz melded with the click of metal.

Maggie pushed the heavy door open just wide enough to slip inside. It slammed shut behind her. The dull emergency light further up the corridor cast pulsating shadows ahead. No outside light ever penetrated the Capitol's attic, at least not here at the base of the building's iconic dome. The absence of windows throughout the Committee's space made it impossible for her to orient herself to the outside world. Did her office face the National Mall to the west or the Supreme Court to the east?

Maggie's hand swept across the wall until her fingers found the switch. She resisted the urge to call out, "Anyone there?"

There was a short cut through the hearing room ahead. By Congressional standards, it was a small, plain space. No marble, lush carpet, or oversized portraits of congressional giants. But the room had what it needed—soundproof walls, secure phone lines, and no listening devices. Regular security sweeps ensured that the information discussed behind these doors would not be overheard by prying ears.

Of course, there was little the security staff could do to prevent a committee member from blabbing national security secrets to the nearest reporter. Some congressmen leaked out of ignorance, not fully comprehending the importance of the information in their possession. Those Members could be rehabilitated, indoctrinated into the rules of secrecy. Rarer, but far more dangerous, were Members who saw every microphone as a tool to enhance their public exposure and demonstrate their importance to anyone who gave a damn.

Maggie continued through the Committee's excuse for a kitchen—a coffee machine, refrigerator and microwave—past a conference room, and into the hall leading to the main office suite. The place was empty all right. Every light was out.

She turned into her office and stopped short. The candid photo on her desk gleamed with sunny color. She and Steve sat together on a Cape Cod jetty, his arm draped casually across her shoulder. He was tan and strong; she was freckled and serene. Everything good in her life was captured in that one moment.

Maggie bit down on her lip and fled further up the hall. *Not now.*

Ahead was an open space housing several desks for the committee's administrative staff. Normally, she'd stop to chat with at least one of the women, but their desks sat empty on the weekend. Besides, her destination was the vault, where the Committee stored its most sensitive intelligence. Just past the administrative area sat the copy machine, the committee security officer's desk, and the entrance to the vault. Another combination lock secured a massive, fire- and blast-proof door. She signed her initials to the log sheet and spun the dial. The door groaned open under the force of her full body weight. She punched in her pin again. Failure to do so promptly would send an alert to some poor soul charged with monitoring secret alarms all over Washington, D.C.

Maggie felt vaguely guilty. Using government documents for personal purposes was not exactly allowed. She paused for a moment, thinking of Steve, of shrapnel tearing through his body, shattering muscle and bone like a hammer to glass. Not only did she have a right to be here, she had an obligation. To Steve. To the truth. With a deep breath, she stepped into the vault, not sure exactly what she hoped to find.

The real treasure trove of American intelligence—outside of the CIA, of course—was found in this obscure room tucked in a remote corner of the U.S. Capitol Building. Before her stood rows of floor-to-ceiling sliding steel shelves, boxes spilling over with unfiled documents, and obsolete files stacked in line, waiting patiently to be shredded and burned. She exhaled noisily and pushed hair away from her face, unleashing the stale scent of last night's wine. *Wine in my hair?* A headache nagged—she never should've opened that second bottle of red. The thought of curling up for a nap in her office was eminently appealing, but this could be her only opportunity to find what she needed.

Maggie scanned the stickers on the shelves. She reached for the first folder dated 2003 and flipped through the documents inside. There was nothing on Russia or Chechnya. *Why isn't this stuff better labeled?* She shoved the folder back in its slot, tearing a nail in the process. Her fingertip turned red. "Damn it!" she muttered, wiping the blood on her well-worn hooded sweatshirt.

The next folder was more promising. There had been three committee hearings relating to Russia in the past year. It would take hours to go through all the documents, but with any luck, they might offer up a clue. She flipped to the bottom of the stack, pulling out a thin folder. It contained an intelligence report alleging that Chechen rebels were training in al-Qaeda camps in Pakistan and eastern Afghanistan. Underneath the report was a staff memo to the CIA requesting a briefing for Richard Carvelli. Her breath quickened. The topic was Chechen involvement in Russian arms smuggling.

Interesting. A few months before Steve deployed to Tbilisi, Carvelli had been part of a congressional delegation to Georgia and several other former Soviet republics. If memory served, that CODEL had been focused on economic development in the small countries bordering Russia, not on national security issues. Maybe, she mused, his visit had sparked an interest in Russian arms trafficking. Carvelli certainly liked to portray himself as a national security expert. In fact, he'd made several recent speeches on the House floor about the threat from weapons of mass destruction, vowing to insomniac C-SPAN watchers that he'd stop at nothing to prevent terrorists from acquiring these doomsday weapons. Perhaps the CIA briefing he'd requested was part of his self-serving crusade to save the American people.

Or maybe . . . Something clicked in her memory. She turned and gripped the cool steel handle on the gunmetal gray file cabinet in the corner. Inside lay the most sensitive intelligence documents in the Committee's possession. If anyone walked in on her rifling through them, there could be serious trouble. Even as a trusted, highly cleared government official, Maggie was expected to uphold the "need to know" principle. Unless she had a verifiable need to know and the specific clearances for certain information, she had no right—professional, legal or otherwise—to access it. But she'd started down this path when she'd accepted the NSA cable from Kate. There was no turning back.

The combination came to her immediately. She pulled the drawer open, her ears primed for the slightest hint of an any movement in the office. Licking her dry lips, she ran her index finger across the files. There were covert action notifications for programs in South America, the Middle East, the Far East. She flipped through them quickly. Where was it? *There.*

The Presidential Finding ordered the CIA to intercept illicit arms shipments going from Russia to terrorist groups and rogue countries—*without* linking the activity to the U.S.

"Steve?" she whispered. Had this been *his* job? Maybe he'd been running this operation. And Takayev was the agent doing the dirty work. Intercepting weapons shipments. The NSA wouldn't have known about such a sensitive operation, which would explain why the cable linked Takayev with Chechen terrorists instead of identifying him as a CIA asset. And maybe—

"Hello? Anyone here?" a voice called from somewhere out in the main office.

She slid the document under her sweatshirt, closed the drawer, spun the combination lock, and ducked behind the vault door. Without thinking, she swatted off the light.

"Officer said someone opened the office for me. Hello?" The male voice was familiar. Maggie berated herself for turning out the light. She couldn't look more suspicious if she tried.

"Well this works out fine," the voice said, just outside the vault. She flattened herself tighter against the wall. Her heart thumped. When the light came on, she pressed her lips together to suppress any sound that might expose her. Through the crack between the door and the jamb, Maggie could see part of a man's back. She heard the shuffle of paper and then the rattle of a metal drawer.

"Really?" he muttered under his breath. "When did they start locking this damned thing?" He banged a fist on the cabinet.

Maggie shrank away from the crack as he stomped out the door. Her chest was about to explode. She gulped in air as his footsteps faded, then stole out of the vault, peering slowly around the corner. There was light coming from the chairman's office. But it couldn't be him—he was back in his congressional district this weekend.

She inched down the hall. The man was on the phone, leaving a message for someone. "I need your help. Call me as soon as you get this message, the cell's on." *His cell phone?* No one, not even the highest and mightiest member of Congress, could bring a cell phone, or any potential transmitting device, into Committee spaces. After a minute, he spoke again. "Hey, it's me. Listen, I'm having a little trouble getting everything together on such short notice, but I'm launching the next offensive today. I think you'll like the results." He paused to listen. "Have I ever let you down?" Another pause. "All right then, relax. The documents are at my house. Give me an hour . . . Yup, I'm leaving now."

The desk chair protested under the man's shifting weight. He mumbled something unintelligible, giving Maggie just enough warning to slip under the secretary's desk that stood outside the committee chairman's office. *The next offensive?* Her heart pounded. *Documents at his house?*

It sounded like he had walked past, but she remained hidden under the desk until the distant thud of the front door jolted her. What the hell was going on? She wound her way back down the hall to the entrance and popped her head out the door.

"Hey, Jim. Did your visitor leave?"

He nodded, looking up from a crossword puzzle. "Mr. Carvelli? Yup. Didn't say a word to me, though."

The name hit her with a wallop. Carvelli? What was he doing here? "I didn't speak to him either. By the time I realized he was in the office, he was on the telephone and I didn't want to disturb him." Maggie tilted her head. "Did he know I was here?"

"Not if he didn't see you. He didn't ask who opened the office. Why do you ask?"

"Oh, it's not a big deal. It's just that he would be concerned if he knew I came into work so soon after . . . Steve." Her mind scrambled to weave a story. "Mr. Carvelli lectured me at the funeral to take some time off before returning to work and I'd hate for him to find out I was here. Aacck!" She threw her hands up in feigned exasperation. "I know everyone means well, but I'm not a child."

Jim chuckled. "Your secret is safe with me unless, of course, he asks me point-blank."

"Of course, Jim. I'm not asking you to lie for me. I just don't want to cause any unnecessary trouble for myself." She sighed, "Everyone seems to think I won't be able to handle . . . life."

"You seem to be handling things fine. But I have to say, I agree with the congressman. You should take some time off."

"We'll see." She forced a smile. "I better go finish my work." Inside, she berated herself for rambling on. She'd have to get better at lying.

As she stepped back into the office, she heard Jim mumble, "You'd think he'd learn how to do this himself."

She pushed the door back open. "You say something?"

"Just talking to myself." Jim said. "It's ridiculous. You know, considering how many weekends he's here, you'd think he'd learn the combination."

"Carvelli?"

"Yeah."

"He comes in here a lot on weekends?"

"That's what I heard from the weekend duty officer. He warned me that I'd probably see Mr. Carvelli. Sure enough, he called to see if the office was open."

"Who usually opens up for him?"

"Don't know, some other staffer, I assume. Let's see here." Jim began flipping through the sign-in log. "Huh, that's funny."

"What?" She stepped fully into the hall. The door crashed shut behind her.

"The sign-in logs from the last two months are here, but check it out. No one signed in for the past couple of weekends."

Jim handed her the paper.

"Maybe he hasn't been in recently," she offered.

He frowned. "That's not the impression I had, but you're probably right."

"I'll ask my colleagues next week, just to make sure people aren't forgetting to sign in."

"Sounds good." Jim put the log back in place.

"Well, enough of this chitchat, officer. I have work to do." Maggie smiled in defiance of the tension coursing through her limbs and stepped back into the office. Someone was letting Carvelli into the office every weekend but not making a record of it. If Carvelli was coming in here at all hours for unexplained reasons, and he had an interest in the covert action files, was it possible he was looking at Steve's mission in Georgia? But why? She tried to connect the dots in her head. There were way too many "ifs" and not enough facts.

Maggie ran back to the vault and pulled the Presidential Finding out from under her sweatshirt, comparing the date on it to the dates

Carvelli had requested briefings. Snatching a piece of paper from a nearby trash bin, she wrote down a flurry of information, folded the note, and shoved it in her sweatpants pocket. Hesitating a few seconds, she rolled up the Finding and slipped it into the pouch of her hoodie.

Hands trembling, she locked the vault and ran down the hall, hitting light switches on the fly. She burst through the front door, quickly punching in her pin and spinning the dial on the lock. "Bye, Jim," she said, avoiding direct eye contact.

"I thought you had work to do?"

"Done," she called.

"Take care of yourself, Maggie."

"I will."

Downstairs, she hurried past the guard, breaking into a full run outside on the plaza. Clutching her purse, she ran hard, challenging her lungs to keep up with her legs. Across the faded lawn, weaving around monstrous, old trees, she ran up to 1st Street, stopping only to avoid being hit by a taxi. The Presidential Finding was burning a hole through her pocket. *What have I done?*

★ ★ ★ ★ ★ ★ ★ ★ ★ ★ ★ ★ ★ ★ ★ ★ ★ ★ ★
★ ★ ★ ★ ★ ★ ★ ★ ★ ★ ★ ★ ★ ★ ★ ★ ★ ★ ★ ★
★ ★ ★ ★ ★ ★ ★ ★ ★ ★ ★ ★ ★ ★ ★ ★ ★ ★ ★
★ ★ ★ ★ ★ ★ ★ ★ ★ ★ ★ ★ ★ ★ ★ ★ ★ ★ ★ ★
★ ★ ★ ★ ★ ★ ★ ★ ★ ★ ★ ★ ★ ★ ★ ★ ★ ★ ★

CHAPTER ELEVEN

February 2001

They lay together in a tangle of sheets.

Maggie ran her fingers through the dark waves of Steve's hair, knowing that what she said next would ruin the moment. But it couldn't wait. "So, about Uzbekistan."

"Don't remind me," Steve groaned as he nuzzled her neck.

Her hands floated down his biceps, and across his muscular chest. Never had she as felt as safe as she did when he held her. She inhaled his crisp, fresh scent. Everything she'd ever wanted was captured in this man.

And now he was about to leave her for the first time. For six long months.

"I know you don't want to talk about it." She kissed him softly on the lips. "But you leave in five days." And I'm terrified, she wanted to add. Uzbekistan, *a former Soviet republic, was struggling with the rise of radical Islam. And Steve was going to be in the middle of it.*

He tucked a curl behind her ear. "I'm going to be okay."

"I know, it's just that . . . What are you going to be doing over there?"

"Maggie—"

"Will you be in the embassy?"

"Sometimes."

"And the rest of the time?" She shuddered at the thought of him being in danger.

He lowered his voice. "There's a target. A woman."

"A woman?" She pulled the sheet up over her chest.

He laughed. "Yeah. She's like sixty years old. Married to a corrupt government official we're tracking."

A wave of relief rushed over her. "Oh. Good. I think?"

He traced a finger along her clavicle. "I'll be counting the days until I get back."

Her eyes grew moist. "How will I know you're okay? Can you call me at a certain time every day?"

He propped himself up on an elbow. "Yeah . . . I can do that. How about first thing in the morning? My time."

"It'll be the middle of the night here."

"If you don't pick up, I'll leave you a message."

She'd sleep with the portable phone next to her bed. "I'll pick up." This was all starting to sound okay. Having a plan in place would make his absence more structured, eliminate some of the worry.

Steve nodded. "I may not be able to call every day."

"I know."

"If you don't hear from me for two straight days, call Warner. I'll give you his home and office numbers."

"Warner Thompson? The Deputy Director of Operations?"

He leaned in and kissed her softly on the lips. "He's my mentor. We're close. And he already knows all about you, Maggie."

"He does?"

"I had to tell someone."

Her heart hammered in her chest. "What if you get kidnapped or something—"

He took her face in her hands and stared deep into her eyes. "If something happens to me, Warner will be the one to tell you. He will take care of you."

"Steve, please—"

"Nothing will happen."

"Promise?"

He kissed her tenderly. "Promise."

CHAPTER TWELVE

The next morning, Maggie trudged across the Capitol plaza through the brisk wind. *Back too soon.* She glanced across the street, unable to see the Supreme Court building through the darkness. Pulling her coat tighter, she forged ahead, shoulders against the gusts. The miserable weather served as a perfect reflection of her mood.

Maggie climbed the Capitol steps and presented her badge to the officer, avoiding direct eye contact. The Crypt was still, its silence reverberating from every gracious curve. There'd be few congressmen around this Monday. Most were still in their districts, except for Carvelli, of course. That meant there'd be even fewer lobbyists around, what with their quarry away. And the tourists? They'd be along after the sun rose.

As she stepped off the elevator, Maggie cleared her throat, alerting the guard to her arrival. "Morning," she croaked as she turned the corner.

"Good morning," he answered, his face sagging from bored exhaustion.

"Open?"

The guard nodded. A quick glance at the sign-in sheet showed that Wendy Carlson, one of the Committee's secretaries and a friend, had signed in minutes before. *Damn.*

She had hoped to get in and out before anyone else arrived for the workday.

Maggie proceeded to her office. It was the last place she wanted to be, but she had to return the Presidential Finding before anyone noticed it was gone.

She ducked into her office, flung her purse onto the desk and stepped back into the hall.

Ahead, Wendy was at her desk next to the chairman's office, frowning at the computer through steel-rimmed glasses. "Maggie! What are you doing here? I thought you'd be out at least another week." She jumped up to hug her friend.

Maggie could barely lift her arms. Weariness permeated every bone. "I needed to get out of the house for a while."

"I bet," she said, nodding in sympathy. "So, all the relatives leave or are they still around?"

"Mom's gone. My father didn't make it." She'd never talked about her deadbeat father with anyone except Steve.

Wendy's eyebrows shot up. Still a Daddy's little girl at twenty-six, she couldn't fathom such a no-show.

"He had the flu, so, much as he wanted to be here . . ." Maggie shifted on her feet. "Did I miss anything big?"

"Work-related, not really." Wendy let the sentence hang. "Buuuut . . . things have been interesting for me."

A conversation about Wendy's love life? Under any other circumstances, she'd welcome another of her friend's salacious tales about life as a single woman in Washington, D.C. They were always good for a laugh. But not today. Still, she couldn't risk raising Wendy's suspicions, so she bit. "Is this the mysterious older man?"

"Yes!" Wendy gushed like a teenager reveling in a new crush. "He is so amazing, and I'm not just talking about the sex."

"Wendy!" Maggie protested, playing along. "I'm not sure I can handle this so early in the morning."

"I can, whenever he can!" She burst out laughing. "Sorry!"

Maggie smiled, pretending to be amused. "That why you're here so early today? Up all night with the new man?"

"I wish." Wendy sighed. "No date yesterday. I went to a family party and had to come in early today to finish putting together the Members' briefing books."

"Well, I won't keep you then."

"Hey, I'm starving. This can wait a few minutes." Wendy dismissed her computer with a wave. "The cafeteria will be open at six-thirty. Wanna walk down?"

Not really. "Sure, just let me hang up my coat."

A minute later, Wendy appeared outside the door to Maggie's office. "Come on. My treat."

They walked down a back stairway leading to the basement. Rarely was anyone seen on these stairs other than Committee staff and VIPs trying to avoid the public. The only tourists encountered were lost ones. "So, when do I find out more about the boyfriend?

Like a name?" Maggie asked, her voice echoing off the metal staircase. "Or are you going to leave me guessing?"

"You know I'd tell you everything if I could. But he's a very public person who values his privacy." With a hint of desperation, Wendy added, "And if he found out I told anyone, he'd probably dump me."

"Is he married?" Maggie had to ask.

"No, I swear. He's a very eligible bachelor, believe me."

"Then why the secrecy?"

Wendy's lips tightened. She pulled open the stairwell door and marched down the hall, leaving Maggie trailing behind.

"Hey, I just don't want to see you get hurt," Maggie called ahead.

Wendy stopped at the cafeteria entrance. "I know. But I don't want to mess this up. My gut is telling me this could be it."

"It? You mean like IT, it?" Maggie suppressed a groan. She'd heard this before.

Wendy beamed. She clutched Maggie's arm, leading her to the counter. "What'll it be?"

"Just an English muffin, butter on the side, and a large coffee."

Wendy chatted aimlessly while they waited at the counter, dropping anecdotes about her new love, what a powerful man he was and how he'd promised to keep her by his side as he ascended the ladder of influence in the nation's capital. "And not only that, he plans to sponsor legislation to help disadvantaged children attend college for free. Isn't that amazing?"

Maggie nodded and smiled through gritted teeth. She was losing precious time, but she didn't want to give her friend a reason to be suspicious, so she nodded in all the right places. They opted for the stairwell on the way up. "Need to burn off this cream cheese," Wendy joked.

Maggie ducked into her office, promising to check back later. There were no voicemail messages. Wendy must have run interference for her all last week. There was also nothing of note in her email. After twenty minutes of shuffling paper, she headed for the vault. Wendy was immersed in her work, and no other coworkers had arrived yet. This was the perfect opportunity.

Inside, the file cabinet was unlocked. Maggie pulled the Presidential Finding from where it was concealed in the waistband of her pants.

"Hey, Maggie." Bill, the Committee's security officer, appeared at the vault door.

She froze. "Hi."

"What are you doing here?"

"I . . . I thought work would be a good distraction," she stammered, clutching the document to her chest. "Just tying up loose ends before I take a few more days off."

"Let me know if there's anything I can do for you."

"Sure." Maggie feigned a smile. She exhaled as his footsteps faded, only to be startled by the sudden appearance of Wendy.

"Ahh!" Maggie gasped, dropping the paper. "Don't sneak up on me like that." Her eyes snapped to the floor, where the Presidential Finding lay exposed. She snatched it and stuffed it into the shredder next to the cabinet. The machine devoured the paper, reducing it to minute slivers in just seconds. Maggie's face was hot. "Thought I'd clean out my safe a little bit before I left. I'm such a pack rat."

Wendy looked at the shredder then back at Maggie. "Would you just get out of here? Go home. Watch Oprah. Drink tea. Go!"

"I'm going." Maggie turned and scurried back to her office. *Calm down!* Taking that document home was a stupid move. Shredding it was even worse. Better to leave now than risk making an even bigger mistake. She logged off the computer, grabbed her coat, and hurried down the hall. Her gut churned. What had she done? What if Carvelli asked to see the covert action files today? Would anyone suspect her? Maggie flew past Officer Jim who'd just arrived for his shift.

"Hi, Maggie," he called out, but she was already at the elevator door before he could utter another word. She pushed the down button three times. *Come on!* She rushed in when the door opened and found herself entangled with Richard Carvelli.

"Well, isn't this a pleasant way to start the day," the congressman said, holding his ground. "Welcome back, Maggie."

She stepped back. "Thanks." She tried to slide by him on the right.

Carvelli shuffled, blocking her. "I expected you to take a longer break after your loss." His breath was warm on her face. "But since you're here, I could use your help on a little project."

"There's plenty of other staff to help you." She turned her shoulder and squeezed by him. In the past year, he'd hit on her several times, like he did with pretty much every female who crossed his path. Today, she was tempted to swing her purse at his head.

He looked over his shoulder at her. "Give it time, Maggie. Things will get better." He sounded almost genuine, but then he added, "Take it from me, the single life ain't so bad."

Maggie felt like retching. Down on the ground floor, she hurried for the exit. Outside, she stood for a moment in the crisp morning air, gasping for breath.

CHAPTER THIRTEEN

Warner poured his fourth cup of coffee. The pot slipped out of his shaking hand, shattering on the countertop. His secretary appeared at once. "Are you okay?" Priscilla asked as she grabbed a roll of paper towels from the cabinet. "Here, let me take care of that."

"Thanks," Warner grunted, wiping coffee splatter off his pants. A piece of glass crunched under foot while the burner hissed with the smell of burnt caffeine. "I need the deputies' meeting memo as soon as you can get it." Dazed by a lack of sleep, he headed to his office, collapsed into the chair, and closed his eyes. It was early afternoon, but he'd been up for twelve hours already.

"Finally," he snapped as Priscilla dropped a file on his desk.

"Someone needs a vacation," she retorted on her way out the door.

You have no idea. He flipped through the file. The NSA cable Maggie had described was not attached. "Damn it!" He popped a few more antacid tablets into his mouth.

"Hey, Warner, what's up?" Barbara Ferguson appeared outside his office. "Three voicemail messages before seven o'clock in the morning? On a Monday?" The Counterintelligence Center chief had two children she saw off to school every day before work. "Sorry it took me so long to come see you. Wall-to-wall meetings this morning."

He waved her into his office. "Barbara, what I'm about to tell you cannot leave this room."

Her lips narrowed into a thin line. "What is it?"

"I heard about the deputies' meeting last week. The NSA cable."

Barbara appeared relieved. "Oh, that. Sure, we discussed it, among other things."

"Fill me in." Warner tapped a pencil on his thigh.

"NSA said that the cable got out to a few of its employees but that it was pulled the next day."

"Why?"

"They said there was a potential counterintelligence issue, but they couldn't provide me with details yet."

"But you're—"

"—the CIA's counterintelligence lead." She rolled her eyes. "Bastards at the Fort are always trying to pull rank."

"As usual." Other intelligence agencies fought against ceding too much of "their" information to the CIA. The bureaucratic turf wars were legendary and never ending. "What about the FBI?"

"The FBI is taking the lead in the investigation." She smirked. "You know what that means."

He knew exactly what that meant. "They're going to lock the Agency out, aren't they?"

She nodded. "Sounds like it."

A trickle of sweat ran down his back. "Steve was a CIA case officer. They can't shut us out."

"Technically, they can. The bombing is considered a crime. That's the FBI's turf. As is investigating whether a U.S. official was selling intelligence." She leaned forward and whispered, "But I couldn't agree with you more. The Agency should be in the loop." She shut the door behind her. "Which is why I snatched a copy of the cable."

Warner flexed his calves, ready to leap from the chair. "Well played, Ms. Ferguson."

"I know." She laughed. "And easy enough. I'm like the invisible woman during these meetings. While they were trading golf stories, I slipped a copy of the cable out of the FBI Director's folder."

"Just like that?"

"Just like that." She lowered her voice. "Obviously, it goes without saying, no one else can know."

"Obviously," Warner agreed.

"In fact, I'd feel better if I gave you the cable for safekeeping. Not that I really expect them to notice it missing . . ."

"I'll lock it in my personal safe." He nodded to the gray Hamilton safe in the corner.

She was back in a flash, handing over a file folder with a red border and TOP SECRET stamped in large black letters. "I have to run to a meeting down on six. If you need anything else, please call." She left and closed the door.

Warner lifted the cover of the file and studied the official cable. It was real. And it included everything Maggie had mentioned.

CHAPTER FOURTEEN

I ce tumbled out of the dispenser with an abrasive rasp. Maggie was out of wine, but hadn't she sworn it off, anyway? Tepid vodka flowed over the ice, splitting it with a crisp crackle. She twirled the ice around with her finger before taking a sip.

She was at a loss—no evidence, no plan, and no answers. It wasn't much past noon, but this called for a stiff drink.

A loud thump came from the door knocker. "No way," she groaned. Could it be Warner? She snatched the refrigerator handle and hid her glass inside behind a jar of jelly.

Thud, thud.

She hurried silently on tiptoe toward the front of the house, slid behind an end table in the living room and pulled back the curtain. That wasn't Warner's car in the driveway. On the landing outside stood a middle-aged man with a generous paunch and an unruly mop of jet-black hair. *Who the hell?* Maggie turned the deadbolt and pulled open the door. "Yes?"

"Maggie Jenkins," the man stated in a guttural accent she couldn't place.

"Yes," she squeezed the doorknob with her right hand.

"I have some information for you. May I come in?" He glanced furtively over his shoulder.

"Information? On what?"

"Please, Miss Jenkins, not here."

Maggie shook her head. "Look, I don't know who you are or what you want, and I'm not in the mood for any kind of—"

"About your fiancé." His black eyes bore into her. "The bombing."

"Who are you?"

"Tamaz Ashkhanadze. I am a political officer at the Georgian Embassy in Washington." His olive-skinned face betrayed no emotion. He held out an embossed, official-looking card.

"The embassy, as in the Republic of Georgia?" She took the card and stared at it, trying to understand.

"Yes. I will explain everything." He stepped forward without invitation, and stood in the threshold now, less than a foot from her. She was a good three inches taller, but the dark circles imprinted under his eyes spoke of at least a decade on her.

The Georgian glanced over at the couch and removed his overcoat.

"Oh, please have a seat," Maggie offered. *What am I doing?*

He settled on the wing chair facing the front door. Though still wary, Maggie shut the door and sat on the couch.

"Well?" Maggie splayed her fingers on her lap. She tried to calculate whether it would be easier to bolt outside or run for the telephone if the man attacked.

Ashkhanadze continued to stare from under thick, unruly brows.

She shifted. "You say you're from the embassy."

He raised an eyebrow in response, then leaned forward, his jowls leading the way. "I am not here on official business."

It was her turn for silence. She was too confused for anything else.

He cleared his throat, but what sounded like decades of smoking still scratched at his voice. "What I have to say, you never heard from me."

"I didn't?" Maggie was growing less frightened and more annoyed.

A scowl crossed his face. "You don't seem to understand, Miss Jenkins. I am putting my life in jeopardy just by being here. Perhaps yours, too."

"Then why are you here?" *Just spill it!*

"Revenge."

Maggie's muscles tensed. *Against me? Steve?* She pushed herself up off the couch. "You need to leave."

He stood. "Miss Jenkins, please sit. I didn't mean to alarm you." A grimace revealed dingy, uneven teeth. His voice dropped. "My brother also was murdered last week."

"I don't understand. Who's your brother?"

Ashkhanadze's jaw tightened. "My brother worked for Georgia's Ministry of State Security." He emitted a noise somewhere between a grunt and a snort. "Our KGB, you might say."

"I'm very sorry." Why was he telling her this? "What was your brother's name?"

He closed his eyes. "Josef."

Silence hung between them. Maggie was at a loss for words, just like the people who came to pay respects at Steve's funeral. "I'll make us some tea." She escaped to the kitchen to consider her options. Asking him to leave was the most logical move, but he might be telling the truth—as a Georgian official, he really might know something about the bombing.

After filling the kettle, she checked the drawer to the left of the stove. Wrapped in a towel and tucked behind the utensil organizer was Steve's loaded .38 revolver. The Georgian seemed harmless enough but just in case the situation went sideways . . .

"Miss Jenkins." He appeared suddenly in the kitchen.

Her left hand jumped to the back of the drawer.

"Please forgive me for this intrusion. I should go. I just . . . It is very difficult."

Maggie couldn't have said it better herself. Everything was difficult now, nothing more so than the act of living. Her grip tightened around the towel. "It's always difficult to lose a loved one . . ."

"I believe my brother knew your fiancé."

Maggie's fingers slid under the towel and brushed against the .38's cool, satin steel barrel. "He knew Steve?" She leaned against the countertop next to the stove, still not used to hearing Steve referred to in the past tense. "In what way?"

"They had a meeting last Monday. At a café in Tbilisi."

Her knees weakened. "At a café?"

The Georgian nodded.

The screech of the kettle gave her a moment to breathe.

"My brother was helping to track weapons going from Russia to terrorist groups. In fact, Josef was a CIA asset."

"Josef Ash . . ." She glanced at the business card she'd dropped on the counter. "Ashkhanadze?" Her mind swirled with contradictory thoughts. This didn't make sense. Steve's asset was named Takayev. She left the utensil drawer open, walked to the table and poured the steaming water into the mugs. "Tell me about Josef." She was desperate to know more.

"He is . . . was my younger brother. Our father died when we were children. Our mother raised us alone. It wasn't easy raising two energetic boys in a foreign land."

"Foreign land?"

"Our father was Georgian. My mother is Chechen."

Maggie's hand trembled as she lowered the kettle to the burner. "So you consider yourself Chechen?"

"No, no. I'm my father's son. Georgian to my soul."

Maggie nodded, not sure what that meant.

"Josef was different. He took more interest in the Chechen side of the family than I ever did."

She inched her way back towards the stove. "Why?"

He stirred his tea and frowned. "Georgians are not big fans of Russia. Josef very much supported Chechnya's fight for independence. Until the Islamists took over and tried to impose their ways on the Chechen people." He slurped from the mug. "Once the radicals started operating in Georgia, he felt like he had to do something about it."

"What did he do?"

"He tried to get Georgian intelligence to focus on the radical threat. But he quickly realized that as long as the Chechen rebels were targeting Russia, our government would do nothing to stop them."

Maggie raised her eyebrows. "The enemy of my enemy . . ."

". . . is my friend. Precisely," Tamaz offered. "In addition, Josef suspected that several of his intelligence colleagues were accepting money from Russian gangsters. The mafia is everywhere. The very men who are supposed to protect our country take bribes to ignore the Chechen radicals in Georgia who work with al-Qaeda and help ship weapons. Weapons that could be used against us." He tapped the table and glared at her with narrowed eyes. "We were a captive nation for far too long. Now we are free, but in name only. The criminals, the Russians, terrorists, they tear us apart."

Maggie slipped onto the chair across the table from him, stilled by his bitterness. "So, he confided in you," she prompted.

"Yes. Last week, he told me he had infiltrated a Chechen cell and was feeding information to an American." Ashkhanadze's skin seemed to sag more under the weight of his sorrow. "Your fiancé was at the café when the bomb went off." He paused as if waiting for confirmation.

Maggie nodded.

"Well, so was Josef. I can only assume that your fiancé was the American Josef was working with."

Up until this moment, she thought she wanted to know everything that had happened to Steve on that terrible day. But now, the facts were like snipers, threatening her from out of nowhere with fresh wounds. She gathered up the mugs and returned them to the counter. "I'm very sorry about your brother." Maggie wanted him to leave. She needed time for her thoughts to settle in the space between emotion. "But I still don't understand why you're here."

Ashkhanadze rose slowly. "I need your help."

She stared, refusing to prompt him again.

He continued anyway. "I want you to pass this information to someone you trust at the CIA."

"Why?" Maggie asked, incredulous. "I thought you said this conversation never happened."

Susan Ouellette

"Tell them that I want to help them discover who killed your fiancé and my brother. And to help them stop the weapons smuggling."

She wanted to laugh. Steve had trained for years to learn how to recruit assets and here she was, an accidental operative, talking with a man who was volunteering to spy on behalf of the United States. "Mr. Ashkhanadze, you're asking me to help you spy on your own country?"

"The way I see it, I am helping to rid my government of the vermin that infests it. My country has suffered so much for far too long." Pain flashed across his face. "I want to find the bastards who murdered my brother."

Maggie felt for Ashkhanadze and his raw anguish, but who knew what the CIA would do with this man and his information? Something told her she needed him more than Langley did. "I'll see what I can do."

"Thank you," he nodded. "I am leaving for home this evening to bury my brother. I hope . . ." His voice wobbled. "They're still trying to identify his remains, but we will hold a funeral regardless. I will contact you next week when I return."

"What's your mother's name?"

He took a step back. "Why do you ask?"

"I—" Maggie scrambled for an answer. "I'd like to send her a letter, my condolences."

Tamaz clasped his hands together in front of his chest. "You're very kind. Her name is Tatiana. Send your letter to the address on my card and I'll be sure she gets it."

Tatiana, she repeated to herself. "Of course." She tilted her head. "By the way, how did you find me?"

"The death notices in the newspaper." He paused, then added, "Thank you for your hospitality. I will let myself out."

"Wait. One more thing. There's a rumor that Steve sold intelligence to the Russians. Did your brother ever say anything—" She couldn't finish the sentence.

The Georgian exhaled. "You know Steve's soul best. Was he capable of such betrayal?" Then he turned and walked down the hall.

Maggie absorbed the question. The click of the front door shook her back into the moment. She grabbed a pen and notepad from a drawer and hastily wrote down the two names she'd learned. Then she ran to the living room window in time to see a silver car with diplomatic plates drive away.

CHAPTER FIFTEEN

Maggie powered on the computer in the upstairs office and opened her AOL account. There were six new emails, the most recent from the bridal shop. A reminder for her upcoming gown fitting. The weight of a thousand what-ifs pressed down on her chest. She inhaled deeply and clicked over to the web browser.

"Tatiana Ashkhanadze."

No relevant results.

"Josef Ashkhanadze."

The hits were all in Russian. She squinted and leaned closer, searching for an obituary. There it was, the third link on the second page. Josef Ashkhanadze, aged 44, resident of Tbilisi. No details about how or where he died. Survived by his brother Tamaz, his mother, Tatiana Ruslanova Ashkhanadze, and his maternal grandmother, Yelena Bulatova Takayeva.

"Takayeva," Maggie breathed. Their mother's maiden name was Takayev. Josef Ashkhanadze and Josef Takayev were one and the same person. She rocked back in the office chair. According to Tamaz, his brother had infiltrated a Chechen terror cell. If true, then the NSA cable reflected only half the story. Yes, Takayev had ties to radicals in Georgia, but not for nefarious reasons. He'd actually been working for the CIA.

She shut off the computer and headed for the staircase. Halfway down it hit her like a wave. She clutched the railing to keep from stumbling. What if Takayev's fascination with radical Chechens had morphed into an affinity for them? What if he'd been turned and was actually working for them? She lowered herself onto a step and wrapped her arms around her knees. What if Takayev had acted as a suicide bomber that day at the café?

She remained seated on the stairs for a few minutes. *Am I overreacting?* There was no evidence that Takayev was a radical. And if she focused on him as the only suspect, she might miss something important. Maggie kneaded her fingers into the knots forming in her neck. A caffeine fix was in order if she wanted to keep sharp.

Downstairs, a cup of tea in hand, she tried to put aside the questions about Takayev. At least for the moment. Over on the couch, she flipped through a jumbled pile of articles she'd clipped from *The Washington Post* over the past several months. She'd meant to go through them and bring the relevant ones to work for her files, but here they sat, still unread and unorganized. A rerun of a military crime drama droned from the TV. If only life imitated art;

all her problems would be solved in an hour. She muted the show, set the clippings aside, and smoothed open the note she'd smuggled from the office vault. She probably should've shredded it along with the Presidential Finding, but here it was, so she might as well try to make sense of things. On October 28th, Richard Carvelli had requested a CIA briefing on Chechen involvement in Russian arms smuggling.

She rifled through the newspaper articles. There. November 1st. Russian President Vladimir Putin claimed that the CIA was arming Chechen rebels. The accusation was absurd on its face. The exact opposite of the truth. The truth that Richard Carvelli had learned from his recent intelligence briefing. But the reader wouldn't know that because five paragraphs into the article, the congressman was quoted as having "grave concerns" over the CIA's alleged interference in Russia's sphere of influence.

"Grave concerns, my ass," Maggie muttered. She folded up the note, shoved it under the couch cushion, and stuffed the newspaper clippings into a file folder that she slid under the coffee table. Maybe it was time for a sanity check.

CHAPTER SIXTEEN

Warner accelerated up Dolley Madison Boulevard. A Dobie Gray song played on the local pop radio station, filling the cabin with sweet guitar and mellow tones. He sang along about games, strains and shames for a minute before switching over to the news station to catch the headlines.

"President Bush indicated Sunday that he opposes extending marriage rights to homosexuals," a radio announcer intoned, "saying he believes marriage is between a man and a woman."

Warner turned right onto his street and eased the gold BMW up the tree-lined driveway. "Bush said it is 'important for society to welcome each individual' but administration lawyers are looking for some way to legally limit marriage to hetero—" The radio cut out with the engine. He pushed the garage door opener that was hooked on the visor and locked the car. The automatic headlights stayed on for a minute, illuminating his way.

"Damn mailman," he muttered as he bent over to pick up a large manila envelope that was leaning against the house. Inside, he dropped his briefcase at the entrance to the den and proceeded to the kitchen, depositing the envelope on the granite island next to the six-burner stove. With its oversized stainless steel appliances, soaring ceilings, and more cabinets than a small army could fill, the kitchen was the perfect space for entertaining Washington's cocktail party circuit. Shannon, his much younger wife—soon-to-be ex-wife—would've loved it. But this wasn't her house, and if he had his way, she would never step foot inside, not after she'd threatened to press for sole custody of the kids. Yes, he worked very long hours. He had to. She didn't seem to understand how important his job was, especially in the wake of 9/11. He'd tried explaining that there were terrorists coming for this country, and that they wouldn't hesitate to take out Shannon and the girls if they had the chance. His warnings and pleas had fallen on deaf ears. She'd filed for divorce back in early spring, citing his prolonged absences and dark moods. "To hell with her," he muttered. But he worried about the girls. He worried she'd win in court and he wouldn't be able to see them nearly enough.

He rummaged through the freezer for a microwave dinner. "Not again," he decided. Take-out sounded like a better alternative, but the only menu he had on hand was from a chain pizza place. He sighed and surveyed the kitchen, catching sight of the manila envelope. There was no return address. In fact, there was no postage on it. *That's strange.* He squatted to bring himself to eye-level with the envelope. It was flat and thin. No obvious bulges. He straightened. Maybe Shannon had dropped off some documents? Maybe, but she preferred to send correspondence through the lawyers or by certified mail. From under the sink he grabbed a pair of rubber cleaning gloves and slipped them on. Carefully, he slid a finger under the flap and opened the clasp. Peering inside, he saw nothing alarming.

He tipped the envelope. Several 3x5 photos spilled out onto the countertop. Warner snatched the top one. There he was in the grainy image, a shot of him lying in his bed in just a bath towel with a naked blond man beside him. His insides seized. It was the man from the moving crew. The one who'd stayed behind for a drink. What was his name? Ted? No, Ed.

The second photo was even worse. Warner, naked now, had his hands wrapped around the man's midsection. He stumbled away, slamming his back into the refrigerator handle. *No. This isn't happening.*

A single sheet of paper, folded in thirds, peeked out from under the photographs. With a shaking hand, Warner reached for it. He opened the paper, smoothing it on the countertop before focusing on the typewritten words.

You have one week to deliver all the intelligence the CIA has on:
1. The Russian mafia
2. Weapons smuggling from Russia

We will contact you before the week is up with delivery instructions. Remember, we will not be patient. If you don't comply, we will deliver copies of these photos to the Director of Central Intelligence, The Washington Post, and your wife.

Warner dropped the note as if it singed his fingers. Pacing the length of the kitchen, he tried to calm his breathing, to think clearly. Moving day had been a picture-perfect but bittersweet late spring day. He was finally free of his angry, demanding wife, but as he left their home for the final time, he'd sensed a chasm opening between him and their six-year-old twin daughters. Given the demands of his job, he knew he'd have to fight for joint custody. If he didn't get it, he'd never again be part of their daily routines, the small events, the shared moments that define lives. If he were lucky, he'd be part of their highlight reels. The dance recitals, the school ceremonies, every other holiday.

After they'd carried all the furniture into his new house, the moving crew had relaxed over pizza and beer before departing. But not the one young man named Ed. They'd toasted his new found freedom. Talked. Had a few more drinks. Laughed. About what, he couldn't remember. It got fuzzy from there. In fact, he had no recollection of Ed in his bedroom. Of that, he was certain. All he remembered was talking to the younger man about the collapse of his marriage. About feeling he had failed to stop the 9/11 attacks. About feeling like nothing mattered anymore. He remembered Ed leading him into the house, his hand on Warner's lower back. Then Ed's arms around him helping him up the stairs. He'd been so alone these last few years. He didn't want to feel that way anymore.

The next thing Warner remembered was waking up in the middle of the night alone in his bed. A pounding headache. Blurred vision. An empty bottle of his best Scotch on the floor in front of the dresser. He'd searched the house for Ed, and then checked his valuables. To his great relief, his belongings were intact, and even more importantly, Ed was nowhere to be found. And never heard from again.

Until now. Until *this*. This would ruin everything. His wife. Oh, would she ever have a field day. A husband cheating with a *man*? A much younger man? A high-ranking government official, entrusted with the nation's most classified information, keeping such a dark secret? *Good Lord.* He'd be lucky to get supervised visits with the kids if these photos surfaced. What would he tell the girls? Would she tell them their daddy is gay? His heart thudded erratically.

He scratched at his cheeks. If the CIA found out, it would be equally disastrous in its own way. *Dammit all.* Even if he ran to the Director today to tell him he was being blackmailed, he'd get fired. Every agency employee knows that hiding secrets makes them a blackmail target, a security risk. If only he'd reported the incident immediately. But how could he have? He didn't really remember what had happened. It was as if hours had been erased from his memory. The morning after, all alone in his cavernous new house, he'd decided it was best to forget about that night. It was a one-time thing. A mistake. Something that would never happen again. Besides that, the country had just gone to war in Iraq. The hunt was on for bin Laden and weapons of mass destruction. The Agency needed him.

Things suddenly felt out of control. An unfamiliar and uncomfortable sensation bubbled up from his stomach. Warner Thompson wasn't one for panic. He was the calmest, coolest person at the CIA. He grabbed the note from the counter.

The Russian mafia? Weapons trafficking? Who would blackmail him? And why? It had to be someone who needed to understand what the CIA knew about the Russian mafia and the illicit weapons trade. He flipped through the photographs again, trying to analyze them as if he weren't the subject. The angles were odd. Looked like Ed had taken the photos, maybe holding a camera above them? But why?

Warner wheezed, the force of the realization slamming him in the chest. He'd been set up. "Russian intelligence," he breathed. It had to be. The Russians were notorious for setting honey traps, dangling attractive young women in front of married American intelligence officers who, if they gave in to temptation, would soon learn the price. In order to keep their infidelity a secret, the targeted American would have to do the KGB's bidding. When Warner was stationed in Eastern Europe, exotic, willowy Slavic women approached him on several occasions. He rather enjoyed their attention but knew exactly what they were trying to do. The last thing he had expected was a male honey trap. Because nobody *knew*. He'd never acted on his feelings. Not seriously, anyway. There'd been that one kiss. A drunken fluke. Many years ago. Long before he'd been married. And the guy died in a car accident only a few months later. Besides, anyone who knew Warner back then knew his many exploits with women. And he most certainly enjoyed female company, even if his eye occasionally wandered to an attractive man.

Warner lowered himself onto a chair at the kitchen table. This had foreign intelligence operation written all over it, but something was off. Why would Russian intelligence care about the CIA's insight into the Russian mafia? They had their own sources of information, their own agents in place. And to dangle Ed in front of him? There was no possible way Russian intelligence could know he might take the bait. His occasional interest was safely tucked away deeply in the closet. No. Something was definitely off. The pieces didn't quite fit.

Who would want to know what the CIA knows about the Russian mafia, he wondered, thrumming his fingers on the table. He straightened. It wouldn't be Russian intelligence. It would be the mafia itself. Because if they were up to something nefarious—and weren't they always—they would want to make sure the CIA didn't catch wind of it and inform the Russian government. But again, how could the Russian mafia, or anyone for that matter, know the temptation he sometimes felt? None of this made any sense.

Warner forgot about ordering food and headed for the den where, with unsteady hands, he filled his favorite Glencairn glass with enough Blanton's to take off the edge. After emptying half of it, his thoughts slowed. He sat on the edge of the desk and ran through the events of the last several days. Steve and his Chechen asset, Takayev, had been murdered. Maggie had come into possession of an NSA cable indicating that Chechen terrorists were trying to buy nuclear materials from the Russian mafia and that a U.S. official was selling intelligence to Russians. And now, someone was blackmailing him into passing on intelligence on the Russian mafia and weapons smuggling. A film of sweat broke out above his lips. This tangled mess was getting too close for comfort.

Three events. Separate. But related. They had to be. There were no coincidences in the intelligence business.

Downing the rest of the bourbon, he closed his eyes. The dots between these events were there, but they weren't connected yet. Too many were missing. He would find them. What other choice did he have?

He refilled the glass, but before he could take his first sip, the phone rang.

"Sanity check? Tonight?" He took a swig. "How about tomorrow for lunch? It's Veteran's Day . . . I'll pick up some food . . . Yeah. Not a problem . . . Uh huh . . . See you then."

The last thing he wanted to do was keep Maggie company. Not with this . . . threat hanging over his head. But he'd promised himself he would take care of her now that Steve was gone. He moaned. This was adding up to the worst week of his life. And it was only Monday.

CHAPTER SEVENTEEN

Maggie brushed crumbs dotting the countertop into the sink full of dishes. A knock on the door interrupted her halfhearted attempt at housekeeping. She hurried across the floor, her slippers clearing a path through fallen petals from the funeral flowers.

"Coming!" She hadn't bothered to change from sweats into something more presentable.

Her outfit wasn't up for company, but she needed to bounce some things off Warner's spymaster brain.

"We have to stop meeting like this," she said without a smile through the opened door.

Warner raised a plastic grocery bag. "Lamb kebobs. Hot from the oven, or whatever they cook them in." He stepped in the foyer, giving her a quick once over. "You look . . . comfortable."

She turned without a word. Warner followed her into the kitchen. If he noticed the wine glass still in the sink from Saturday night, he didn't say anything.

"So, how's everything?" Warner pulled the food cartons out of the bag.

The tangy scent of yogurt sauce flooded her senses. Taverna was nothing more than a hole in the wall, but it was her favorite restaurant. She and Steve used to go there at least once a week. She wondered how Warner knew. "I don't know. I'm numb."

Warner scooped some rice onto paper plates. "It's going to take some time."

"That's what they say." She stared directly into his eyes. "Any updates on the investigation?"

"No, nothing new yet."

His eyes. Something behind his eyes. What was it?

They sat.

Maggie pulled the lamb and vegetables off the skewer. The meat practically melted off. She took a bite and closed her eyes.

"Good, isn't it?" Warner said between mouthfuls.

"That's putting it mildly. I don't think I've ever had a bad meal there." Something made her feel on edge. Warner seemed distant, like he didn't want to be there. Was her grief too much to handle? "I've been thinking," she said, giving in to her need to feel him out. Was what she'd seen in his eyes real or imagined?

He tilted his head, "'bout what?"

"How well do you really know Richard Carvelli?"

He wiped his mouth with a napkin.

"We were in the same fraternity at Yale, but I wouldn't exactly call us friends. These days, just colleagues of a sort, occasional adversaries on certain intelligence matters. I don't particularly like him, but he can be a useful political ally once in a while."

"Was he a pompous jerk in college?" She sipped her diet soda.

"Come to think of it, he really wasn't. In fact, he ran a couple of campus fundraisers for inner city charities. Raised a lot of money, if I recall." He spooned more rice onto his plate. "It seemed to be a true passion for him. Probably because of his background."

"His background?" Maggie was on the right track. She could sense momentum building for her final questions.

"Most of us in the fraternity came from money. Carvelli didn't. It was something he was embarrassed about, I think." Warner paused for another mouthful. "Truth is, a few of the guys let it be known they didn't want to associate with him, but they were the exception. Most of us didn't care where he came from. Even so, I don't think he ever felt like he measured up. It was like he couldn't get past his past, if you know what I mean."

Maggie almost nodded in sympathy. How unnerving to have something in common with that man. Her father had destroyed her capacity to trust anyone. Friendships and relationships fell to the wayside because she assumed everyone would betray her eventually. She realized why, but she couldn't get past it. Then came Steve. He'd been the only one able to break through the wall around her heart.

"So why the sudden interest in Carvelli's frat boy days?"

She swallowed. "I'm just trying to figure him out. I've been thinking about that counterintelligence problem. Haven't you?"

Warner blinked slowly before answering. "Where are you going with this?"

Steve had been good at giving non-answer answers, too. Maggie could see that he'd learned from the master. "Here's my theory. I have nothing to base it on except for the fact that Carvelli is very engaged in matters relating to Russia and weapons proliferation. He attends all the briefings and hearings and has requested what seems like a disproportionate number of personal briefings on these subjects. He knows more about these issues than any other congressman I know." There. She'd laid her cards on the table, just not all of them.

"Carvelli?" Warner abandoned his fork. His jaw twitched slightly to the left side every few seconds. "You think he's what? A spy?"

"You told me that a U.S. official is selling intelligence to the Russians. And the NSA cable seems to confirm that." Maggie raised her eyebrows. "Maybe it's Carvelli."

Warner placed his fork on the table. "Of all the people in Washington, D.C. . . . . Richard Carvelli? I dunno, Maggie. That's a little farfetched."

Her face fell.

"I mean, yeah, he likes to portray himself as a foreign policy whiz. It gets him on Sunday news shows from time to time. Just wait until he's a senator. His mug will be all over TV."

"Wait, what? He's running for the Senate?"

"I can see it. His ego's getting too big for the House. The Senate's the next logical step. Then maybe on to the big house."

"The White House? You've got to be kidding. God help us all," she choked. "Honestly, I think I'd move to Canada—" She cut herself off. He'd done it again—changed the subject. She steered the conversation back. "So, you really think I'm off base on Carvelli?"

Warner pursed his lips. "I think you're under a lot of stress. And I want to help you. Protect you. Which is why I think you should give me your copy of the NSA cable. You don't want to get caught with a document you shouldn't have."

"Get caught? By who?" Her face flushed. "What, are you going to report me?"

"You know you shouldn't have it."

"Oh, right, and I'm sure you've never bent the rules." She scoffed. "Mr. American hero, Warner Thompson, here to save the day."

A muscle in his neck twitched. "It would be in your best interest to give me your copy of the cable."

"My best interest?" She sat back in the chair and folded her arms. "Not until you tell me what you really know about what happened in Tbilisi."

Eyes narrowed, he pushed the chair back from the table and stood, filling the breakfast nook with his height and authority. "You already know everything I can tell you."

"Look, Warner, I know all about the FBI taking over this investigation. They're trying to shut you out, aren't they?"

He flushed. "The FBI will not run this investigation."

"But as of right now, they're running it, aren't they?"

"I will get to the bottom of Steve's murder if I have to do it myself."

She shoved her plate away. "Then why won't you tell me what's going on? You're hiding something, I just know it."

He jabbed a finger in her direction. "I'm not the one hiding something."

"What's that supposed to mean?" Her temper began to flare. This was always a dangerous moment for her, the intersection between emotion and control.

"Maggie, give me the cable. I won't ask who gave it to you. Stop this now before you get in serious trouble."

"I don't have it." They both knew she was lying.

Warner leaned forward, knuckles resting on the table. "Clearly, you don't understand the consequences. If there's even one hiccup in this investigation, you may never find out what happened." His voice rose and the lines in his forehead deepened. "Is that what you want? Because if you screw up, the most the Agency will give you is the unclassified story. And that may be total bullshit."

His eyes bore into hers, but she'd be damned if she surrendered the only piece of the puzzle she had.

He slammed his fist into the table. "Hand it over!"

"What is wrong with you?" She jumped up from the chair, spilling the remaining rice all over the floor. "You know what," she fumed, "I don't think you're even investigating his murder. No, I smell a cover up. So much for your loyalty to Steve. The little brother you never had, my ass."

"Don't you dare question my loyalty!" he hissed, taking a step toward her.

Maggie retreated until her back bumped into the refrigerator.

"Just give me the damned cable!"

"Get out. GET OUT!" she screeched. "You son of a bitch. Get out of my house. Now!"

His cell phone rang. He ignored it, but it stopped his advance. "Think long and hard about what I said." Warner turned and left without another word.

Maggie worked to control her breathing. What the hell had just happened? It was like a switch had flipped inside him. *No*, she decided. She absolutely wasn't going to sit around and wait for answers. If she was ever going to learn who killed Steve, she'd have to figure it out herself. If Steve was dirty, she'd be the first to find out and the only one to ever know. But if Steve was clean, she'd take down everyone trying to smear him.

Even Warner.

CHAPTER EIGHTEEN

O n Thursday morning, Maggie exited a taxi outside her
hotel in Tbilisi, the capital of the Republic of Georgia.
Located along the city's main boulevard, the nearly
century-old hotel had recently been restored to its pre-Soviet
glory. She briefly took in the lavish stone façade and large columns
framing the main entrance. Inside, surrounded by marble pillars
and a soaring, ornate ceiling, she frowned at the sight of herself
in the large mirror running the length of the side wall. Fatigue
was written all over her pale face after two marathon layovers at
European airports. Her outfit—stretch pants and an oversized
sweater—made her appear even more world weary. Topping off

the look, she'd covered her red curls under a plain, black headscarf in an attempt to blend in with both traditional *babushkas* and local Muslim women who no longer camouflaged their religion under Soviet garb.

Her room was as modern and clean as any in a western hotel. It took all her strength not to collapse on the bed. Sleep would have to wait. Inside the white-tiled bathroom, she freshened up the best she could and slid a lycra travel pouch around her waist. Steve had purchased it for their honeymoon travels across Europe. Trying not to dwell on the fact that that trip would never happen, she stashed her passport, a credit card, a scrap of paper covered in notes, and a pile of American and Georgian currency inside. She practiced slipping a hand under her shirt and opening the pouch zipper in one, smooth move. So long as she chose a quiet moment, it wouldn't be noticed, not even in a crowd. A final glance in the bathroom mirror confirmed that the tight-fitting pouch was invisible under the outdated blue blouse she paired with her oldest jeans. Blending in, looking less western was the goal. The less attention she drew, the better.

Outside, another taxi took her from the hotel to the apartment building on Moskovskiy Prospect where Steve had lived. Maggie couldn't be sure, but she seemed to recall him mentioning that all CIA station personnel lived in the same building, both for convenience and security. From the sidewalk across the street, as if trying to keep a respectful distance, she stared at the old building, absorbing every detail in its chipped façade. Dull, sand-colored concrete panels, stacked vertically one atop the other, reached skyward for six or seven stories. Metal-framed horizontal sliding windows marked each floor in drab symmetry. The overall effect was melancholic. She tried to picture Steve coming out the door, a cautious bounce in his step, alert eyes scanning the neighborhood. Across the street, people hurried in and out of a small coffee shop where Steve probably grabbed a cup to warm him for the brisk walk to the embassy. Did any of the regulars there notice that he hadn't been in for over a week?

Maggie straightened her shoulders and adjusted her headscarf as she crossed the road. Georgian police and security forces seemed to be on every corner, their eyes nervously scanning for protestors who'd been agitating to overthrow the government. The protestors had a point. Based on a CIA report she'd read recently, it seemed that Georgia's president, the former Soviet foreign minister until that country collapsed twelve years earlier, had rigged parliamentary elections. Knowing Steve, he would've been in the thick of the demonstrations, talking to protestors, gathering as much information as he could.

She tugged open the glass door to the apartment building. Inside, a stooped old babushka was mopping the lobby floor. "*Izvenitiye, menya,*" Maggie said softly, not wanting to startle the woman, whose dark eyes squinted back at her through deep wrinkles. "*Vyie znaete etovo cheloveka?*" Maggie offered a photo of Steve, hoping the woman would say she recognized him.

The woman took the snapshot in her gnarled hand. "*Da, krasivie amerikanets.*" She handed the picture back and resumed mopping, splattering the murky water on Maggie's shoes.

The handsome American. She tried to put together the Russian words rattling around in her brain. She wanted to ask if the woman had noticed unusual visitors or anything else out of the ordinary, but too little practice over too many years had left her without the necessary words. In the Soviet days, this woman would've reported encounters with a foreigner to the KGB, not out of a sense of patriotism, but out of fear. Maggie doubted this was the case now. All the same, she decided not to ask too many questions. The last thing she needed was Russian intelligence, or whoever the hell it was who ran things here, following her around. And it probably would be the Russians, she thought. They were always meddling in their neighbor's business, fomenting separatist movements even while they spilled Russian blood in an attempt to quash separatist sentiment within their own borders. With a final glance back at the disinterested babushka, she slipped out the exit.

The street map she'd picked up at the hotel showed Antonelli Street was not far away. Eight minutes later, she stood eyeing the U.S. Embassy from her vantage point across the street. The CIA station—that's where Steve had worked—was housed in the attic. The building itself was exactly how she'd pictured it, as stately as a nineteenth-century palace.

The American flag she was used to seeing raised in front of gray, boxy, concrete government buildings looked incongruous before the sweeping balconies and the grand edifice. And there was something else. The embassy was set right against the street, offering those inside no protection from a terrorist bomb. *It's only a matter of time.* She understood why the State Department had snatched up the first available properties in the former Soviet republics at the end of the Cold War. But in its haste to establish a presence amidst former enemies, the government had set up its civil servants for possible catastrophe.

Maggie breathed in the cold morning air to shake off images of recent embassy bombings and darted across the street, avoiding both pedestrians and a speeding car. She climbed the stairs, surprised there was no Marine Security Guard contingent outside, ready to fend off anyone with evil intent. At the door, a lone Georgian militiaman stood, a gun holstered safely at his side. Inside, she found herself staring at a bulletproof glass pane that shielded an efficient looking, middle-aged Georgian woman. She was an FSN—a foreign service national—one of thousands hired by the U.S. government to help run its embassies and consulates around the world.

The woman peered at her through the glass. "Yes, hi, um, do you," Maggie paused, wondering if the woman spoke English. *Of course she does,* she scolded herself. "I have an appointment."

"With whom?" the woman asked, leaning toward a microphone.

"With . . ." She didn't know Peter's CIA cover name. She couldn't very well blurt out his real name and blow his cover. Then again, maybe Belekov was his cover name? She had no way of knowing. Maggie hadn't thought this far ahead. *Now what?* "I can't believe this. I've forgotten his name. I'm so embarrassed."

The woman stared back, expressionless.

"A tall, blond gentleman."

"His name?"

This was going nowhere fast. *Some spy you'd make.* "I apologize. My appointment is actually tomorrow. I'll come back then."

She turned and walked back outside. The cold morning air nipped at her cheeks. How was she going to find Peter? She could stake out the embassy, but that probably wouldn't go over well with security. She could chat with the apartment babushka to confirm that Peter lived there, too, but even if he did, she didn't want to wait for him all day.

Maggie turned up her coat collar and headed down Antonelli Street. Two blocks up, she spotted a bus terminal. She hurried over to the adjacent payphone and grabbed the receiver. With her free hand, she fumbled in the travel pouch around her waist for odd-sized *tetri* coins and a scrap of paper containing Steve's phone number at the CIA station. Maggie deposited five coins, punched in the phone number, and hoped the call would go through. It took three tries, each requiring more money, before she heard a faint ringing on the other end.

"Hello," an American-sounding voice said.

"Hi, is Steve there?"

There was a long pause on the other end. Then, "This is Steve."

Maggie's breath caught into her throat. If only it were. She swallowed. "Hi, Steve. I hope you can help me. I'm actually looking for one of Steve's friends. He's tall, blond hair. Early thirties."

"Who is this?" the man asked, his voice flooded with suspicion.

"Maggie," she gambled, hoping it was Peter on the other end, not the Station Chief.

"Maggie?" The voice came as a hoarse whisper.

"Yes. Is this Steve's friend?"

"How are you?" His voice softened.

She smiled to herself. *Bingo.* "I'm all right. Actually, I'm just a few blocks away."

"What?" Peter sounded shocked.

"I need to talk to you." She was careful to avoid saying his name over the open line in case anyone was listening.

"Why didn't you call me first?"

"I didn't have time before I left." That was true, in part. She hadn't planned anything about this trip, except for what hotel she'd stay in the first night. She'd always been a list person, thinking through every detail and possible eventuality before she made a move. But all the planning she'd done for her life with Steve had been a waste. So now she was operating on impulse. That and instinct. "Come meet me."

"I can't."

Maggie's fatigue fueled sudden irritation. "Well, damn it, can you squeeze me in for dinner?" She hadn't traveled thousands of miles to be put off by him.

Peter sounded taken aback by her tone. "Yes, of course. Dinner at 6:00? I can pick you up. What hotel?"

"I'd rather not say over the phone."

"Understood. But how will I find you if you won't tell me."

"I'll find you."

"Really?" He exhaled loudly. "How?"

"You'll see." Some spy he was. It didn't occur to him that she knew where CIA employees lived?

"If you say so. You know, you shouldn't be here."

"Why not?"

"There's nothing new."

"Please, spare me the party line. I know that you know more."

"What?"

"The note," she replied with an edge in her voice. "The one in my purse."

He cleared his throat. "I have to go."

"Don't hang up on me," Maggie shouted into the receiver.

"The note was a mistake. So just calm down, alright?"

She imagined Peter's impossibly blue eyes turning from Caribbean blue to dark North Atlantic ice. She struggled to rein herself in, but a potent mixture of fatigue, grief, and anger propelled her to push further. "A mistake? Who told you to say that? The big boss?"

"As a matter of fact, he—" Peter stopped himself. His tone softened too quickly. "Let me rearrange some things and I'll come meet you now."

"No."

She needed more information first. Information superiority—the underpinning of all recent U.S. military victories—was vital to her maintaining an edge over Warner, Peter, and anyone else who tried to hide the truth. Besides, given the turn in this conversation, it wasn't at all clear whether she could trust Peter.

"Ten minutes, I can be there in ten minutes," he pleaded.

This was not the reaction she'd expected from a seasoned case officer. "I'll see you tonight." She dropped the receiver back in its cradle.

Maggie strode down the sidewalk away from the bus terminal, not sure where she was headed. She just needed to walk. What had she been thinking, showing up here, unannounced, unprepared, barely a week since an American CIA operative had been killed? Peter had no choice but to be evasive over an open phone line. Nonetheless, something about the conversation had been strange. Peter's clipped sentences, his initial refusal to meet with her, then his sudden change in tone and urgent need to see her had triggered an internal alarm. She didn't know him very well, but her gut dictated that she avoid him; the rest of her obeyed.

She continued on for several blocks, scarcely taking in the bustle of the ancient city, stopping long enough to pull the scrap of paper from the concealed pouch. Her hand trembled as she unfolded it again. Dima's restaurant, the place where Steve had been murdered, was on Perovskaya Street. She needed to see it for herself.

The taxi ride there was considerably less harrowing than her ride from the airport, but she noted with dismay that no one here seemed to obey traffic lights. *Hail Mary, full of grace.* She gripped the door handle tightly, as if that would protect her from an oncoming car. The taxi veered suddenly, coming to a screeching halt outside a small, dark café nestled amidst a long row of bars and clubs. Across the street stood two large casinos adorned with flashing neon signs. They looked as out of place as she felt.

"Dima," the driver said.

She paid him, opened the door and emerged from the car. Her eyes were drawn to the right of the building, where two men were shoveling shards of glass from a large pile into a dumpster. Twisted metal bars were stacked neatly to the right, like a pile of kindling gathered for a campfire. Why was the rubble still here, more than a week after the bombing? Maybe the police had needed time to sift through the wreckage for evidence. Or maybe the cleanup wasn't a priority. The dead were already dead. The mess would keep.

Maggie tilted her head back and inhaled deeply. Overhead beams that must have supported the atrium's glass ceiling cast linear shadows on the blood-stained concrete floor below. An oversized oval-shaped blot lay to the left. Smaller stains formed concentric circles around the larger one, finally fading into pinpricks of brown. This had to be it, the spot where Steve bled out. Her heart thudded slowly, heavily, as if time were grinding to a halt. Maggie stepped closer to the space where, a little over a week ago, diners chatted over coffee while watching the city pass by outside. Closing her eyes, she could almost hear the sound of patrons laughing, sharing stories and secrets.

Then came the concussive blast, the sucking of oxygen inward toward the explosion. Shattering glass. Everyone screaming. The dying moaning in agony. Steve, calling for help, calling for her until he could speak no more. She knelt at the spot and placed her hand on the cold, stained concrete.

The workmen glanced at her, then got back to work. The glass made a tinkling sound as it fell, like champagne flutes shattering in slow motion. They'd rebuild, she realized. A new, gleaming atrium. Eventually, no one would remember what happened here. And another piece of Steve would be erased from the world.

People jostled past, their heads down against the cold. She ignored them, lost in the painful realization that this was the place where Steve had taken his last breath.

Maggie squeezed her eyes shut, trying to picture him the way she remembered him instead of the way she imagined his last moments. It was impossible.

A bus hissed to a stop, pulling her from her thoughts. To the left stood the original part of Dima's café. The exterior cement block wall showed no signs of trauma from the blast, save for a gutter on the far eave that dangled precariously. After a final glance at the piles of metal and glass, Maggie walked into the restaurant with uncertainty as her escort.

Her eyes adjusted to the dim light inside the empty cafe. It was too early for lunch and even for those who began their day with a drink. She turned in a slow pirouette, trying to imagine the place when it was full of life.

The stale smell of cigarettes and a tired odor of booze permeated every corner. Several round wooden tables for four were scattered along the back wall. The bar dominated the front of the restaurant, extending the length of the room. Mismatched stools stood empty, waiting to be pulled into service. She slid onto the end stool, imagining Steve ordering a beer, probably a local brew. Maybe a band played over in the far corner at night. They wouldn't have known any of the songs, but if they'd come here together, they would've danced.

The slam of a door behind her startled her to her feet. A dark-haired man dressed in even darker clothes stood in the middle of the room. His ample mustache twitched, his eyebrows rose in curiosity.

"*Dobre dehn,*" Maggie offered. She couldn't remember how to say "good morning," so "good day" had to suffice.

"*Dobre utro,*" he replied.

Yes, good morning! "*Vyie govoritye po-angliskiy?*" She crossed her fingers, hoping his answer would be "yes."

"A little English," he nodded, approaching her.

"Are you the owner?" *What do they call them here?*

"My name is Ergan. Who are you?"

"Just a tourist. Are you the proprietor?"

"Proprietor, no. But I work, ahh," he searched for words, "I am *dva.*" He held up two fingers, which she took to mean that he was the manager, perhaps.

"I've heard good things about this restaurant."

He smiled thinly, looking uncertain. "*Khoroshaya yeda?*"

"Yes, very good food."

"Thank you."

"A friend dined here just a week ago." She gestured toward the door. "What happened outside? There's glass everywhere."

His shoulders sagged. "You didn't hear the news?"

Maggie glanced around the room, seeking the courage to proceed. This was risky. Steve would be angrier than hell that she'd put herself in potential danger, but he'd also be cheering her on. Squaring her shoulders, she offered him the snapshot of Steve. "Actually, I did hear. I'm looking for information on what happened to my friend. How he died." The words spilled from her mouth. "Did you see him here?"

Color vanished from Ergan's face.

He ran to the entrance and looked around outside as if he expected an invading army. He returned to his spot before her, anger flashing from his eyes. "What you want?" he hissed.

Maggie grabbed his right forearm. "Do you know who set off the bomb? What have the police said?"

"I don't know anything." His left hand gestured wildly toward the spot where the bomb had detonated. "There's been enough trouble here."

"But, this is my husband," she waved the photograph. "*Moy muzh.*"

The edges melted from his expression. "I'm so very sorry, miss." The man glanced furtively over her shoulder. "But you must go." He turned and walked through the rear door next to the bar.

She stood abandoned, but only for a moment. Hurrying after him, she pushed aside the swinging door that led into the kitchen. *Where'd he go?* "Hey, please. Just a few questions!" Silence. Maggie swallowed her fear. "Did you know Steve?" Nothing. "Or Takayev?"

A sudden clattering of dishes disrupted the quiet. Maggie whirled around in time to see Ergan lunge out from beside an enormous refrigerator. Seconds later, a dishrag stuffed in her mouth and another pulled tightly around her eyes, he shoved her into a closet. She struggled to her feet, knocking over a bucket of moldy smelling liquid in the process, and yanked the rag from her mouth and the blindfold off her head. Her heart beat wildly in the total dark, but she managed to keep full panic at bay. Anyone who would forget to tie her hands couldn't be all that intent on harming her.

She slid her hands along the wall, seeking a light switch or a doorknob. She found the knob. The handle turned, but the door was blocked by something. *Damn!* Maggie could hear her captor shouting in what sounded like a mixture of Russian and Georgian. The only word she could make out was "Takayev."

CHAPTER NINETEEN

Warner nearly ran down Priscilla as he burst into the office suite. Her silver hair was pulled back neatly in the customary bun. A peacock blue cashmere cardigan hung loosely over a white silk blouse. Priscilla always looked perfect, an attribute Warner could rely on no matter what crisis consumed the Agency. Or his life.

"There you are. I've been looking all over for you."

He scanned his mental calendar. "Don't tell me I'm late for a meeting?" It was only 7:00 a.m.

"There's an urgent call for you."

His stomach dropped. "What now?"

"He says he's your lawyer, but he wouldn't give me his name and he didn't sound—"

Did something happen to the girls? Warner dashed to Priscilla's desk and pushed the white blinking button. "Warner Thompson."

"I trust you received the envelope and your instructions." The voice was male, the accent British, but not authentic. The man was not a native English speaker.

Warner's knees went weak. "Who is this?"

"Don't be coy. Do as instructed and those photos will not see the light of day. The deadline is firm."

"How did you get this number?"

Priscilla materialized suddenly at his side, her forehead lined with concern. *Act normal.* "Yes, let's meet before you draw up the final divorce papers."

Priscilla drifted off to the file cabinet across the room. He lowered his voice and turned his back. "How did you get this number?" The CIA's switchboard operators were not supposed to let just anyone through to Priscilla.

"We have connections in very high places."

"I want to speak directly with Ivan Nikolayevich."

"Who—"

"Never mind, I'll call him directly."

Click.

The caller didn't seem to get the reference to the head of Russian intelligence. Everyone in the business called him Ivan Nikolayevich. If Russian intelligence was behind the blackmail, the caller would've laughed at his request, not hung up on him.

A cold sweat came over him. He knew how to deal with adversaries in the intelligence world. But if this was the mafia, it was entirely new territory. The question was, how to proceed?

Should he appear cooperative to buy time? Be defiant to force a confrontation? He slammed the phone down and stormed into his office. It would come to him. He'd worked his way out of far more dangerous situations during his days in the field. But he had nothing to go on here. And so much to lose.

Warner sat on the edge of his desk and tried to steady his hands. Not only did he have to figure out who killed Steve before Maggie self-destructed, he had to find out who was blackmailing him and destroy them before they destroyed him.

"Priscilla," Warner called from his office. "Get the New York station on the line?" He forced calm into his voice that he didn't feel. The deadline was firm—one week to produce highly classified intelligence, or they'd ruin him. Why the accelerated timeline?

Priscilla appeared at his office door. "Everything all right?"

"Just the ex. She can't stop tormenting me."

She grimaced. "She always struck me as a bit conniving."

"You've got that right . . . The New York station—what's the Chief's name up there, the new guy?"

"Baker. Grant Baker."

"Could you get him on the line?"

"I'll try, but it's early. Not everyone shows up to work before the sun rises."

"You do."

"Only because you do, Warner."

He pasted on a smile. "I'm heading to New York to rally the troops." From time to time, he'd kept information from her for security reasons. But he'd never outright lied to her. Until now.

"Today?" Priscilla frowned at the prospect of planning the necessary logistics on such short notice. "But the Director's plane is booked for days," she protested.

"Don't panic. I thought I'd take the express train up. I'll need a first-class ticket, and I'd like to leave as soon as possible." Given the state of airport security, the train trip might be faster than flying out of Reagan National. Not only that, the train probably was more secure than any commercial flight. Unless and until the TSA adopted El Al's security procedures, U.S. commercial flights would remain a serious terrorist target. If the American public knew what he knew . . .

Priscilla interrupted his thoughts. "But what about security? You can't just hop on the train without—"

"Yes, I can, Priscilla. Have one of our guys in New York meet me at Penn Station. I'll be fine by myself on the train. No need for the entire security detail to travel with me on a quick daytrip." He had to do this alone. There was no way his old KGB nemesis would meet with him if CIA security were tagging along. Besides, this trip had nothing to do with the New York office. He didn't want anyone to know who he was meeting and why.

CHAPTER TWENTY

At noon, Warner stepped off the train onto a platform in the bowels of Penn Station. Just outside of Baltimore, he'd phoned the New York station to tell them there'd been a slight change of plans—he'd be arriving at 3:00 instead of 12:00, and he'd get himself to the office.

Escaping the underground station, he stepped out into the crisp November air on 34th Street. Christmas decorations already hung everywhere, serving as holiday makeup to cover the scars borne by the city, still visible two years after the attacks.

He had nearly three free hours, more than enough time to catch up with the Russian. It'd been years since they'd last squared off, back when it was CIA versus KGB. Now, he needed help from his old adversary—information on the Russian mafia, the group most involved with supplying illicit weapons to the international black market. And if you wanted intel on the Russian mafia, there was no better source than Yuri, a man who had enriched himself after the Cold War as an advisor to sketchy Russian businessmen. Warner didn't care that he essentially ran one of the more notorious crime families in New York City. That was irrelevant to the situation at hand. Yuri had the insight he needed. He'd know if the Russian mafia was behind the blackmail photos. And he'd know something about the bombing, too. Warner hailed a cab.

Some forty-five minutes later, he arrived in Little Odessa in the Brighton Beach section of Brooklyn. He glanced at the storefronts around him, wishing for a moment he was actually in Moscow or St. Petersburg. The Soviets had been the Cold War enemy, of course, but since his college days, Warner had loved Russia's rich culture. Tolstoy, Dostoevsky, Chekov, and the list went on. The Bolshoi ballet. The Winter Palace. Endless streams of ice-cold vodka. He'd availed himself to as much of the culture as possible when he was stationed in Moscow in the 1980s. In retrospect, he wished he'd spent even more time on the finer things in Russia. But duty called, so most of his time had been spent recruiting and running Soviet spies, often to great success. His crowning achievement had been recruiting the senior KGB officer who'd provided critical details about the ascent of a young Mikhail Gorbachev to the apex of Soviet power in 1985. To this day, no Russians, not even Yuri, knew about the traitor in their midst.

Inside Café Arbat, he found Yuri smoking a cigarette at a dimly lit corner table. The sixty-year-old Russian gave him a suffocating bear hug, topped off with a sharp clap on the back.

"Warner! You haven't changed since Gorbachev begged the *putschists* to let him live." He laughed a low, deep laugh.

1991. "Has it been that long?" He sat. "How are you, you old commie bastard?"

"Life is good, Warner. You ever think I'd be living the high life in the belly of the capitalist beast?"

Warner shook his head. "It's a different world, you're right about that." His expression sharpened. "I lost a good case officer a couple of weeks back. He was one of the best." It was all he had to say. Yuri, a high-ranking KGB official until Boris Yeltsin fired him, would understand.

"In Georgia?"

Warner nodded.

"I heard."

"He was a talented kid. You would've liked him."

Yuri responded with a sorrowful shake of his bald head. "I'm very sorry, my friend."

"You know anything about it?"

He shifted in his seat. "There is a woman. Supposed to be the best assassin around."

"Russian?"

"No. *Nevesty Allaha.*"

"A Bride of Allah?" Warner scanned the restaurant and lowered his voice. "You think a Muslim woman killed him?"

"If nobody saw who planted the bomb, then yes, it might've been the elusive *Muslimah*. A Chechen. No one I know has ever seen her, but the rumor is that she's young, beautiful, and stealthy as hell."

A waitress interrupted, depositing a large serving of blini and vareniki and two tumblers of vodka in front of them.

Warner ignored the food, opting for the vodka. A female assassin hadn't been on his radar. He tucked the lead away for later. "I need a favor."

"From me?" The Russian threw up his hands in mock amazement. "What could an old man like me do for you?"

"The mafia, Yuri. I need information."

"You think I'm mafia?"

"Yuri—"

"I'm more of a . . . facilitator, you might say. I have people everywhere. Military. Government. Business. When they need information or want to buy or sell this or that, they come to me." He brushed his palms together. "I assure you, I am a legitimate businessman. Ask the FBI." He let out a belly laugh that shook the table.

Warner laughed back, but inside felt no humor. Here he was sitting with a known mafia boss, mocking the FBI's inability to infiltrate Russian crime gangs in America's largest city. "Look, I don't give a damn about how you make your money. What I need to know is between us."

"Warner—" Yuri blew a puff of smoke in his face.

"I'm serious. This is all off-line, my own investigation." He stared into Yuri's pale blue eyes. "This matters to me on a very personal level."

The Russian's eyebrows shot up. He leaned forward. "Go on."

"There's a U.S. official who may be feeding intelligence to Russia. Perhaps to the government, or the military. Or maybe to the mafia." Yuri's expression remained unchanged, so he continued. "And the rumor is the case officer we just lost might have been the leaker."

"What does this have to do with you?"

Warner scrambled. "This case officer was my protégé. I fast-tracked him up the ladder, gave him all the best overseas postings. He was one of the best." He stared at a point over Yuri's shoulder. "If it turns out this officer was dirty, my career is over."

"If you lose your job, we could always go into business together." Yuri's mouth curled into a smile. "Maybe call it 'Cold Warrior Consulting.'"

He was getting nowhere with this conversation. Time to cut to the chase. "Yuri, I may be in deep shit. I received a strange phone call . . ." It took everything in his power to keep his voice steady. ". . . demanding intelligence on the Russian mafia in exchange for clearing my case officer's name." He would never trust an old KGB man with the actual truth behind the blackmail attempt. Giving Yuri leverage over him would be foolish. Shading the truth, concealing his motivation, and probing for information was the much wiser course.

Yuri dragged on the remains of his cigarette stub. He extinguished it and shoved several blinis into his mouth before clasping immense hands across his enormous belly. "I have had no contact with any American traitor. As for my competitors . . . perhaps I've heard rumors to that effect." He paused to finish chewing. "The question, my friend, is whether I should share them with you."

"Look, I'd owe you one."

Yuri raised an eyebrow. "I'll remember that . . . I have a source. A Russian who grew up in Chechnya. Young fellow, definite mafia ties. And I suspect he personally knows the notorious female assassin. Maybe he knows about this U.S. official. Maybe—"

Warner's pulse quickened. "Maybe what?"

"Remember when the sides were clear? Russia versus America." Yuri shook his head. "Now we have people like this young man who believe in nothing. He's slippery. Doesn't care who he works for as long as it's the highest bidder."

"I need to talk to him."

"I will speak with him first." Yuri locked eyes with Warner. "He may be inconsequential. But perhaps he knows things about your potential traitor. Or about the people threatening you. In the meantime, you do realize what really should keep you up at night?"

"What?"

"The fact that the Islamists are plotting the next 9/11. Only a bigger, more devastating attack." He took a swig of vodka. "Perhaps using Russian nuclear materials."

Warner folded his hands together and scanned the surrounding tables. "Believe me, Yuri, I worry about that possibility all the time."

"This is more than a remote possibility, comrade. It's a certainty." He signaled the waitress for a refill, accepted a fresh tumbler and set it down. "In fact, I stopped a deal last year."

Warner lowered the glass from his lips. "Stopped how?"

"I eliminated the problem. Enough said, *da?*"

He studied the Russian through narrowed eyes. Yuri appeared to be telling the truth. "Who sells the nuclear material to the terrorists?" They locked eyes. "Is it the mafia?"

Yuri scowled and thumped a meaty fist on the table. "If there's one thing I would never do, it's allow the sale of nuclear technology to the jihadists. They will be the death of Russia."

Warner softened his tone. "What about one of your rivals? Would they sell nukes to terrorists?"

"Perhaps." Yuri leaned in. "I've heard that a few tactical weapons are missing. But this is not the time or place for such a discussion."

Warner's eyes widened. A trickle of sweat ran from under his arm.

"I hope the Agency is keeping an eye on the Chechens."

Warner cocked his head. "I thought your side had control of the Chechnya situation."

"We did when I was in charge. But not now." He lowered his voice. "There's a Chechen terrorist cell in Georgia. You'd better pray, my friend, that this group wasn't involved in your case officer's murder."

Warner took a final sip of vodka. "Because . . ."

"Because this cell has trained with al-Qaeda. I'm certain they are cooperating."

"In what way?"

The Russian exhaled. "In every way."

CHAPTER TWENTY-ONE

Maggie felt around in the darkness of the closet for something she could use as a weapon. Through the thin wall, she could hear Ergan on the phone, shouting about Takayev. The mere mention of Steve's asset's name had hit a dangerous and unexpected nerve.

Her fingers touched something cool and smooth on the wall. *A window? Not likely. A mirror? Maybe.* Maggie slid her hand down the slick surface until it met with a knob and after that, a cold, hollowed-out bowl. She turned the knob, releasing pent-up water with an urgent gush. She shuffled away from the door to the back of the closet where she'd fallen into cleaning supplies just minutes before. Grabbing the splintered wooden handle of a mop, she moved back to the mirror. Under the circumstances, she was willing to trade seven years of bad luck to save her life.

With a swift thrust of the mop handle, the mirror shattered. She froze. There was no noise from outside the closet; the shouting had ended.

Stepping toward the sink, her shoes crunching on broken glass like boots on crisp snow, she reached gingerly for the basin where she found a long sliver. She cried out as one of the jagged edges bit into her index finger. The glass fell to the floor with a clink. Maggie stuck her finger in her mouth. The metallic taste of her own blood told her she was bleeding a bit too generously. She found the faucet without further injury and ran the cold water over her hand, biting down on her lip to absorb the sting. She felt a large slit running across the tip of her finger. *It's okay*, she assured herself, letting the water flow another minute. More carefully this time, she found another chunk of the mirror and placed it in her travel pouch but quickly decided it needed to be more accessible. She slid it between the pages of her passport and stuffed both in her coat pocket.

Maggie listened, ear to the door. She tried to open it again. It moved slightly, but not nearly enough for any light to seep in, never mind for her to squeeze out. Bracing for impact, she threw her entire weight against the door. Her shoulder protested with a jolt of pain; the door stood resolute. "Hey!" she shouted, without thinking. "Hey!" again, louder. Maggie groaned at her fate.

Moments later, there was movement. And voices, more than one. Maggie couldn't understand a word. She couldn't even figure out if her captor was in the group. The air inside the closet felt thick with her own breath. She had to get out. She pounded on the door. The conversation outside stopped.

The door rattled, then swung open into the kitchen. Blocking her escape route were two men—Ergan and a dark, husky man. Behind them stood two other burly, bearded men. Beside them stood a slender young woman with wide, olive-colored eyes and lush black hair that cascaded over her shoulders. Although petite, the woman projected more authority than the men. Maggie looked from one to the next, noticing with dismay that Husky stood with his jacket pulled back on one side, revealing an occupied gun holster. The slice of glass would do her little good against that. The others were probably carrying, too. Steve had told her everyone in Georgia was armed. Everyone, that was, except her. She stuck her wounded hand inside her coat pocket.

"What do you want?" she asked, trying to control the panic pulsating in her throat. Ergan and Husky looked at the woman, who stepped closer.

"Perhaps I should ask you the same question, miss," she replied, surprising her with a slight British accent.

Maggie stared for a moment. "Look, I'm an American," she began, before stopping herself. Her citizenship wouldn't get her anywhere in this situation, except possibly in deeper trouble. "I don't know what this man wants from me." She eyed Ergan. "Please—"

The woman nodded to Husky, who tugged off Maggie's coat before she could react. The chunk of mirror and her passport fell to the floor. Ergan stepped behind her, catching sight of the destruction she'd wrought in his closet. He grunted something—in Georgian, she presumed—to Husky.

The woman, meanwhile, picked up Maggie's passport, and yanked off the headscarf, unleashing a tangle of hair. "Margaret Mary Jenkins." The woman's tone was cold and low. "What brings you to Georgia, of all places?"

She sensed the trap being set. Of course, Ergan would've told them about her inquiries into the bombing. "I was engaged to be married to an American diplomat who was murdered here." Her knees felt suddenly flaccid.

"So, if he's dead, why are you here?"

Maggie winced, still not used to the word "dead."

"I had to see it, the place where he died," she whispered. "Please, let me go. I won't come back."

The woman muttered something to the men, who slid next to Maggie, grabbing an arm each with rapid strength. "What are you doing?" She tried to struggle free, knowing already that her effort was a waste. Their hands ran along the sides of her body, up and down her legs and then under her blouse where they discovered and removed her travel pouch. Maggie twisted her torso in a vain attempt to wriggle free. "Let go of me!"

The woman smiled. "Ever seen the Georgian countryside?"

Not more than twenty minutes into the ride, the road became unbearably bumpy. Maggie's head banged against the side of the truck with every lurch. She couldn't steady herself, not with her hands tied behind her back and her cut finger throbbing. Worse still, her riding companion was Husky, who either spoke no English or cared not to. He stared at her, no expression other than apparent boredom, as if kidnapping foreigners was routine. Through a small window into the cab, she could see the woman seated between the other two men.

Maggie couldn't even begin to imagine where they were taking her, much less why. Every clichéd threat she could think of—*You'll never get away with this! I know powerful people!*—fell flat in her own ears. She'd surprised herself by remaining relatively calm in the closet, but now the bravery was melting away. Her palms itched and her ears rang. The odor of diesel fuel filled the air, poisoning her every breath. The only thing she could think to do was to run at her first opportunity. Based on the terrain that tossed the truck about like popping corn, she assumed they were well into the countryside. Maybe she could find refuge in an abandoned farm or dacha somewhere. If she could escape.

Husky shifted in the wheel-well seat across from her. She closed her eyes, unable to concentrate on formulating an escape plan. What seemed like an hour went by, but it could've been more. Or less. She'd be a horrible witness. Or spy. Her powers of observation seemed to have abandoned her. Finally, the van slowed to a stop. Husky rose to a stooped stand, looming over her like a hungry bear. She heard the groaning thud of the passenger doors and waited, muscles tensed.

The back door opened to a field of overgrown grass littered with jagged rocks. A majestic stone-faced mountain with snow-tipped peaks rose in the distance. A dilapidated house that appeared to sag to the right stood before them. Remnants of white paint clung to the wood siding. There were no other structures in sight. One of the men stepped into the van, material for a blindfold in hand. "No," she shook her head. "It's not necessary. I won't do anything." Husky grabbed her while the other man tightened the band across her eyes. She'd never liked the dark, and always slept with a nightlight on when Steve was away.

The men guided her out of the van. She landed with a thud in the soft mud and tried desperately to get her bearings. It was still daytime, but she had no way to discern east from west, north from south. They started leading her, chattering unintelligibly to each other as if they were on a stroll in the park. Maggie stumbled, then tripped again.

The men had only a loose grip on her. She made a sudden move, tugging one arm free from the rope, then reaching for the blindfold. She unveiled one eye before the men seized her arms, pulling them back with such force that she howled in pain. They retied her hands and pulled the blindfold back over her eyes.

"Take this thing off!" she shouted, partly from pain but more in anger.

The men continued pushing her along, but then the woman spoke. "This is for your own protection, Miss Jenkins. Be patient."

Patient? She struggled against the vise grip on her forearms. "Could you get these thugs to ease up a bit?"

The woman ignored her plea. The group fell back into silence. Less than a minute later, Maggie was led up steps. A door shut behind her. There were new voices. *Two more of them,* she thought. She stood still, feeling trapped and utterly helpless.

Someone led her away. "Sit here," the woman ordered, guiding her down onto a chair. She pulled off the blindfold.

"There will be people looking for me. People you don't want to mess with." The woman did not appear frightened in the least. "What's your name? Can you at least tell me that?"

"Zara."

"Zara, why am I here? I don't understand what you want from me."

Zara stared at her, revealing nothing. "Stay here." With that, she turned and left the room, closing and locking the door behind her.

Maggie's desperation was blooming into panic. Her eyes darted around her new cell, a small room with only one door and a boarded-up window. Chipping plaster hung in flakes from the wall. A single light bulb in the fixture above her cast a sallow glow over the scuffed wide-plank floor. There was another wooden chair and a round, three-legged table in the corner near the door. If only she'd gone sightseeing instead of to the café. She banged the back of her head against the wall, wishing she were just about anywhere else.

When no one came to see what the thudding noise was, she stood and twisted her neck from side to side, trying to soothe knotted muscles. Her stomach complained of hunger, her mouth begged for a drink. She walked over to the door and pressed her ear to it. The men were speaking Russian, but once again she was lost in a world divided by language. In her state of fatigue, she couldn't be sure, but she thought they said something about turkey. And the trimmings. It was almost Thanksgiving, but why would Chechens be talking about an American holiday? Her Russian was lousy, so maybe she'd misunderstood. Then she heard them laughing and could've sworn they said, "axis of evil." In English. *What the hell?*

A rattle in the doorknob sent her running back to her chair. Zara entered with two men she hadn't seen before. Both sported black beards and camouflage pants and jackets. Zara stood directly in front of Maggie, the two men flanking her like oversized Dobermans.

"We have some questions for you. You can make this easy or not. It's up to you."

How did I get myself into this mess?

One of the men dragged the empty chair over for Zara. She sat, leaning forward. Maggie felt the woman's breath hit her face.

"Who are you working for?"

"What are you talking about?"

Her olive eyes bored into Maggie.

"Listen, I went to Dima's because," Maggie cleared her throat, "because that's where my fiancé was killed. That's it. I'm not working for anyone other than myself."

"So, you came all the way from the United States to see where your boyfriend died?"

"Yes."

"Hmmm," she tossed her hair then reached into her jacket pocket. "Who's this man?" She flashed a photograph of a man who resembled Zara's flank-guarding friends. Black beard, dark eyes, an angry look. He stood on a rocky ledge, an intimidating weapon slung across his chest.

"I have no idea," Maggie answered. It was the truth. She'd never seen him before, but she was beginning to think she knew exactly who he was. *Takayev?*

"We'll have to try this again later," Zara snapped as she stood. She nodded to the man on her left who promptly produced another blindfold.

"Zara, please! Some water?"

Zara stood silent as the man flattened Maggie's eyelids with the cloth. As the footsteps began to retreat from the room, she called out, "Wait. I know more!"

"You've remembered something?" Zara asked from across the room.

"Could you take this thing off, first?" Maggie implored.

Zara ignored her plea to remove the blindfold. "What is it that you wish to tell me?"

"Nothing."

"Very well." The door shut with an echoing thud.

She licked her lips, grimacing as her tongue stung the cracked skin. What did they want from her? She tried to calm her thoughts and analyze the situation. Perhaps cooperating, maybe giving them intelligence, even if she made it up, would gain her some freedom of movement. And with that freedom, maybe she could figure a way out of the place.

She stood and shuffled sideways, sticking out her left elbow as much as the rope would allow, using it as a buffer against unseen obstacles. She hit a wall and turned around backwards, feeling for the door with her hands. She found the knob and pressed her ear against the wood but was unable to detect anything more than a low murmuring from the other side.

"Zara!" she shouted, kicking the wall. Moments later, she heard footsteps approaching, then a rattling. She took several steps back to avoid being hit by the swinging door.

Powerful hands seized her shoulders and shoved her full-force across the room, where she fell into a heap against the wall. "Ah," she cried at the pain shooting down her neck into her lower back. Then came a swift kick to the thigh. "Stop!" she screamed, which only encouraged another kick, this time to the ribs. She curled into a protective ball, and waited for the next blow. Mercifully, he departed, leaving Maggie struggling to breathe evenly.

"Perhaps I should've warned you," Zara purred, her smooth, feminine voice a stark contrast to the brutal assault. "My men don't like trouble. Freedom fighters don't have the time to waste on annoyances like you."

She unfurled her legs and struggled to a sitting position. Her ribs were on fire, her leg throbbed. "Freedom fighters?"

"Come on, who do you think we are?"

That's what I'm trying to figure out. "You're Chechen, aren't you? At first I was thinking Georgian, but I'm pretty sure that Georgians wouldn't treat an American this way."

"Georgians are like lost little lambs, bleating and crying for someone to protect them from the big, bad bear. They're cowards. At least Chechens will fight the Russians for freedom."

"I understand. I think the Russians have been far too brutal in Chechnya."

"Shut up. I didn't ask for your opinion. So until you have something useful to tell me about Takayev and why you're really here, I'll let my friends handle you."

A rush of air hit Maggie as Zara turned to leave.

"Wait!" Her mind scrambled for some kind of leverage. "My government will pay you for information on al-Qaeda."

"Blood money?" Zara scoffed.

"No, it's not that. Not at all." Her mind flashed back to one of the intelligence reports she'd read in the vault. She shouldn't be sharing this information with a foreigner, but she had to do something. "We know that Chechens have been training with al-Qaeda."

Zara was silent. She'd struck a nerve. Might as well throw a Hail Mary to try to rattle her even more. "And we know about the axis of evil."

Her captor remained mute. *Direct hit.* But what, exactly, had Maggie hit? She didn't know what the axis was, but obviously it was significant.

"Al-Qaeda isn't your friend. The CIA knows exactly—"

"Why would I trust a word the CIA says?" Zara strode over and grabbed Maggie by the hair, pulling her to a stand. "Tell me about Takayev."

Maggie tried to break free. "Dammit, let go!"

Zara yanked her hair again. "What do you know about Takayev?"

It took several painful breaths to get her voice under control. She could forget about her career in intelligence. She was about to break every rule she hadn't already broken since Steve's murder. "My fiancé worked for the CIA," she began. Her legs went weak and she fell to the floor.

"Get up!" Zara commanded.

Maggie couldn't help herself back up with her hands tied and searing pain beating her body into submission. "I can't." She braced for another blow. But Zara relented, pulling her up by the arms then shoving her into a chair. The woman's strength surprised her.

She focused on a small sliver of light filtering through a gap in the left side of the blindfold. "He worked for the CIA in Georgia and recruited Takayev as an asset to provide information to the U.S. government."

"How do you know this?"

"The CIA told me after my fiancé was killed. They said he was murdered while meeting with an asset. I assume that asset was Takayev."

"What information was Takayev giving to your government?"

"I don't know."

The air in front of her stirred as Zara bent over to move in closer.

"I swear I don't know anything for a fact."

"Then what do you know that's not a fact?" she intoned, her mouth close to Maggie's ear.

Her mind scrambled. "The rumor was that he was providing information on drug trafficking in and out of Russia."

"Drugs?" Zara exploded. "We are Muslims. Not possible! Try again."

Maggie wasn't about to backtrack on her own lie. She'd elaborate, clarify. "No, what I meant was that he was providing information on drug smuggling into Russia, by the mafia, by secular Chechens. Maybe others." *Stop babbling!*

"I thought your government cared only about terrorism, not drugs," she rejoindered, her tone accusatory.

"There are links. Terrorists use drug money to buy weapons, fund training, and all that. But in this case, the CIA was concerned about Russian mafia activity being funded by drug money." *Will she buy it?*

Zara sounded calmer. "Takayev never indicated that he had any knowledge of drug trafficking."

She tried to straighten herself in the chair but had to slump forward to breathe steadily. "You knew Takayev?"

"It's quite fortunate that you've stumbled into us, Maggie. You see, despite all the odds, Takayev survived."

"He survived the bombing?"

"Yes. But he's missing. And now you're going to help us find him."

CHAPTER TWENTY-TWO

W arner left Café Arbat, weighed down by a sense of foreboding. He had more to worry about coming out of the meeting than he'd had going in. Despite his strong suspicions, there still was no concrete information proving that the Russian mafia was blackmailing him. On top of that, he had to track down some Chechen assassin, a woman with ties to al-Qaeda, who possibly was the person who murdered Steve.

Then there was Yuri's source, a Russian who not only might know the assassin, but might also have information on the American traitor. And last, but certainly not least, Yuri had warned him, if rather elliptically, about terrorists buying Russian nuclear weapons to use against the United States. All that in less than an honest day's work.

He walked several blocks to Brighton Beach and stared out over the water. A stiff wind accelerated off the cresting waves. Further down to the right, a couple huddled into each other as they plodded along the sand. The cold air helped focus his mind. On a personal level, figuring out who killed Steve and who was blackmailing him were paramount. But his professional responsibilities couldn't take a backseat to anything. Warner inhaled the salt air and flagged down a cab.

The taxi dropped Warner outside a gleaming glass-walled office building, one of the tallest in the city, a new distinction born of September 11th. Inside, the CIA's New York station hid in plain sight behind the logo of an innocuous investment firm. Once through the doors, he cleared a metal detector checkpoint along with dozens of harried office workers. On the nineteenth floor, he exited the elevator and went down two flights of stairs to another elevator bank. Inside, he swiped an ordinary-looking ID card over a glowing crimson button on the wall. The elevator reopened on the twenty-second floor. He approached frosted double-paned doors, fully aware that security cameras had picked up his image, alerting the guard inside to his arrival. The reception lobby looked like any other in the building. Sofas and plush chairs were scattered around the room to welcome large groups of businessmen who would never materialize. The logo on the front desk read simply, *Westman Associates*.

The young woman behind the desk jumped to her feet after a quick glance over her shoulder at a mirror, behind which security officers, no doubt, were stationed. "Sir?"

"Hello," he approached. "Warner Thompson." He extended a smile and a handshake.

"Yes, sir. I'll let them know you're here."

Thirty seconds later, a pale Grant Baker, Chief of Station, New York, hurried into the lobby. Warner felt a bit guilty about the panic he'd surely incited in the CIA's largest domestic office.

"Mr. Thompson, welcome!"

Poor boy, Warner mused, *I've thrown off his entire day.* "I got in a little early. Hope it's not any trouble."

"No, of course not. Not at all," the COS chattered. "Come on back. I'll show you around."

Warner tried not to grind his teeth through a meet 'n greet with the rest of the station personnel followed by a briefing on the latest domestic contacts.

It was common knowledge that the CIA couldn't operate within the U.S. against its own citizens, but the New York office was part of the National Resources Division. Recruiting foreigners in the U.S. to become CIA assets when they returned to their home countries was a specialty.

"Nice briefing," he told Baker when they'd moved to his private office. "We're getting some outstanding reporting out of this station."

"Thank you, sir." Baker appeared relieved to get a passing grade.

"But I tell you," Warner offered, "I've been thinking that we might be missing something. Maybe something big."

Baker edged forward in his chair. A full head of brown hair and a round, chubby face made him appear much younger than he was. "Can you be more specific?" He came across like an over-eager rookie.

"Do you have any inroads into the Russian mafia?"

"Not at the moment. It's my understanding that the station was working a few leads, but we obviously changed focus after the

World Trade Center and Pentagon attacks. Now, most everything we investigate is terrorism-related."

"Precisely my point, Grant. Terrorists need weapons. But what they really want are the tools of mass destruction. Chemical, biological, nuclear."

Baker nodded in agreement.

Warner continued. "Where do terrorists look for these weapons of mass destruction?"

"Russia?" Baker answered, the obedient student. "Among other places."

"Exactly. And who is selling these weapons in Russia?" He answered his own question. "The mafia. Corrupt military officers. Sometimes working together. I think it's time we reconnect with the Russian mafia here in New York to see if we can get some insight."

Baker sat back in his chair, eyes alert.

"Put out some feelers. I'd like to know about any local contacts, communications."

Baker nodded. "You might want to talk to Randy Taylor, one of our officers here. It's his second posting to the station and I understand that he had some mafia contacts a few years back."

"Sure, bring him in."

Randy Taylor was a nondescript man who stood about six inches shorter and twenty pounds heavier than Warner did. "Mr. Taylor, Grant here tells me you've had some contact with the local Russian mafia."

"Until about a year ago, I was in regular contact with a prospective asset. Didn't exactly thrill the FBI," he snorted.

"Nothing pleases them," Warner added. "But hey, if he's a foreign national on our soil, and we beat the suits to him, that's their loss." He chuckled, not feeling the least bit amused. "Do you have the files on your contact here?"

"Hard copies didn't survive the World Trade Center attacks."

Among other things, Warner thought. The New York office had been destroyed two years ago, on September 11th.

"I have reasonable facsimiles in the form of computer records. But, unfortunately," Taylor continued, "I lost a lot. Most of my notes, impressions, and so on from my last meetings with the prospect were destroyed."

"I'd like to take a look at what you have."

"Now?" Taylor asked.

"Please," Warner commanded. He needed to find out if this mafia contact knew anything about weapons trafficking. Or about the blackmail campaign.

After several minutes, the case officer returned with a folder full of paper.

"Would you like me to discuss each report?"

"Not necessary," Warner said pulling the folder across the table. "I'll skim through these myself to get a feel for what kind of targeting we were doing back then. I wasn't exactly focused on the Russian mafia at that time, so I could use a good refresher." He gave a half smile, teeth concealed behind tight lips.

"Okay, then, sir. I'll be right down the hall if you need me," he offered, backing out the door.

"Ah, Randy?" Warner said, looking up from the folder.

"Yes?" he popped his head back in.

"Do you know where this asset is now?"

"No," he replied, paling, "but I'm sure we could find him."

Warner turned back to the documents without another word. Taylor disappeared.

The asset had been given a code name, even though he hadn't been fully recruited. Warner flipped through the pages detailing information that RS-WATCHMAN had offered to Randy Taylor during the courtship phase of the recruitment.

WATCHMAN had begun providing sketchy information on the structure of his uncle's mafia organization. A young émigré to the United States, he acted as a gopher for the organization, running all over the metropolitan area for whatever was needed—guns, cash drops, coffee, anything. He was being trained to serve as a lookout during high-level meetings and operations. But WATCHMAN was not satisfied, he claimed, living the life of a criminal. He wanted opportunity, his own source of income to bring his extended family over to the U.S. And he didn't want to risk arrest or his life working for the mafia. So he turned to the U.S. government, hoping for cash and a chance to start life as a young American. The CIA had made no promises, but had offered him something that resembled hope.

"Hmm," Warner mumbled. He would track down WATCHMAN. If the CIA's reporting was accurate, this man could be bought. If Warner offered him enough money, and this asset had access to higher ups in the mafia, maybe he'd get some answers about who was bribing him. And whether Steve's Chechen asset really was involved with trafficking nuclear materials. Of course, all of this might lead nowhere, but it was the only lead he had.

CHAPTER TWENTY-THREE

"Takayev is still alive?" Maggie gasped. "But the CIA said—"

"It seems your CIA is wrong more often than it's right," Zara replied. "My sources say he's alive. I believe them, not you."

There were two possible explanations for this news. Either the CIA mistakenly believed Takayev was dead, or someone was lying. But who? Zara, Warner, or Peter? She thought of the man's grief-stricken brother, Tamaz, who had come to visit her. Did he know that there was no need for a funeral?

"I don't understand," she said.

"There's nothing for you to understand."

Zara called out to her men. Two of them dragged Maggie from the room and deposited her on a hard chair. Zara untied the blindfold, but kept her wrists bound. Maggie's eyes darted around, gathering information to devise an escape plan. She was in the kitchen of what she now assumed was a small farmhouse in the Georgian countryside. The sliver of a view she had out a window showed craggy terrain mingled with overgrown vegetation.

The guerrillas spoke to each other in rapid-fire Georgian. There was no understanding them. Straight ahead was a refrigerator so old that it reminded her of her grandmother's antique ice box. To her right sat an ancient stove that looked lonely from years of neglect. Only a compact microwave oven on the counter hinted that modernity had permeated the house's walls. Zara filled a glass of water from the sink and brought it to Maggie's lips. Particles floated in the water, but she gulped it down. "Thank you." If Zara was going to play nice, she'd reciprocate. To stay on Zara's good side was to stay alive.

"So, where is he?"

"Takayev? I have absolutely no idea."

"But you came looking for him. Did you not?"

Maggie stole a quick glance at the heavily armed men looming a few feet behind Zara.

"No. I had no idea he was alive. I came to find out what happened to my fiancé because I didn't believe the story I was being told. And, I . . . I thought if I could find information about who Takayev was and how he knew Steve, then I could get to the bottom of this. It's the only way I'll be able to move on." *Move on? To what?*

"Why don't you believe what your government told you?" Zara dragged a chair across the uneven floorboards and sat before her.

"The details of the story don't fit. Steve would never meet an asset in a public café. That's not the kind of risk he'd take." She exhaled. "I don't know any more than that."

Zara seemed to take a moment to think. She stared, olive eyes fixed on a point somewhere behind Maggie's head. "What does the CIA say about Takayev?"

"How would I know? I've never seen his file. And I thought he was dead." She suddenly remembered that Peter Belekov had told her the night of Steve's wake that they hadn't identified Takayev's remains yet. It never occurred to her that he might have survived the blast. Knowing what she did about how Steve had died, she couldn't understand how Takayev hadn't. "I thought . . . maybe . . . he was a suicide bomber. That he was the one who killed Steve."

"Takayev?" Zara laughed. "Smart guy but not the martyr type."

If Takayev had been a suicide bomber, he'd certainly be dead, too. Right? Unless he got cold feet at the last minute and tried to escape the blast. "What are you going to do if you find him?"

Zara snorted. "Kill him, of course."

"You're trying to find him just so you can kill him?"

"We have to. Now that we know he's been working with the CIA, he must pay for his betrayal."

Horror flooded through Maggie. All her yammering about Steve had revealed too much. She'd basically condemned Takayev to death.

To be fair, she had thought he was dead already, but her sense of guilt didn't care about logic. Even if he deserved to die, she didn't want it to be her fault.

"I can tell that you're sad about your boyfriend."

Maggie turned away.

Zara grabbed her chin and forced it back to center.

"But I can also tell that's not why you're really in Georgia. Someone sent you. Who? And why?"

Maggie's heart thumped. "Have you ever lost someone, Zara? Someone who changed your life? Who was your life?"

Zara laughed. "Do you think you are the only one who has lost a loved one in a conflict? You Americans are so naïve. You feel protected and safe because you're far away from the theater of war. The rest of the world does not have that luxury."

"War? My country is not at war with anyone in Georgia. And my fiancé was not a soldier. He was killed by terrorists."

"Half of my family was murdered by Russians. None of them were soldiers either."

Maggie winced. "This isn't a competition."

Zara's eyebrows shot up and her eyes narrowed.

Maggie backed off, softening her tone. "All I'm saying is that I had to come here, to see for myself what happened to Steve. Can't you understand that? You must understand that."

Zara crossed her arms.

"Steve was the only man I ever loved. I thought I'd been in love before." Maggie paused.

Zara tilted her head, listened.

"There was this guy in college," Maggie continued. "He had a serious girlfriend back home. And I had no idea. It was humiliating when I found out."

"That's nothing. Men do that sort of thing all of the time."

"Even to you?"

"There was a boy. Nikolai. I called him Kolya." Zara's gazed dropped to the floor. "We were young. Teenagers. My brothers tried to keep us apart."

"Why?"

"He was Russian." She sighed. "We had to sneak out to meet."

"Forbidden love?"

Zara smiled. "Yes. But then we got caught and my brothers never let me out of their sight. They told me they'd seen him kissing another girl, one with a terrible reputation."

"Was it true?"

She shrugged. "Probably? Maybe? His family moved away soon after. He'd write and sometimes call, but eventually I realized we could never be together."

"Just because he's Russian?"

"Among other reasons." Zara lit a cigarette and inhaled lustfully. When her face emerged from a cloud of smoke, she leaned forward, elbows on knees. "Cigarette?" She waved it in front of Maggie's nose.

"Don't smoke."

"You Americans, so puritanical."

Maggie stared at her. This woman was unpredictable, too good at keeping her off balance.

Zara huffed a command to her henchman, who grabbed Maggie and dragged her over to the sink. They stuffed her blindfold in the drain and turned the water on full force. "What are you doing?" her voice rose, cracking with a hint of hysteria.

"You look thirsty."

She watched the sink fill with water. *They're going to kill me.* The realization passed quietly through her. It would be so easy to give up, to let it all go. Without Steve, it didn't really matter if she lived or died.

One of the men forced her head into the sink, crashing her skull against the spigot in the process. Maggie managed to hold her breath before her face hit the shallow pool. The guerrilla had her hair entwined tightly in his fingers. She couldn't move. Her lungs grew hot, panic surged. She kicked her legs to the side, lashing out in vain. She had to inhale. She opened her mouth just as he pulled her back up.

She gasped in as much air as she could. Wet spirals of hair clung to her face. Maybe she had nothing to live for, but this was not how she wanted to die.

"Well?" Zara spoke from behind her.

"Well, what?" she shot back, her voice hoarse, deadened by too little oxygen and too much stress.

Zara barked another order. The man obeyed and shoved Maggie's face back under water. She counted as slowly as she could to keep from panicking. When she reached twelve, she had to fight. Her lungs protested the incoming water, but it had nowhere else to go. Her body heaved, slamming into the sink's edge. Then the man pulled her out.

She coughed, desperate for an honest breath. As the water came back up into her mouth, she turned her head and spewed it onto one of the torturers.

He swung an arm in retaliation, but Maggie managed to dodge him just as another man burst into the kitchen, shouting and waving his weapon. The men readied their guns and ran from the room, forgetting about their American captive. Zara remained, standing alert, a handgun drawn.

"What's going on?" She felt a glimmer of hope. Perhaps the chaos would offer her an opportunity to escape.

"Sit!" Zara pointed her gun at the chair.

Maggie obeyed. Zara paced around her, glancing into the next room and, she assumed, out the window.

"Is someone here?"

"Shut up!" she shouted over her shoulder.

"They're here for me."

Maggie knew whatever was going on outside had nothing to do with her. Peter wouldn't know she was missing yet. And no one else knew she was in Georgia.

"I said, shut up!"

Zara came toward her, gun aimed at her face. She tipped Maggie's chin with its cold barrel, then dragged it along her jawbone all the way up to her temple.

Maggie squeezed her eyes shut. There was one more thing she could try. It was her last hope.

"I don't know where Takayev is," she gasped. "But I know someone who does."

"Who?" Zara demanded.

"He works in the American Embassy. He used to work with my fiancé." She tried to shake off the wet curls that were plastered to her cheekbones.

"What's his name?" Zara's tone remained urgent.

"I really shouldn't be telling you this." Zara pressed the gun even tighter against her head. *Good.* She didn't want to seem too eager to cooperate. "Okay, okay. His name is Peter. I don't know his last name."

"How do we contact this man?"

"We have to call the embassy."

Zara's laugh came out more like a growl. "Amusing. You want us to call the U.S. Embassy?"

"I don't know how else to get in touch with him."

"Where does he live?"

"He might live in the same apartment building as my fiancé. I don't remember the name of the place, but I know where it is."

"Do you have a picture of this Peter?" She eased the gun away from Maggie's temple, keeping it pointed at her.

"No. I mean, I hardly know the guy, only his name. But I met him a couple of times back in Washington."

"What does he look like?" Zara stood a few feet in front of her, the weapon finally lowered from its menacing aim.

Forgive me, Peter. "He's tall, I'd say around six feet, maybe a bit more. In shape, definitely. But it's his hair and eyes that will tell you who he is. White blond hair and blue eyes, kind of faint blue, but intense."

Zara shook her head. "Faint but intense eyes? You think my men could be bothered to search for someone with a description like that?"

"I could try to find him for you, maybe even lure him into a trap."

"Why do you want to hurt this man?" Zara looked at her with suspicion.

"I don't want to hurt him, but if he can help both of us, then we can agree to forget about everything that's happened today."

"Forget everything?" Zara scoffed. "We'll never forget all the blood that's been shed fighting Russian oppression. We'll get our revenge."

"But I have nothing to do with any of that."

"That's not how I see it, I'm afraid." She focused her gaze on Maggie. "You're American. The U.S. government, the one you vote for, had one of its men turn a Chechen brother against us. Every American has something to do with that."

"Zara," she began, incredulous. "That's like saying that if you harm me, every Chechen, every Muslim in the world is responsible."

"Isn't that the very basis of your war on terrorism?" Zara sniffed.

"We're targeting terrorists, not—"

A sudden commotion outside tore Zara from the debate over to the window in the next room. Maggie stood and crept closer to try to catch a glimpse. Zara shouted harsh words and bolted for the front door. Maggie stood, stunned. She listened for a moment to see if she was really alone. Automatic weapons fire erupted outside. She hurried to the window. One man ran by. Another, who stopped not far from the window, waved his arm toward the back of the house. Had Georgian security come to rescue her? Who could have sent them? Peter? No, still too early for him to suspect that she was in trouble. Warner? He didn't even know she was in Tbilisi. No, these people were not here for her. They wore all black, but she couldn't see any identifying insignia on their clothing. It sounded like they were speaking Russian, and, based on the blond hair and fair skin of the man closest to the house, they weren't Chechens.

Whether they were here to rescue her or not, they could be her way out. She ran to the kitchen and tugged open the drawers with her still-bound hands. No knives, only a lone screwdriver. *Everyday objects can be useful tools, especially in dire situations.* Maggie recalled the words of her instructor at The Farm.

Even though she'd joined the Agency as an analyst, she'd taken an operations overview course, designed mainly to impress new analysts with the bravado of the Directorate of Operations. She leaned to one side to lift her hands into the drawer and began to work the screwdriver into the knot between her wrists. She fumbled, cursing at herself. At any moment, Zara would realize she'd left Maggie unguarded.

The gunshots sounded more distant, and there was still no sign of Zara. *What if she got shot?* The prospect of it horrified her only because if she were left to the mercy of Zara's henchman, there was no telling what the end of her life would be like. She redoubled her efforts to manipulate the screwdriver into the knot. One minute later, the first section of rope was undone. The rest of the operation was over in seconds. She shook her freed hands, opened the front door, and peered out. She could hear shouting in the distance but couldn't see anyone. This was her chance.

She dashed out the front door into the field, looking for cover, which was nowhere to be found. The air felt thin, the ground jagged and unforgiving. The dilapidated prison of a house stood drooping behind her. Overgrown brush crawled over barren stones for miles around. Ahead, occasional trees, probably older than Maggie by decades, were scattered in a random pattern.

She paused. Where were all the attacking gunmen? Maybe they had retreated. *Keep going.* She picked up her pace, looking for the road they'd taken only a few hours earlier. With each step, she felt more confident she'd escape, but less sure that she'd be found by anyone who could help her. She hadn't been running since before Steve died. She drank in the cold, thin air, imagining him beside her, easily keeping pace.

And then . . . over there, in the brush, one of the attackers was lying on his side, gasping for breath.

She slowed to a stop.

He caught sight of Maggie and raised his hands in surrender. A semi-automatic rifle lay near his feet. His black shirt was tied into a makeshift tourniquet high on his right thigh.

With one eye on the gun and one on the man's hands, Maggie approached.

"*Pomogi mne,*" he pleaded.

He needed help. She kicked the gun away and squatted next to him. His well-defined chest sported two tattoos—a crucifix on one side and a Russian flag sprouting hundred-dollar bills on the other. "Do you speak English? *Angliyskiy?*"

Confusion clouded his face. "American?"

"Yes. Russian?"

He nodded. "My leg." Blood oozed through his pants from under the tourniquet. A sheen of sweat covered his chest and face.

"Are you military?"

"*Nyet.* Is business."

What kind of business would these Russians have with the Chechens?

"Help?" he implored.

There was nothing she could do for him. Not out here in the middle of the Georgian countryside and not in his condition. "What kind of business?"

"Weapons."

"Did you come to kill them?"

He shook his head. "Money."

He closed his eyes and grimaced. His entire pantleg was now soaked.

She studied his tattoos. Russian criminal gangs had specific tattoo designs much like drug cartels. "Are you *mafiya?*"

His eyes fluttered open as he whimpered in pain.

"Shhh," she soothed. "It's okay. I'll stay with you until help arrives."

He raised his head from the ground. "America." Deep breath. "Attack."

"What? An attack?"

His gaze lost focus. "Al-Qae—"

She grabbed his shoulders. "Did you say al-Qaeda?"

His head flopped to the left.

"What attack? Is this about the axis of evil?"

Sharp cracks erupted behind her followed by an intense buzzing that sounded much too close. She froze momentarily and looked back, catching sight of one of her captors firing in her direction. With one final glimpse at the dying Russian, she grabbed his gun and scrambled, keeping as low as she could until she put more distance between her and the Chechen. She lengthened her stride, but not enough to avoid the tree root reaching out to grab her foot. As she tumbled, her head hit a rock jutting from the ground, and the world went dark.

CHAPTER TWENTY-FOUR

W arner returned to CIA headquarters early Friday morning. Instead of taking the private elevator from the garage to his seventh-floor office suite, he opted for the main entrance. To his right was the white marble Memorial Wall. He paused, his eyes focused on the spot where the 84th star soon would be added. Steve's star.

Upstairs on seven, Warner found Priscilla, a cup of coffee in hand, her computer already humming. He needed her to get his password for the asset database. For the life of him, he couldn't keep track of all his IDs, PINs and the like, particularly for those systems he rarely accessed. He wasn't supposed to share his passwords with anyone, but Priscilla wasn't just anyone. And the infraction seemed so minor compared to his more recent transgressions.

"Here it is, Warner. By the way, I just got a call from Betty . . ." She trailed off, brow furrowed. Betty was the secretary for the Director of Central Intelligence—the DCI. "The Director needs to see you ASAP. Something major. You'll probably have to go to the Hill later this morning."

The Hill, again, he moaned inwardly. "Did they say what it was?"

"No, but Betty said the DCI was swearing up a blue storm."

He stopped a curse from escaping. "Fine, I'll go down in five." If the DCI was in such a state, it'd be wise to give him time to cool down. He went back to his office, password in hand, and sat at the computer.

Others with access to this database were privy to information on assets with whom they had a direct relationship. But as Deputy Director of Operations, Warner had access to everything. He scrolled down the screen through the list of current assets. Nothing. Then he toggled over to inactive recruits.

WATCHMAN: Nikolai Sergeyevich Petrov, DOB =1978 (est.), St. Petersburg, Russia.
BACKGROUND: Petrov grew up in Grozny, Chechnya, where his father served as a Soviet military officer in the North Caucasus Military District. Despite the Russia-Chechnya conflicts, he maintains close ties to friends in Grozny. In 2000, Petrov emigrated to the United States, and resides in the Brighton Beach section of Brooklyn, New York (exact address unknown). The nephew of a Russian mafia boss, Aleksandr Ivanovich Plechenko, is being groomed to take on greater roles of responsibility within the organization but claims to want a safe way out of the mafia.

A Russian who grew up in Chechnya? Just like Yuri's source. It couldn't be a coincidence. Not anymore. He typed an email to Randy Taylor: "When you track down the man we discussed yesterday, contact me immediately." Nothing like an email from your boss's boss to scare you into action.

"Ahem," Priscilla cleared her throat outside his office. "You best be going."

"I'm going already." He stood and brushed past his secretary.

Two doors down, he entered the DCI's office suite, putting on a relaxed air he didn't feel. "Morning, Betty. The world falling apart again on our watch?"

A heavyset woman with hair dyed a garish blonde scowled at him. "Don't mess with him today, Warner. He's in no mood." She buzzed her boss. "DDO is here."

"About damned time," barked the voice over the intercom.

Warner pushed open the door to DCI Thomas Hargrove's office. Hargrove didn't look at Warner, preferring, it seemed, to maintain a furious pace back and forth in front of a window overlooking the naked trees outside.

"Tom?" Warner asked. He knew Hargrove's pacing could go on for more time than he could afford to waste.

"Unbelievable, Warner. They're going insane on the Hill." He continued to march along the same well-trodden path.

"What happened?"

"I just got the call a half hour ago." The DCI finally stopped long enough to squeeze his head with his palms. "The House Intelligence Committee wants to freeze all funding for CIA operations in Russia and the former Soviet republics until we deliver a full damage assessment."

"Damage assessment?" Warner breathed.

"Tbilisi. Who killed Steve Ryder and why?" Hargrove stopped pacing. "Why don't we already know this?"

Blood pulsed in Warner's temple. "I'm working on it day and night, Tom."

"You need to be on the Hill today and be prepared for them to hit you on this *Washington Post* story about the CIA selling weapons to Chechen rebels."

"It's a complete fabrication."

"Obviously, Warner."

"Then why hit us for it?" He threw his hands in the air.

"Who the hell knows. Just fix it." He banged the glass-top desk. "Today!"

If only it were that easy. "I'm on it."

The DCI waved his hand, dismissing Warner without a further word. He sprinted back to his office. Although he'd been away from his desk for only ten minutes, Priscilla already had handled the logistics of briefing slides and transportation. He was due to testify to the House Intelligence Committee at 10:00 a.m. sharp and would be expected to report back to DCI Hargrove upon his return.

He groaned. There were a million other things he needed to do. At this rate, it was only a matter of time before those photos of him showed up in the newspaper.

He tried to shake off the desperation. It was time to focus on getting through the day. He clicked the computer mouse. There was an email reply from Randy Taylor.

Got your message, sir. I recall the name of a few places
WATCHMAN used to hang out, eat, etc. I will try to track him
down today. RT

"It's a start," Warner muttered to the screen.

At five minutes to ten, Warner ducked into the men's room just off the elevator in the U.S. Capitol Building's attic. He checked the stall. Empty. In front of the full-length mirror, he pulled back his overcoat and suit jacket. A wet oval was expanding under his right arm. He looked back at the man he didn't recognize. *Sweating a bunch of congressmen?* If only they were his biggest concern. He turned to the sink and splashed water on his cheeks, careful to avoid the perfect hair sweeping across his brow. He blotted his face with a paper towel that felt more like tree bark.

He breathed in the antiseptic smell of the newly mopped floor. The fog began to lift. He was Warner Thompson, a decorated CIA case officer who'd risen to the top of his profession. He'd get through this.

Ensconced in the Intelligence Committee hearing room five minutes later, Warner paced before the congressmen, his right hand in a pocket, the left rubbing his chin. If ever he felt like an actor, today was the day.

"Ladies and gentlemen," he gestured to the Members. "As you know, and in no small part thanks to your support for the CIA, particularly the Directorate of Operations, we have scored some impressive victories against terrorists around the world. Your ongoing support for our extraordinary budgetary and operational needs has been instrumental in these successes." Flattery got you nowhere short of everywhere in Washington, D.C.

"But as you also know, these achievements have come at a high cost." He stopped directly in front of Chairman Nelson's seat.

"Since the beginning of the Global War on Terror, we've added too many stars to the Memorial Wall that honors CIA employees killed in the line of duty. We have . . ." His voice caught in his throat as Steve Ryder's face flashed through his mind. He froze, blood rushing in his ears.

"Mr. Thompson?" Chairman Nelson asked, leaning forward. "Are you okay?"

Warner's eyes darted behind the congressmen, scanning the staffers who watched him with a mixture of uncertainty and curiosity. Maggie wasn't among them. *Good.* She hadn't been in good shape when he left her house the other night and was in no way fit to return to work yet.

A member of his entourage cleared her throat, another shuffled through papers. He turned to the witness desk and gulped from a glass of water.

"Yes, sir, I'm fine. Excuse me, scratchy throat." The muscles in his neck tensed to the snapping point. "As I was saying, we have lost lives, but for a necessary cause." He recovered sufficiently to continue, but with much less flourish. "Despite these losses and the increased danger to our operations officers in the field, we have young people beating down our doors to get in on the action. These people need intense training because our operational needs are urgent, and our caseload has grown exponentially." He turned to the screen on the wall behind him, nodding to the budget analyst sitting at a laptop, who promptly clicked to the first slide.

A door slammed shut in the far end of the room. "Please excuse my tardiness, Mr. Chairman. I hope I haven't missed too much of this critical hearing." Congressman Richard Carvelli took his seat. To Warner, he looked drawn, the circles under his eyes more pronounced than usual. His skin was pasty, and his tie was askew.

Warner's prepared remarks took only minutes to deliver. The bottom line, he told the gathered men and women, was that shutting down active operations could result in more lost intelligence, more danger to U.S. national security, and even more deaths. Not only was it possible, it was necessary to continue all intelligence operations while simultaneously conducting the Tbilisi damage assessment.

"Mr. Chairman, may I ask a question of our witness?" It was Carvelli.

"The gentleman from New York may proceed."

"Did the CIA notify Congress that it has been selling weapons to Chechen rebels?"

Warner straightened his tie and locked eyes with Carvelli. "The CIA has not and never would sell weapons to Chechen rebel groups. The *Washington Post* report alleging so is based entirely on an anonymous source who is telling outright lies."

"I remind the witness that he is under oath," Carvelli sneered.

Heat swept up Warner's neck to his face. Why was Carvelli questioning his integrity? What did he have to gain from attacking him and the CIA? He couldn't let this man get the upper hand.

The chairman banged the gavel. "May I remind you that you are speaking on the record, Mr. Carvelli. You might want to think twice about impugning the reputation of a CIA official who has always been forthcoming with this committee."

Warner nodded to the chairman. "As I was saying, there is absolutely no merit to *The Washington Post*'s report. The truth is quite the opposite, in fact. The Agency is actively monitoring illicit arms sales around the world, including any that might involve Chechen rebels."

Carvelli remained silent during the round of questioning that followed Warner's briefing. He seemed suddenly subdued, less the attack dog than the petulant child. Twenty minutes later, Warner saw him slink out the hearing room's side door without a backward glance.

Warner wrapped up the briefing, shook the hands of all the important congressmen, and followed the rest of the entourage out of the Capitol Building. As they wound their way around newly installed concrete bollards, his phone rang.

"Warner Thompson."

"There's been a change in plans."

Warner's breath caught at the sound of the fake British accent. He waved the others on. First they called him in his office, now his cell phone? Weren't these numbers supposed to be private?

"We will pick up the first delivery this evening. Leave the package in the mailbox three houses down from yours."

"Three houses down?"

"We expect only the highest quality, most updated, most relevant intelligence."

"I need more time. The deadline isn't for four more days."

"As I said, change in plans."

Click. The line went dead.

Warner stared at the phone.

"Mr. Thompson!" It was the driver waving at him from the waiting car.

He hurried over. "I apologize," he mumbled. "Urgent business."

He sat in stony silence on the ride back to Langley. Priscilla gave him a raised eyebrow but asked no questions when he returned to the office. At his desk, he began to shuffle through email, but was interrupted by the phone.

"It's Randy Taylor," Priscilla informed him. "New York office."

"Taylor," he grunted into the receiver.

"Yes, sir. I think I've found him."

Warner felt a flicker of hope.

"I found out he frequents a particular bar in Little Odessa. I'm going tonight to see if he shows."

"And if he doesn't?" Tonight might be too late.

"I'll let you know. He spends time down in Washington, too, so I can't guarantee I'll find him at the bar. But at least I can ask around."

Warner bit down hard on his tongue to stop himself from cursing. "How can you not know where this guy is?"

"Well," Taylor began, sounding apologetic, "he always contacted me when he wanted to meet. And after September 11th, we sort of lost contact."

"What exactly are they teaching case officers these days? You let an asset control when and how his handler contacts him?" Warner scoffed.

"Potential asset, sir."

"What?"

"WATCHMAN wasn't a fully recruited asset. He had very restrictive conditions for our meetings, so I felt like I had to—"

"Spare me the excuses," Warner interrupted. "Just find him and call me on my cell phone." He ticked off the number and slammed down the phone. "Rank amateurs!" he yelled at the walls.

"You talking to me?" Priscilla called from her desk.

Warner ignored her and began searching through the database of human intelligence reports, the ones compiled by overseas operatives. These HUMINT reports were scrubbed of information that could reveal anything about the actual source—the human spy who'd betrayed his own country to provide information to the United States. Maybe he could find a few relatively benign reports to get the blackmailer off his back for the time being. The problem was, even if he passed on useless information, he'd still be committing espionage by providing Agency documents to someone outside of the U.S. government. He grumbled in frustration. No way could he do that. Too risky. The only option was to create fake reports that looked authentic enough to pass close scrutiny. The problem was, he'd never forged such documents himself. *No time like the present to learn a new skill*, he mused.

He scanned through several HUMINT reports, jotting down notes about their format, subject matter, and language. This would be the easy part. He'd written and read these sorts of reports his entire career. More problematic was the prospect of forging documents from the National Security Agency. If the blackmailer had a background in intelligence, he might be able to spot a fake NSA document.

Warner began typing furiously, creating assets and information out of thin air. He calmed himself with the reassurance that, his integrity aside, he was giving away nothing of true value. He waited to print off the documents until Priscilla had stepped away from her desk, then tucked the pages into his briefcase. Next up was searching through online intelligence reports that he could alter enough to make them appear authentic. He ended up with three documents about the Russian mafia. He tapped a pen in frustration. Analytic work was pure tedium.

Warner scratched at his forehead, but his thoughts were interrupted when he noticed the blinking message light on his secure line. He picked up the phone and listened.

"It's Peter. Maggie Jenkins is in Georgia. Unfortunately, she's gone missing."

CHAPTER TWENTY-FIVE

Maggie woke to a pain searing across her forehead. Her hands and feet were bound, her eyes covered in darkness again. Her stomach lurched with the slightest movement of her head.

"Help . . ." A moan came from her throat. She ran her fingers along the ground. A rough, cold surface. Indoors? The last thing she remembered was being outside with the injured man. The Russian. Had the Russians taken her somewhere?

A swell of vertigo overtook her as she tried to sit up. Her throat burned with thirst, her body with despair. What had the Russian said? An attack? Jumbled thoughts sought order. Maybe she was confusing their attack on the farmhouse with an attack somewhere else?

She rolled onto her side and drew her knees to her chest for warmth. The Russians wanted money. Yes. That was it. For . . . for what? For weapons. Probably guns. Or ammo. Maybe both? Something important niggled at the edge of her mind, just out of reach. Al-Qaeda kept popping into her head. It made no sense. She twisted her wrists in an attempt to loosen the rope binding them together. The effort led nowhere.

Muffled sounds of activity came from somewhere nearby. Were they speaking Russian? She strained her ears, willing herself to focus. No, definitely not Russian.

"Oh," she groaned. It was the Chechens. The escape attempt had failed. The Russian must be dead by now, and with him the rest of his warning. *America. Attack.* It came rushing back. He'd tried to warn her. Something about al-Qaeda.

What time is it? For all she knew, something between twenty minutes and twenty-four hours had passed since the assault on the farmhouse. The more time that passed, the less time she had to stop whatever was coming. Her body begged for rest, but her mind refused to comply. *Attack. America. Al-Qaeda.*

"Zara!" she called weakly. She inch-wormed her way forward, seeking a wall or the door. When her knee hit something solid, she drew her legs back and kicked. "Zara!"

Stomping nearby. The creak of a door. And the movement of air in front of her face.

"I ordered my men to shoot to kill if you tried to escape. You should be dead."

"Then why am I still alive?"

"For one reason. I think you know something of value to us."

Zara's tone was so calm, almost kind, that it was confusing. Didn't she just say she ordered them to shoot her? Or did she say her life was valuable? The throbbing became rhythmic. "I'm so thirsty."

"I need more information."

"Okay," Maggie managed to whisper before everything faded into black again.

She awoke to find herself propped up in a chair. The pain was even more intense now. Her empty stomach rose, but she swallowed hard, forcing back the swell. Someone put a cold glass to her mouth. She opened, eager for a drink, but lost most of it down her shirt. On the second attempt, she managed to drink.

"Thank you," she whispered.

"You're ready to talk now?" It was Zara.

"Yes."

"Excellent. Now tell me again why you're in Georgia and what your fiancé was doing with Takayev?"

Maggie heard what sounded like moaning from the next room over. "What's that? Is someone hurt?"

"It's of no consequence to you."

She sensed an opportunity to buy some time. "I know first aid, maybe I can help." It wasn't exactly a lie, but her knowledge of emergency medicine was limited to treating sprains and minor cuts. "My mother is a nurse." Now that was a lie.

Zara walked out of the room without a word. When she returned minutes later, she pulled off Maggie's blindfold. The dim light of the room felt too bright. She squinted against the pain.

"One of my men is badly wounded and we have no medic here. We can't move to another place until Dhokar is stable."

"Who attacked us?"

"Us?" Zara sneered.

She probed. "What happened out there? Those men were Russian."

"It doesn't matter. They're all dead."

Maggie tried to keep her expression neutral. *All dead?* Blood pulsed at her temples. What if there was no way out? What if she'd botched her only chance at escape?

The man in the other room moaned again. "Let me help." She held her breath. "Please." Maybe she could find a way. Maybe if she helped Zara, another opportunity for escape would materialize.

Zara knelt down and untied her feet, then her hands. She had to help Maggie stand and even then, the room seemed to tilt violently to one side. Maggie groaned.

Zara looked at her with a hint of concern.

She managed a weak smile and took a step to follow her from the room. Across the hall on a cot lay one of the bearded men, breathing in irregular gasps.

Dark blood seeped through a makeshift bandage pulled tightly around his midsection. She was no expert, but it looked like this guy had only minutes of life left in him.

"My brother," Zara nodded to the cot.

"Dhokar . . . your brother?"

Zara blinked rapidly and left the room, stranding Maggie with two men looming over her. She steadied herself against the wall, noticing for the first time that it was pitch black outside. The stinging smell of gunpowder and shredded flesh convulsed her senses. She shuffled over to the dying man and pinched an unsoiled corner of the bandage, lifting it gently to peer underneath. The entry wound was smaller and cleaner than she'd expected. "We need to get the bullet out," she said to the men who spoke no English. "I need a knife." She made a sawing motion with her hands.

One of the men left the room. The other blocked the doorway, his left hand resting on the butt of a Kalashnikov. Maggie took Dhokar's pulse, stalling for time and hoping it looked like she knew what she was doing. She had no clock to judge by, but his heart rate felt too slow. "Water?" she asked. *"Voda?"* Surely he spoke Russian. He nodded, but stayed at his post.

Dammit. She needed some time alone with the gravely wounded man. Maybe in his delirium, he'd reveal something she could use against Zara.

"Dhokar," she whispered. "English?"

His head moved a fraction. A nod?

The man guarding the door shifted. Maggie glanced back. *"Voda! Seychas!"*

This time, the Chechen took her words as an order and disappeared into the hall.

"Listen, Dhokar, the CIA knows everything about Zara. I will protect her, but only if you tell me what you know about the attack."

He blinked, panicked eyes honing in on her face.

"The CIA will kill your sister if you don't help."

He flinched. His parched lips fell open.

"Tell me about the attack against America."

"Oni—" He coughed.

"They? They what?"

He settled and closed his eyes.

Maggie gently patted his cheek. "Dhokar, the axis of evil. What does that mean?"

A weak smile broadened his face.

She grabbed his shoulders. "What about al-Qaeda?"

The first captor returned with the knife, followed by the second with a saucepan full of water. Maggie released her grip on the dying man when Zara appeared behind them. She took the knife from the first captor and walked it over to Maggie.

"If I can get the bullet out, we may be able to stop the bleeding," Maggie explained. *Unless, of course, it has pierced his liver, or intestine or whatever else is in there.* "Do you have a lighter or something to sterilize the knife?"

Zara pulled matches from her shirt pocket. It took five of them to sterilize the knife to Maggie's satisfaction. She turned it in her hand. It was a slim stiletto, something she pictured these men using to slit a throat. As she leaned over Zara's brother, her knees buckled. "I'm alright," she assured Zara who steadied her from behind.

Zara pulled over a chair for Maggie, who sat and leaned forward, elbows on her knees. She knew the man would die if nothing was done, but she didn't want to be the one Zara blamed for his death. "God help me," she muttered under her breath.

She turned to Zara, who stood with her arms crossed tightly. The men behind her still had their guns trained on Maggie. "How long has it been since he was shot?"

"Ten hours." Her raspy voice betrayed her exhaustion. "Maybe more."

She calculated. When the skirmish with the Russians broke out, daylight had just begun to fade. If Dhokar had been shot around six o'clock last night, it had to be around four in the morning, give or take an hour. Peter Belekov had expected her to make contact with him the evening before. Even though they'd made no firm plans, he should be concerned enough by now to start looking for her. She just needed more time. She closed her eyes for a moment, not believing what she was about to try.

She held the knife in her right hand, steadying her wrist in her left palm. Pushing the tip of the knife against the side of the wound set free a fresh gush of blood. Dhokar groaned. The room swam, but came back into focus after she took a couple of deep breaths. "I need some clean towels or shirts. Anything to staunch the blood when I go in."

She probed again, not yet ready to search for the bullet. Zara appeared with two black t-shirts.

"This all you have?"

Zara nodded in reply. Her brother's breathing was becoming more labored.

As Maggie sliced around the wound in a circular motion, Dhokar howled in pain and twisted his torso away. Zara rushed to his side and barked a command to her men. They knelt beside their gravely injured comrade, straightened his body, and took hold of his arms.

Zara whispered in her brother's ear, then nodded at Maggie.

Taking another deep breath, Maggie inserted a finger into the wound, where soft, warm flesh glommed onto it. She couldn't feel a bullet. There was no hope for him. The charade was about to end.

She extracted her finger, wiping it on the corner of a t-shirt, which she then pressed down on his abdomen. "I'm sorry, Zara, I can't feel the bullet." She was at a loss for words. She wondered if Dhokar could hear them talking and if Steve had heard the frightened screams of those around him as he laid bleeding to death. Dhokar's breathing quieted. Maggie stood and stepped away. Zara fell to her knees, resting her head on her brother's gently falling chest.

Maggie knelt beside her, placing a hand lightly on Zara's back. "Is there anyone we can call for help?"

Rocking back on her heels, Zara sniffled. Her voice was soft. "Nobody who could get here in time."

"What about family?"

Zara stood, stretched her legs, and sat in the bedside chair. "No."

Maggie dragged another chair to the opposite side of the cot.

Dhokar's body suddenly convulsed. Then he gasped. Maggie grabbed his wrist and felt for a pulse. It was slow but still steady.

"Shhhh, Dhokar, I'm right here," Zara soothed. Looking at Maggie, she added, "He feels hot."

She nodded and took the last clean t-shirt into the kitchen, soaked it, then hurried back and laid it across the man's forehead.

Dhokar's breathing was lighter, his face more relaxed.

"What's going to happen to him?"

Maggie's mind scrambled. She'd never seen anyone die. And every time she looked at him, all she could think about was Steve suffering in his final moments. "I think his breathing will become shallower. He might even seem to gasp for air. But I don't think he'll be in pain."

Zara's olive eyes brimmed with tears. She leaned closer to her brother's face, whispering softly to him in Russian.

Maggie was certain that time was running out. "You sure there's no one you can call?"

"My mother's dead."

"I had no idea, Zara. How long has she been gone?"

"Three years. The Russians bombed the school where she taught." She stroked her brother's face. "That's when everything changed."

"Is your father—"

Her expression hardened. "Still alive the last I heard."

"Wouldn't he want to know?"

Zara looked sideways at her, her face partially obscured by her hair. "I don't care what he wants. After what he did to Dhokar, he's dead to me."

Maggie leaned forward in the chair. "What did he do?"

Zara's face softened. She swept damp hair away from her brother's eyes.

Maggie placed a hand on Zara's. Zara pulled away. Her shoulders stiffened, then drooped. "Dhokar . . . he's the baby of the family. So smart." She sniffled. "Wanted to be a doctor."

Maggie studied Dhokar's face. "So, what happened?"

"Russia happened. They've destroyed Chechnya! They've killed our people, smashed our buildings, attacked our women." Her eyes flashed. "Dhokar changed . . . after our mother and brother died. I tried to convince him to stay in school, maybe go to medical school abroad where he'd be safe." Zara stared vacantly at the floor. "Instead, he joined the jihad."

"And then?" Maggie prompted as she placed a hand on Dhokar's chest. The faint thud-thud of a heartbeat pulsed below.

"When Dhokar disappeared one day without saying goodbye, our father was furious." She rolled her eyes. "He was never furious about his family members being slaughtered, but he was about Dhokar's disappearance?"

"He must've been so worried."

"Ha! Maybe, but what he did . . ." She shook her head and studied her brother's face. "I followed my father one day. He said he had a meeting. But there were no jobs, no meetings. I was suspicious."

Maggie nodded, not wanting to interrupt.

"I overheard him asking a Russian intelligence officer to help him find Dhokar. He said that his son had been radicalized and disappeared. My father is so . . . naïve," she huffed. "He didn't understand what he'd done. Russians kill, not capture, anyone they consider radical. It was up to me to save my baby brother. I knew where he'd gone, so I joined him."

"At a training camp?" Maggie breathed.

"It was an easy decision. My father is weak. No courage. I chose honor. I chose Dhokar."

Zara's eyes locked with Maggie's. "I'm supposed to honor my parents, but—"

"I don't blame you." Maggie took a deep breath. "My father is a terrible person. I'd never choose him over someone who meant more to me."

Zara sat back and tilted her head.

"The more he drinks, the more vicious he becomes. Who knows how many affairs he's had."

"But would he ever betray you?"

The question caught Maggie off guard. "He wasn't the father he should've been."

Zara raised an eyebrow. "Your father neglected you. Mine betrayed me."

Maggie couldn't argue; she knew her life seemed privileged by comparison. "I'm really sorry, Zara."

Zara nodded, then a shadowed descended across her face. "He will pay for this."

"Who?"

"My father." Her gaze flitted around the room. Peeling paint, broken floorboards, dim lighting. "We wouldn't be in this god-forsaken place today if my father had kept his mouth shut. He dealt Dhokar to the enemy."

Dhokar shuddered, his eyes flew open, focused on nothing.

Zara leapt to her feet. "Help him! Do something!"

Maggie again felt for a pulse. It was so weak. "Zara—"

"*Nyet,* Dhokar, *nyet!*" She threw her arms around his chest and buried her face in his neck.

Dhokar's breathing was suddenly rapid and shallow, the air rattling inside his chest.

"Let me try CPR!" Maggie blurted.

Zara dragged herself off of him and watched as Maggie began compressions. It was too late. Dhokar took a final desperate breath and went still.

"Nooo!" Zara howled.

Maggie ran to her side and caught her as her knees gave out. She lowered her into the seat and clasped her hands. "I'm so sorry."

Zara shook her off and began a wordless, keening wail. Maggie fled the room. Perhaps now was her chance to escape, but her head still ached to the point of vertigo. She touched the dried blood near her temple and discovered a wide gash. Without food or water, she stood little chance of getting away, never mind surviving in the countryside on her own. Maybe she'd have the strength tomorrow.

Maggie slipped into the kitchen. All but one of the men were in the other room with their slain comrade. She turned to the sink and splashed water on her cheeks. The runoff was an orange-brown mix of dried blood and dirt. Her stomach lurched, begging for sustenance. Inside the hulking refrigerator was nothing but bread. She nodded to the man, the loaf in her hand. He looked disinterested, so she tore off a chunk and chewed on a hardened corner. "Dhokar." She shook her head.

He offered a cold stare before turning his attention to loading bullets into a half dozen empty magazines.

Maggie's eyes widened. Were they preparing for another attack? Or were those bullets meant for her? Waiting to see what Zara's plans were might prove to be a fatal mistake. Her hands suddenly shaking, she dropped the bread and slipped into the hall, swiveling her head from left to right. To get to the front door, she'd have to go left past the room where Zara and the others sat huddled around Dhokar's body. Instead, she turned right and sprinted toward the back of the house, sure there was another way out. And then she saw it. The back door.

Ten more feet and her hand was on the doorknob. She fumbled with the deadbolt and tugged open the door, hesitating a moment to take in the darkness. How long until sunrise? It didn't matter, she decided.

With one foot out the door, two hands clamped down on her shoulders. She struggled and tried to twist free. He held fast, his rancid breath hot on her neck. Maggie jammed the heel of her shoe down his shin and stomped on his foot.

He roared, spun her around and swatted her across the face. The room blurred around the edges, then light faded to dark.

CHAPTER TWENTY-SIX

The throbbing vessel in Warner's temple felt close to bursting. Maggie went to Georgia? And now she was missing? Peter's voice on the recording was calm but laced with a touch of defiance. Despite Warner's explicit instructions to keep him informed of everything, Peter had waited God knew how many hours to tell him Maggie was in Tbilisi.

What the hell was she doing? It didn't really matter so long as Peter found her immediately. If he didn't, Warner would have to call in reinforcements—the Chief of Station and, *heaven forbid*, the Ambassador. The last thing he wanted was for them to start poking around in this mess.

Warner gnawed on a loose cuticle. He couldn't believe she'd actually done it, traveled halfway around the world to find out what Warner couldn't tell her. "Maggie," he grimaced. Most likely she'd gone to Georgia to find the people who'd killed Steve. Or maybe to track down his asset's family or the Chechen rebels he associated with. *Foolish girl.*

He dug furiously through scraps of paper that had accumulated in a growing heap on his desk over the past few days. He needed Peter's secure cell number. He found it, dialed the number, then shoved the paper into his pants pocket.

"Peter."

"Yeah," he sounded out of breath.

"Where the hell is Maggie?"

He cleared his throat. "I was hoping maybe you'd heard from her?"

Warner closed his eyes and counted backwards from ten. "Do you mean to tell me that you're just waiting for her to show up somewhere? Or hoping that she'll ring me up for a chat?"

"Of course not," Peter protested. "I just thought—"

"I don't give a damn what you think. Just find her."

"I've been looking. In fact, I think she stopped by the apartment building this morning. I woke the cleaning woman who lives on the first floor and she said she'd talked to someone matching Maggie's description."

"That gets us nowhere!"

"I . . . I know, and I'll blame myself if anything happens to her."

"Spare me the sentimentality, Peter. You were supposed to keep me updated!" The last word came out in a shout. Warner squeezed the phone so hard his knuckles turned white. "What about Takayev's family? Can you find them, ask them if they've seen her?"

"I could try?" It came across like a question.

"Try? Just do it, Peter," he ordered. "Find Maggie. Do not tell the Station Chief or anyone else in the Agency what you're doing."

"Yes, sir."

"And if you fail to find her," he added, "I will request that the Agency charge you with the willful mishandling of your duties. And if turns out that your pathetic incompetence contributed, in *any way*, to Steve's murder, you will pay."

Silence was all Warner got in response.

"Keep me updated. Hourly." He hung up the phone and pounded a fist into his forehead. He had to get out of here before things got worse. At least he could kick the walls in the privacy of his own home. He slid the rest of the forged documents into his briefcase and grabbed his overcoat from the coat rack. "Priscilla, I'm leaving. See you tomorrow."

"Go home and relax. Have some tea," she called.

If only he could live in Priscilla's world.

As he pulled in the driveway twenty minutes later, his cell phone rang.

"It's me," Peter said.

"Let me talk to her."

"I don't, she's not—"

"Do you not understand the meaning of the word urgent?"

"I went to Dima's, to see if she'd been there. I have been cultivating the manager as a possible source. He seems to have ties to all sorts, including at least one group of Chechen fighters."

Warner waved his hand in a rapid circle, mentally urging Peter to get on with it. "And?"

"I showed him a picture of Maggie. The guy got hostile and had some goons throw me out."

"All very exciting for you, I'm sure, but are you any closer to finding her? Let me answer that for you. No."

"No disrespect, but, actually, I think I know exactly where she is."

"Where?" Warner ventured.

"I can't tell you. Not yet."

CHAPTER TWENTY-SEVEN

When Maggie came to, she found herself back in her room, her coat thrown over her as a makeshift blanket. The room was black, except for the sliver of light reaching under the closed door. Maggie stood and stole over to the door. Out in the hall there was movement, the men speaking in short phrases and thumping about as if preparing to leave. She turned the knob. *Unlocked.* Opening the door a crack, she heard Zara's voice drifting from somewhere in the hall.

"No, Ahmed, you listen to me! You didn't deliver the money on schedule. No money, no materials. And just wait until the Russians find out their men are dead."

Maggie opened the door wider and peered out. To the right, near the front door, stood Zara, holding a large black phone with a thick antenna protruding at an angle from the top. *A satellite phone.*

"I suggest you offer them twice their asking price to smooth things over . . . Look, the original delivery has already been made . . . Yes . . . Mexico . . . Right, for the holiday. But if you want more this week, you have no choice." She ran a hand through her thick black hair. "Get us the money, Ahmed, and we will get you what you need."

Zara whirled around suddenly and caught sight of Maggie.

"Who's Ahmed?"

Zara lowered the phone to the floor and advanced up the hallway.

"Is he al-Qaeda?" Maggie asked, retreating a few steps. "What's the money for?"

Zara pushed her against the wall. "You'll find out," she hissed, her breath hot on Maggie's face.

"You're planning an attack, aren't you?"

Zara smirked.

"What's the axis of evil?"

The front door slammed. Then there was shouting. Two of Zara's men ran past them toward the back of the house. Gun shots erupted. Zara looked left then right as she unholstered her pistol. "Don't you dare move or I'll kill you." She pressed the muzzle against Maggie's shoulder.

Maggie nodded and watched as Zara turned heel and raced after her men. *The Russians again?* Maggie ducked back into her room. *Escape or hide?* Zara had made it clear what would happen if she tried to escape. Would the Russians think she was with the rebels and kill her? She closed her eyes and saw Steve. The bright smile. The impossible blue eyes. He'd wrap her in his arms and smuggle her to safety. She leaned against the wall, trying to control her breathing and formulate a plan.

"Maggie!" someone shouted.

She froze.

"Maggie!" A male voice.

She slid over to the doorway and caught sight of a tall, blond man. "Peter?"

He whirled around. Relief washed over his face. "Yes, yes, it's me. Look, I shot a few of them, but I don't know how many more there are. Take this."

He shoved something into her hand. The light from the hall glinted off cool metal.

"Ever fire one?"

Maggie nodded. "Steve taught me to shoot." She squinted at Peter, the fog finally starting to lift from her head. "How did you find me?"

"That can wait. We have to get out of here."

"Okay." She ran her fingers along the barrel of the gun.

"This way." He peered out into the hall and motioned for her to follow him to the front door.

The house was silent, but as soon as they stepped outside into the dawn's weak light, shots rang out around them.

"Stay there," Peter hissed.

Maggie crouched on the crumbling stone porch steps, watching as Peter disappeared around the side of the house.

"Where do you think you're going?"

Maggie popped up and whirled around. *Zara.* The Chechen woman stood inside the house no more than ten feet away, pointing a rifle directly at Maggie's chest.

"Drop the gun," Maggie ordered as she raised the semi-automatic pistol. "I will shoot," she added to convince herself as much as to threaten Zara.

Zara steadied her weapon. "You should know that I'm a highly trained assassin. Guns, bombs, you name it." She laughed. "You should've seen the chaos at Dima's."

A loud humming filled Maggie's ears. "Wait . . . what?"

"When I killed Steve. It was chaos." She shrugged.

Maggie staggered sideways. "You killed him?" Her arm went limp. The hand holding the gun dropped to her side.

"I was only following orders, Maggie. I had no idea Takayev would be there, but now I understand why he was. Your fiancé turned him against his own people."

"Orders? Whose orders?" Maggie whispered, lips trembling.

"That doesn't matter." A smile spread across Zara's face. "He deserved to die. They both did. And as soon as I find Takayev, I'll finish the job."

Maggie tried to move, knew she should *do something*, but she was frozen, transfixed by the gun barrel. And then Zara closed one eye and adjusted her aim. Some internal switch flipped. Maggie turned, dove away from the house, and tumbled down the cracked stone steps to the rocky ground below. A burst of bullets flew overhead.

Peter reappeared and, leaning into the house, fired several rounds. "Get up and run. Now!" he shouted.

Maggie pushed herself to a stand and, without much aim, fired up through the open front door. A shriek came from inside. She fired several more rounds, then ran away from the house, her chest low to the rocky ground, lumbering forward, arms flailing to help her battered body keep its balance. The pistol slipped from her hand.

"Keep going!" It was Peter, sprinting toward her. In one deft movement, he snatched her gun from the ground and shoved her forward.

After another fifty yards, she stopped and looked back. In the distance, was that someone running away?

"It's Zara! I have to go back!" She lunged for the gun, knocking it out of Peter's hand. She dove for it as it clattered off a large boulder protruding from the ground.

Peter shoved her aside and snatched the sidearm. "She's dead. We've got to get out of here." He tucked the gun into his waistband and yanked her up from the ground.

"No!" She thrashed against him. "I have to kill her. Let me go, Peter!"

He stopped and put his hands on Maggie's cheeks. "She's dead."

"But I saw someone running away!" She blinked. Her head was pounding.

"Wasn't her. I shot her. Now, let's go!"

She nodded and ran, energy coming from an untapped reserve of adrenaline.

"My car is that way, down the hill."

Maggie tried to keep pace with him, despite her body's protest. Up ahead sat a dusty blue Ford sedan. She threw herself into the passenger seat. Peter gunned the engine and careened off before she'd even slammed the door shut. Her heart beat wildly in her chest. A quick glance behind showed no one in pursuit.

"All clear."

He took the next curve far too quickly. The car fishtailed violently.

"Slow down, Peter!"

He ignored her, driving like a bandit for another mile before suddenly swerving off the road and coming to a quick stop behind a cluster of shrubs.

Still no one in pursuit. She turned to him. "You saved my——"

"What the hell were you thinking, Maggie! Why are you here?"

"I had to see for myself."

"See what? Where Steve died? Good grief, Maggie. A bombing site is not a tourist spot. These people are terrorists!"

"Don't you think I know that?" she yelled. "They held me hostage. Beat me." Suddenly she couldn't keep it together anymore. "They killed Steve. Murdered him!" The tears she'd been holding back burst out of her.

She could feel Peter's arms around her, his soothing voice consoling her.

"I know. They're dead now. They can't hurt you anymore."

She freed herself from his embrace. "Even the woman inside the house?"

Peter nodded. "Yes, I shot them all."

"You sure? The woman with the black hair?"

"Yes, I promise." He eased the car back onto the road. "She's dead."

CHAPTER TWENTY-EIGHT

A few miles into the trip, Maggie asked "Is this the way to Tbilisi?"

Peter nodded and tossed her passport and travel pouch onto the dashboard.

"Where did you find those?" She snatched the pouch. Her money and credit card were gone.

"I searched a couple of rooms before I found you. These were sitting on the kitchen table. That's when I knew I had the right place, but I had no idea if you were still alive."

"You got there just in time. I think they were getting ready to move to a different location. You really did save my life. So, thanks."

"No need for thanks, Maggie."

She gave him a weary smile.

"First thing I want to do when we get back to Tbilisi is call Warner. I need to talk to him."

"About what?" He gripped the steering wheel so tightly it made the veins on his hands bulge.

Maggie looked at him sideways. "Well, first of all, he has no idea where I am. And I heard the Chechens—"

"Maggie," he interrupted before pausing briefly. "Listen, I don't know the whole story yet, but I think Warner will do whatever he can to stop you from discovering the truth."

"Why?" She shot more questions at him before he could answer. "What did your note mean? Who's not telling me the whole story?"

"Who do you think?"

"I . . . I don't know." She squinted against morning sun as it rose ahead of them on the narrow road.

"Think about it. Who has access to all the information? Who has the most to lose if the truth about Steve comes out?"

Maggie frowned. Warner had virtually unlimited access to classified information. Yet he hadn't shared any of it with her. And over lunch the other day, he'd gone from avoiding her questions to outright screaming about the NSA cable. What if he knew something he wasn't telling her? What if he could've prevented the bombing but hadn't?

"It can't be him," she breathed.

Peter shot her a look.

"You think Warner is the one hiding information from me?"

Peter raised his eyebrows and pursed his lips. He accelerated, passing a rickety GAZ-53 farm truck rumbling along at half their cruising speed.

"He wasn't himself the last time I saw him," she said as much to herself as to Peter.

"How so?" He drummed his pointer fingers in a random beat on the steering wheel.

"He was . . . I don't know . . . just something in his eyes. He looked wounded. Or off in his own world. It seemed like he'd changed overnight."

"Hmm. Not surprising."

Maggie shifted in the seat and studied Peter's profile. "What's that supposed to mean?"

The corners of his mouth twitched upward into a grin. "He was aware of Steve's collusion with Russian intelligence, you know. But he did nothing about it. Makes me wonder . . ."

Maggie's gut tightened. "There's no proof—"

"Trust me. There's plenty."

She rolled the travel pouch into a twisted ball of fabric. "It can't be what you think it is, Peter. Steve didn't collude with Russian intelligence. In fact, he was actively working against the Russians."

"I know you want to believe that, Maggie."

She stared out the passenger side window, trying to sort through wildly conflicting thoughts. They'd been driving for at least half an hour. Shouldn't there be more signs of civilization the closer they got to Tbilisi? "Look, Peter, I know what Steve was doing here. I know all about the Presidential Finding."

Peter's eyebrows shot up. "Which one?"

"The one directing the CIA to intercept weapons going from Russia to terrorist groups."

Peter stared straight ahead, eyes squinting, gaze fixed on the road.

"And Warner? He may be a lot of things, but—" She tried to shake her head, but the pain stopped her.

"Maggie, I understand why you can't imagine Steve and Warner being involved in anything illegal. I couldn't believe it myself. The truth is painful, but the sooner you accept it, the sooner you can move on."

"Move on? Why does everyone keep telling me to move on? I just buried Steve last week!" Her voice rose. "I am here to find the truth, and nothing, not one single thing, points to Steve being a traitor. Despite what everyone says." She stared out the window. Stark, jagged, rock mountains rose from the ground around them, fierce protectors designed to keep the country's inhabitants safe from the outside world. "Please just take me to the hotel."

"I can't. It's too dangerous."

"Why," she snapped. "Who's out to get me now?"

He turned to her. "I told you, I don't trust Warner."

"I never told him I was coming here."

Peter flushed. "Maggie, he's CIA. Do you really think he wouldn't be keeping tabs on you? It wouldn't be hard for him to figure out where you are."

Maggie stared at him. "But why would he be looking for me?"

"Because he knows you won't rest until you know the truth! In fact, he called me. And I told him you were here."

"Why would you do that if you don't trust him?" Nothing Peter said was making any sense.

"I don't know. I wasn't thinking? He's my boss? I was worried when you didn't call me back or show up at my apartment last night? Listen, my colleague, my best friend, was just killed in a bomb attack. Do you think things are business as usual around here?"

"Steve wasn't your best friend." Maggie felt like a petulant child wanting to set the record straight, and yet, somehow, she couldn't bear the thought that Peter walked around claiming closeness to Steve.

Peter stared at her, his eyes dark as ink. "You have no idea what's going on, Maggie. Case in point—you got yourself kidnapped," he snapped.

"Well, if you know everything, then why don't you enlighten me?" Tension crept up her shoulders into her neck. "Just how the hell did you find me out in the middle of the Georgian countryside anyway?"

Peter slammed on the brakes and turned to face her. "Would you rather I hadn't looked?"

His voice had taken on a dangerous edge. She retreated. "Look, I'm exhausted. I just want to go home."

No response.

"Peter, I can handle Warner. I don't need you to defend me. I need to warn my boss—I think something big is brewing."

"The only thing that's brewing is your imagination." He glared at her. "And the only thing you need to do is get on a plane back to Washington. Let the professionals handle this."

"Fine with me." It wasn't fine. She had considered telling him about the Russian assault on the farmhouse. About the indications, vague as they were, of some sort of imminent attack. About Takayev still being alive. But something about Peter's demeanor set off alarm bells in her head. Something was wrong.

They drove on in silence for a few minutes.

"How do you know Richard Carvelli?" Her question was fueled by nothing but instinct.

"Who?"

"I saw you talking to him at the wake."

"I talked to lots of people at the wake," he snapped.

"I think he's involved in something criminal."

"Criminal?"

"Yeah. Intelligence related."

He threw his hands up off the steering wheel in dramatic frustration. "Then why don't you call the FBI or something."

Maggie studied his face. Tension lined his forehead. "It was pretty obvious that you and the congressman know each other. In fact, it looked like you were having a serious disagreement about something."

"I don't know anything about him other than that he's a congressman. I know nothing about his foreign dealings. And if I did talk to him at the wake, I can't remember what it was about, alright?" He stared daggers at her.

"Foreign dealings? What's that supposed to mean?"

"Nothing. You know, Steve said you were a bit unstable, but I had no idea."

She buried her hands in her coat pockets. It took every ounce of self-restraint she had not to slap him. She couldn't—he was her only way back to Tbilisi. She stared out the window. They hadn't seen a single car since they passed the old truck. In fact, the road signs for Tbilisi had disappeared, only to be replaced by ones for places she'd never heard of. Were they east, west, north, south?

"How long until we're in the city?"

He ignored her question, driving on in silence. The car slowed to a halt a few minutes later. He took the keys from the ignition and opened the door. "Get out."

The car was parked on a craggy ledge, mid-way up a steep incline. On the road far below a lone car passed. Beyond that, in the far distance, several small houses dotted the grassy landscape. A hawk soared above, its lonely cry the only sound echoing off the surrounding rocky outcrops.

"Where the hell are we, Peter?"

CHAPTER TWENTY-NINE

Warner paced along the cobblestone walkway in front of his house. First Peter Belekov had withheld critical information, and then he'd hung up on him. *Sonofabitch!* He was tired of reacting to everyone else's moves. He snapped a branch off his prize rose bush and threw it to the ground.

Warner climbed into the BMW, thrust it into reverse, and began the now-familiar drive to Maggie's. With her missing in parts unknown, he'd do whatever it took to track her down. Steve would've expected no less. The best place to begin was her house. During the ten-minute drive, Warner convinced himself that breaking in was entirely necessary.

He was, after all, trying to help—her and himself. He was saving lives. And asses.

Upon arrival, he parked across the street, several houses down. He reached into the glove compartment and pulled out the toolkit before scanning the area for curious neighbors. All was clear. Warner conquered the front door lock in under two minutes. If common criminals knew how to do what he did, no one would be safe at home.

At first glance, the house appeared neat, but it certainly wasn't clean. Two unwashed mugs sat in the sink along with a small plate, a half-eaten cookie, and a crimson-stained wine glass. Dried grains of rice littered the kitchen table. Warner took the stairs to Maggie's bedroom. Dirty clothes were strewn across the far end near the closet, and clean laundry remained folded in a basket on her hope chest. It looked like she'd packed and left in a hurry. A pile of unmatched socks lay entwined with a pair of jeans on the floor in front of the dresser. What had she been wearing when he brought over lunch? He picked up the jeans and reached into the pockets. Empty. Warner sat himself down on the edge of the bed. The sheets on the right side were drawn back in restless disarray; the ones on the left were pulled tight, tucked in, undisturbed.

He slid to the floor and threw up the comforter, peering underneath the bed. Nothing but a few scattered magazines and a lonely t-shirt. He rustled through some drawers, resigned to finding nothing. In the master bathroom, he spotted a portable telephone resting on the vanity. Next to it was a scrap of paper with a list of barely legible dates. *Josef and Tamara Ashkhanadze* was scrawled across the bottom.

"Who the hell are they?" he asked himself in the mirror. The names sounded Georgian, but Warner had never heard either of them. He picked up the phone, dialed *69, then repeated the number to himself. Her last call had been to a number in D.C. He dialed.

A woman answered in slightly accented English, "Good afternoon. Embassy of the Republic of Georgia, how may I direct your call?"

On a hunch, he said, "Josef Ashkhanadze, please."

"You mean Tamaz Ashkhanadze?"

Warner glanced at the paper. He frowned. "No, Josef. Or maybe Tamara?"

"I'm afraid the only person here with that last name is Tamaz Ashkhanadze. He's not in the office this week. Perhaps someone else can help you?"

Warner hung up. What was Maggie doing contacting the Georgian Embassy? Was it innocent, perhaps for visa or travel information? He pulled the cell phone from his belt clip and called Priscilla. "Hey, there. I forgot to check one more thing before I left. Should I know someone named Tamaz Ashkhanadze? He's with the Georgian Embassy."

"Ashkhanadze," Priscilla murmured. "Hold on a minute."

Warner heard her flipping pages.

"Warner, I'm looking for my embassy directory, it's here somewhere. Where on earth did it go?"

Warner massaged his temples with his free hand. *Come on, Priscilla.*

"Can't find it anywhere. Let me check this list here. Let's see . . . Gambia, Georgia, here it is, our list of their acknowledged intelligence personnel. What's the name again?"

"Ashkhanadze. A-S-H— "

"Got it. Tamaz Ashkhanadze."

"Is there a Josef Ashkhanadze?"

"No. Only a Tamaz. He's listed as a political officer."

"Thanks, Priscilla." He hung up, wondering if the two men were related, or perhaps even the same person. He walked out of the bathroom, through the bedroom, and into the hall. The adjacent room was empty except for a few boxes of books. The room at the end of the hall was the office. Warner invited himself to sit at Maggie's computer.

As he booted up the machine, he compiled a mental list of potential login passwords. But then the screen brightened and, just like that, he was in. No password required. He frowned. She should know better, especially given her experience in the intelligence world. Pausing for a moment, Warner recalled his last face-to-face conversation with Steve, just days before he deployed to Tbilisi. He had confided how worried he was about Maggie's safety while he was overseas. She never locked her car, often forgot to lock the house, and opened the door for anyone who knocked. Steve loved her innocence, her belief in the goodness of others, her certainty that nothing bad would happen to her. But it also caused him great anxiety. So much so that he'd asked Warner to keep an eye on her while he was away. That request weighed heavily on him now. Maggie was alone and vulnerable in a foreign country, and there wasn't a damned thing he could do about it. Not yet, anyway.

Warner quickly scrolled through her emails. Nothing helpful. No clues. He searched U.S. papers for the name "Ashkhanadze" but came up empty. Then he searched in the *Moscow Times* online edition.

Warner gave a low whistle and blinked at the screen. Josef Ashkhanadze died in Tbilisi . . . on the same date as Steve. But that wasn't his asset's name. It was Tak-something, wasn't it? Whatever

Maggie was doing, she was steps ahead of him, further than he could've imagined. He deleted the history file for the day.

He called the Georgian Embassy back again, explaining that it was urgent that he speak to Mr. Ashkhanadze. "He left for Georgia Monday evening, sir. Perhaps someone else can help you?"

Warner declined assistance. Maybe Maggie was with this Ashkhanadze character. Peter said she was still missing but that he was pursuing leads. Maybe Peter knew Tamaz, too? If so, then Ashkhanadze might just be more than just a diplomat. He might be an intelligence officer. He dialed Peter's cell number, determined to retake control of the situation. No answer.

"Dammit!" Warner cursed and kicked at the air.

CHAPTER THIRTY

P eter grabbed her by the elbow. "Let's go."

Maggie tugged her arm away. "I'm not going anywhere. Not until you tell me what the hell is going on."

This time there was no escaping as his hand wrapped firmly around her wrist. She stumbled behind him as he dragged her up an incline. A ramshackle wooden shack staggered into view from behind a knotted tree that sprouted from the ground at on odd angle. A lonely plume of smoke curled up from a crumbling stone chimney on the near side of the structure.

"You ready?" Peter asked, his tone suddenly all business.

"For what?"

"Inside are the answers you're seeking," Peter replied without further elaboration.

He pulled at her coat as if she were his pet on a leash, leading her the final twenty feet to the house, where he twisted open the doorknob. She followed him into the shack, blinking her eyes to adjust to the dim light.

Peter dropped her arm and disappeared into a back room. To her left was a kitchen straight out of the 1940s—an ancient cast iron stove, cracked linoleum flooring, peeling yellow paint on the walls. Down the hall, she heard Peter speaking in Russian. Another male voice answered, but she couldn't follow the conversation. She looked back to the front door. A sudden surge of energy came and went quickly. If she was going to run, now was her chance. But Peter would catch her. He had a car. She was battered, exhausted, and in the middle of nowhere.

"Maggie!" he called. "There's someone you need to meet." He leaned out of the back room and waved her down the hall.

The small room beyond the door held a sagging cot and a kerosene lantern that stood alone on a simple wooden table. At the foot of the bed was a small wood stove. A half dozen logs lay haphazardly on the floor beside it. On the cot sat a man whose dark, tousled hair framed a chiseled face that was defined by a jagged scar running along the right cheekbone. He sat hunched forward, large hands supporting his weight on the cot. Beneath a rugged military green jacket, he wore a tan shirt marred by a dark brown stain of dried blood. His left wrist bore a handcuff that was tethered to the wood stove by a long chain.

The man raised his face, his great black eyes taking in all of her. Maggie felt momentarily dazed but knew, at once and without a doubt, that Zara had been right. Takayev was very much alive.

Only, unlike Zara and possibly unlike even Peter, she knew his real identity—Josef Ashkhanadze.

Maggie held his gaze then stole a furtive look at Peter who stood beside her, arms crossed, expression neutral. Why wasn't he uncuffing him? Takayev was Steve's asset. The CIA's asset. Did Peter consider him dangerous? "You're Takayev," she whispered.

He nodded, his eyes flitting between Peter and her.

Peter smiled. "And this is Maggie. Steve's girlfriend," he added flippantly.

Fiancée, you jackass. She focused on Takayev, then advanced toward him. "He needs a doctor."

Peter's arm shot out, stopping her in her tracks. "He's fine. I left him with food, water, painkillers. And I checked on him when I got back from Washington."

Takayev glared at Peter.

"At least uncuff him," she pleaded.

Peter tapped his lips with his right index finger. "No can do. This is a very dangerous man."

"But he's—" Doubt crowded Maggie's mind. Zara had said that Takayev betrayed her, that he worked for the Americans. But what if that had been a ruse? What if Zara wanted to find Takayev because he was integral to their plans for an attack? Her breath caught in her chest. But . . . no, that made no sense. If Takayev was on Zara's side, he wouldn't have been at the café that day, especially if he knew there was a bomb. Maybe he'd learned about Zara's involvement in an impending terrorist attack. And maybe he'd been planning to warn Steve when they met.

She turned her attention back to the cot. "I don't understand. Everyone in Washington thinks you're dead. Your bro—" She stopped short, wary of revealing any information to anyone.

"He's clearly not dead. In fact, I saved his life."

"You *saved* him?" She shook her head in disbelief. "You told me you never saw his body!"

Peter shrugged. "I happened to be nearby when the bomb went off. What was I supposed to do? Leave him there at the mercy of a third-world hospital?"

Nearby? He just happened to be nearby when the bomb went off? She inched away from Peter. "Why didn't you tell anyone Takayev was alive?" Her voice rose. "You didn't think it was relevant to the investigation into Steve's death?"

"Calm down, Maggie."

"His family is grieving. For God's sake, Peter, his funeral is today."

Takayev paled. "Today?"

Maggie nodded.

"The funeral may be for him, but obviously, they won't be burying his remains."

Maggie gasped. "Then whose are they?"

"A mixture of parts from the other people who died at the café." He smirked. "You'd be amazed at what you can accomplish simply by throwing American dollars at government officials around here. Just like that," he snapped his fingers, "they identified some of the remains from the bombing as Takayev's."

Her jaw dropped. "I don't understand why you are hiding him, Peter."

"If I'd let Georgian officials take him, we'd never get to the bottom of what he and Steve were up to."

What?

"You can't . . . you can't just take someone prisoner and interrogate him," she sputtered.

"Sure I can," he replied breezily. "I work for the CIA, remember? You think they'll be displeased when I tell them I uncovered a traitor or two within the ranks? I don't think so."

Maggie waved her hand in Takayev's direction. "You should've notified Langley immediately. They would've arranged for a team to come in and question him."

Peter leaned against the wall and studied her. "You're saying I should've let Warner lead the interrogation?" He nodded toward the cot. "If that had happened, our friend here would've mysteriously died during the process. Case closed. Truth buried. Steve's name stays clean, Warner keeps his job, and we never find out the damage Steve did by selling secrets to the Russians, the Chechens, or whoever the hell he was involved with."

Takayev spoke, his voice raspy, laced with anger. "You're a liar."

"Shut up," Peter barked.

"You're making no sense, Peter. Are you saying Steve was in cahoots with his asset to . . . do what exactly?"

Peter flushed and pushed himself away from the wall. "This is why I'm interrogating him."

"It's all lies, Maggie," Takayev said, his voice stronger.

"I said, SHUT UP." Peter lunged at his prisoner, pummeling him in the midsection where dried blood stained his shirt.

Maggie clawed at Peter's jacket. "Stop it! You're going to kill him."

Peter twisted right then left. Maggie lost her grip and stumbled back a few steps.

Turning his attention to her, Peter growled, "Don't you dare grab me like that again."

Behind him, Takayev was doubled over, gasping through clenched teeth.

Maggie tried to defuse the situation. "He's no good to you dead, Peter."

The CIA officer straightened his jacket and ran fingers through his tousled hair. "I know what I'm doing."

"Here's what I don't understand," she ventured. "Someone tried to kill Steve and Takeyev at the café, right? Who? Who set off the bomb?" She knew it was Zara. Did he?

Peter tilted his head to the side.

"If Steve was selling intelligence to the Russians, it probably wasn't them. If Steve and Takayev were working with Chechen radicals, it probably wasn't them, either. You don't cut off the hand that feeds you. So who was it, Peter? The CIA? Why? Or is there someone else you're not telling me about?"

Peter's eyes darted between Maggie and Takayev, who was now sitting up straighter. "Takayev was using Steve, only he was too stupid to know it. Once the Chechens got the information they needed from Steve, they decided to kill him." He pointed to Takayev. "He placed the bomb but was too slow to get away before it went off."

Maggie turned to the cot, sudden confusion coursing through her.

"*He* told me to meet him at the café," Takayev croaked.

She blinked. "Steve?"

"No. Peter."

"I don't understand. Wasn't Steve your handler?"

Takayev nodded. "Peter said Steve was in the middle of something big and had asked him to set up a meeting on his behalf."

"Steve and I covered for each other all the time," Peter said flatly. "It wasn't a big deal."

A sudden ringing filled her ears. Peter set up the meeting at the café. Peter just happened to be nearby when the bomb went off.

Her face grew hot.

"Not a big deal? Steve's dead. Because of you." She advanced on Peter. "You sent him there!"

He shoved her, sending her tumbling back to the dusty floor. "Are you accusing me of knowing about the bomb?"

"Well, did you?" Maggie shrieked.

"You know, Maggie, I was going to drive you back to Tbilisi, but you're asking far too many questions."

She righted herself, turning slightly to the side to protect her midsection in case he came at her again. "Too many questions?"

He shook his head as he paced the small space like a caged animal. "Everything would've been fine if you'd just let professionals like me handle this."

Blood thrummed behind her eyes. "Steve didn't sell information to the Russians, did he?"

Peter grinned. "My sources say he did."

In her peripheral vision, she caught Takayev shaking his head. "It wasn't Steve."

Peter sucker-punched Takayev in the gut, leaving the man gasping for breath again, his face contorted in agony. "If you don't keep your mouth shut, I'll beat you to the edge of your life."

Maggie rushed to Takayev's side. She put one arm on his back, the other on his arm.

"He. Set. Us. Up." Takayev's words came out in pained gasps.

Rage coursed through her body, giving her a sudden surge of strength. In one deft move she pivoted and hurled herself at Peter's midsection. Air left him in a loud exhale as he tumbled backwards, hitting his head on the wall.

Maggie scanned the room then grabbed a chunk of firewood from the floor. Already, Peter was straightening himself, shaking off the blow. She swung, hitting the side of his head with a firm *thunk*. He collapsed onto the floor, unmoving.

"Keys?" Takayev implored, raising his cuffed arm.

Maggie searched Peter's coat pocket. She grabbed his wallet and rifled through it. Several credit cards, VIP cards from two Tbilisi casinos, and a large wad of American dollars and Georgian Lari banknotes. She tucked the wallet into her jacket and checked the other pocket for his keys. "Got them!" She hurried over to Takeyev, fumbling through several until she found a small one that slipped right into the lock.

The cuff fell from Takayev's wrist, revealing a circle of raw red skin underneath. "We must go."

Peter moaned on the floor.

She helped Takeyev up from the bed. He shuffled with a limp, but when Peter groaned more loudly, he picked up the pace.

CHAPTER THIRTY-ONE

Maggie waited for Takayev to lower himself into the passenger seat. "You okay?"

He grimaced and nodded. She felt around under the seat, hoping Peter had stashed a mobile phone there. No such luck, but her fingers brushed up against the cold steel of a Makarov 9mm semi-automatic pistol. The one she'd dropped at the farmhouse. After tucking it into her waistband, Maggie started the engine and felt her tension ease. "How far to Tbilisi?"

"About 100 kilometers." Takayev directed her to a two-lane road that had suffered from years of neglect, but at least she was finally headed in the right direction.

She placed a hand on his arm. "We're safe now."

"Safe?" He turned his head, laughing. "He's CIA. He's prepared. There's an old car behind the shack. It still runs. The key's in the kitchen. He'll be after us in no time."

Now he tells me. Maggie checked the rearview mirror and pressed down on the accelerator. "What happened that day?" A lump formed in her throat. What she really wanted to ask was how Takayev had survived when Steve hadn't.

"Like I said, Peter phoned saying that Steve needed to meet with me but wasn't able to call. He was out on an operation or something, so Peter set up the meeting for him."

Maggie reached to the console to turn up the heat. The cold Georgian morning was nipping at her nerves. "Did Peter give you any other details?"

"No, just that Steve needed to give me some important information."

"And then?" She glanced at him, taking her eyes off the road for a moment.

"And then, I got to the restaurant and saw Steve sitting by the front window in the atrium. He was surprised to see me."

"Why?"

"He was expecting Peter. Steve said Peter had asked to meet him there for breakfast. Steve had no idea I was going to show up instead." The story tumbled from his mouth. "We both knew instinctively that something was wrong and decided to leave. He walked to the counter to pay as I headed for the exit, but moments later—" Takayev's voice caught in his throat. He cleared it. "Moments later, glass flew at us from every direction. There was so much smoke." He ran his hand across his face. "The next thing I remember was someone dragging me into a car."

"Peter?"

"Yes," came the muffled response.

"Why was he there?"

"I . . . I don't know."

"Did he say anything?"

"I don't remember."

"Why did he keep you alive after the bombing?"

"I suppose he panicked when he saw that I was still alive. He hid me away so I couldn't tell anyone that he had set us up."

Maggie studied her passenger. "If he was trying to kill you at the café, why didn't he finish the job and kill you once you got to the shack?"

"Maybe he thought he could use me as a bargaining chip."

"Bargaining with whom?"

"I don't know." Takayev shrugged. "I'm sure he would have killed me eventually. I know too much."

Maggie gripped the steering wheel so hard that her engagement ring pinched her finger. "You know too much about what?"

"I know that Peter sent both of us to the café where a bomb went off."

Maggie had been dealing in assumptions and vague theories since the moment she'd learned of Steve's murder. Now, she needed facts, incontrovertible facts.

"But that doesn't prove anything. Even if Peter sent you both to the café, it doesn't mean he knew of the bomb. If he needed you dead for some reason, you'd be dead, too."

Takayev closed his eyes. His voice was weary. "I had never met Peter until the moment he pulled me out of the wreckage. I can't psychoanalyze him for you. All I know is that he set us up. He wanted us dead."

"So you think he knew about the bombing?" Her voice was barely above a whisper.

"No question." He took a deep breath to steady his voice. "I wish Steve had left right away instead of trying to settle the bill. If he had, he'd still be alive."

She swallowed. It was so like Steve. The idea of leaving without paying wouldn't even have crossed his mind. Even so, she couldn't help but wonder how perfect her life would be if Steve had been less honest and just left without settling his bill. "Let's get you home so you can call your brother."

"Tamaz?"

"He thinks you're dead."

"You know Tamaz?"

She nodded.

A weary smile crossed his face. "He's going to kill me when he finds out I'm still alive. For putting him through all this."

There were still a few hours until the funeral. "I'll talk him out of it."

Josef closed his eyes again.

His version of events made sense, but had Steve really known who he was dealing with in Takayev? Did Steve know about his association with Zara? She ran her hand over the Makarov, wishing she'd checked if it was still loaded before they'd left the shack.

"Takayev?

"Mmh?"

"Zara's been looking for you."

His eyes flew open and he blanched, his olive skin suddenly splotchy and white.

"If she finds me—"

She won't. "Why were you working with her?"

He exhaled.

Maggie stiffened. *Awfully dramatic*, she thought.

"I work for Georgian intelligence. Steve and I often met on official business, but I also gave him information that I didn't give to my own government."

"Why?"

"My government is very corrupt. I don't know who I can trust anymore. I knew Steve would get my information where it needed to go." He placed a hand on her arm. "I trusted him. Completely."

Maggie pressed her lips together and focused on the road. Signs for Tbilisi were appearing more frequently. "Where do the Chechens fit in?"

"The government has been ignoring Chechen activity here for a long time. Our leaders don't want to give Russia another excuse to meddle in our country, which they would, if they knew the extent of rebel activity in Georgia. About a year ago, there was an uptick in the number of al-Qaeda operatives coming to Tbilisi." He scrunched up his face in disgust. "They were trying to recruit young Chechen men to their cause." He raised his hands to his shoulders. "I couldn't sit by and watch that happen. I needed to know who they were recruiting, and to what end. So, I infiltrated a Chechen cell, calling myself Takayev."

Zara's cell. "How did you manage to do that?" She'd heard of intelligence agents going rogue, but infiltrating a terrorist cell on his own?

"My mother is Chechen." He looked at himself in the side-view mirror. "I blended in quite easily. I know the people, the customs, the beliefs."

Maggie raised her eyebrows. "So, you ran your own operation against al-Qaeda?"

"With Steve's help and advice. We were a team."

She imagined them huddled together, discussing developments, planning next steps. Surely, Warner had known about this. Why hadn't he told her?

He continued. "Zara has contacts in the Russian mafia."

Maggie's mind flashed to the tattooed, dying Russian back at the farmhouse. *Mafia.* "Why would the Russian mafia work with radicals who are fighting a guerrilla war against their own countrymen?" None of this made any sense.

Takayev sat taller in the passenger seat, confident in his expertise. "Back in the early '90s when the Soviet Union collapsed, criminal gangs ran rampant. They stole and extorted from the state, the military, businesses, and ordinary people. Old communist leaders and military officers seized on the opportunity to enrich themselves.

They took over criminal gangs and leveraged their existing networks to amass huge fortunes. Some of these mafia families were fiercely loyal to all things Russia, but others would sell their souls to the devil for money."

Maggie nodded. His explanation aligned with what she had learned in her days as a CIA analyst. "So it's the latter, the ones who would sell their souls, who might work with Chechen rebels."

"Precisely. These mafia bosses have no morals. They'll sell weapons to militantly anti-Russian groups if doing so results in a big payday." His gaze returned to the countryside whizzing by. "Several weapons smuggling routes go right through Georgia."

Maggie tapped on the brakes. Traffic was getting heavier. "What kind of weapons?"

"Small arms, light weapons like grenades, and so forth." He exhaled. "And lately, nuclear materials."

She glanced at Takayev. Dirt creased the worry lines around his eyes. "Nuclear?"

He nodded, lips pressed together, eyes downcast. "Several mafia families are led by former Soviet military officers who have relationships with active duty Russian officers. The mafia guys wave a whole bunch of cash in front of the Russian military guys, and just like that, some old nuclear waste goes missing and no one bats an eye."

A sense of dread filled Maggie. "Would the mafia really sell this stuff to a group like Zara's?"

"That's what Steve and I were trying to find out. Whether Zara's ties with the Russian mafia were significant enough to give her access to nuclear materials."

Maggie swallowed. Takayev seemed trustworthy, but after everything that had happened in the past ten days, she couldn't be certain.

"What is it, Maggie?"

Then again, she trusted Steve. And if Steve trusted Takayev . . . "I think she was very much tied in. I overheard Zara talking to a man she called Ahmed. She said something about not delivering the materials to him until he sent money. I think the Russian mafia was the one supplying the materials."

Takayev's brow furrowed. "Most members of her cell trained in Pakistan or Afghanistan at some point. They have Arab contacts."

Maggie's pulse quickened. "Which means al-Qaeda?"

Takayev nodded, his expression grim.

Maggie laid the pieces out in her mind but couldn't bring herself to connect them. She focused on the road signs ahead.

Takayev cleared his throat. "You've confirmed everything that Steve and I suspected. Zara was the middleman. She facilitated the sale of nuclear material from the Russian mafia to al-Qaeda. To this Ahmed person."

"Where does Peter fit in?"

"I have no idea," he admitted.

Maggie let it sink it. Peter sent them to the café. Zara murdered Steve. To ensure that she could keep smuggling nuclear weapons. Maggie felt sick. She had tried to understand this woman's plight, tried to save her brother's life. Even traded stories about their fathers. "What's the ultimate target?"

"I was trying to figure that out before all of . . . this." He touched his blood-stained shirt. "The night before the . . . the café, I was with Zara and her men. They were discussing an attack against the United States in the next month or two. I told Steve that morning. He'd heard the same thing, but we didn't feel safe discussing it in public. And then . . . it was too late . . ."

Her throat seized. "Any details on the attack? Anything at all?"

He shook his head as his face crumpled. "No. But al-Qaeda is definitely involved."

Maggie remembered the terror of being in the Capitol Building on September 11th. They'd watched in horror as not one plane but two struck in New York. When the Pentagon was hit, a panicked exodus had begun from Capitol Hill.

A nuclear attack would make 9/11 seem like a fire drill in comparison. "The Chechens' gripe is with Russia. Why get involved with al-Qaeda?"

"For the money."

"The money?"

He winced and held his side as the car hit a pothole. "Al-Qaeda has deep pockets. Saudi money, mostly. The Chechens need cash to buy conventional weapons, so they sell nuclear materials to al-Qaeda and use the proceeds to fund recruitment and training. And to buy weapons to use in their fight against Russia."

"Why don't the Chechens use the nuclear materials against Russia? I mean, wouldn't that force the Russian military to stand down or maybe even grant Chechnya independence?"

Takayev shook his head. "If the Chechens threatened Moscow with any kind of weapon of mass destruction, the gloves would come off. President Putin would level Chechnya. And the rebels know that. They want independence. They're willing to risk a certain level of casualties, but they won't set themselves up for total annihilation."

Maggie hated to admit it, but she wished the Chechens would use the nuclear materials to settle their own scores. The prospect of al-Qaeda using such weapons against the United States was inconceivable. But it was suddenly all too real.

They rode on without speaking as Maggie accelerated into roads slicing through villages that appeared more frequently with each passing mile. They were on the outskirts of Tbilisi, which was more like home than any place she'd been in days.

"What's the fastest way to Moskovskiy Prospect?" she asked.

"Why there? That's not where the embassy is."

CHAPTER THIRTY-TWO

Maggie parked the car along the curb near Steve's apartment building.

"What are we doing here?" Takayev furrowed his brow. "Shouldn't we go to the American Embassy?"

Maggie removed the keys from the ignition and glanced at the rearview mirror again. "We will, after I check out a few things."

Takayev didn't look convinced but followed her into the building's lobby. The little old woman was there, again pushing a dirty mop across a worn and stained marble floor. Maggie approached, keeping her voice low. She flashed a ten dollar bill from Peter's wallet and got the information she needed.

"Who lives here?" Takayev demanded when he caught up to her at the elevator bank.

Maggie gave him a tight smile and pressed the call button repeatedly. "Come on," she ordered the elevator, which finally opened with a tired moan. The stairs would've been faster, but it was unlikely that Takayev could make it up more than one flight.

They disembarked on the seventh floor and turned right down the hall. She'd been able to understand enough of what the cleaning woman had said to figure out which apartment it was. The second key on the ring worked, and the door swung open into a sparsely furnished Brezhnev-era apartment.

"Maggie?" Takayev said.

"It's okay, no one's home." Maggie walked through a little cave of a kitchen into the cramped living room and set the keys down on a small table next to the rotary telephone. She proceeded to open kitchen drawers and cabinets, not sure what she was hoping to find. Something incriminating. Right now, it was Peter's word against hers and Takayev's. She needed solid evidence.

Takayev emerged from the bathroom down the short hall to the right of the living room. He'd washed the grime and dried blood from his face and neck. "This is Peter's apartment?"

She nodded as she rifled through desk drawers in the living room.

"What are you looking for?"

"I don't know. Classified documents he shouldn't have. Correspondence with Russian intelligence. That sort of thing."

"I'll take the bedroom," he suggested.

"I'd rather you find yourself something to eat. This won't take long." Takayev might overlook something important, and not knowing how long it would be until Peter made his way back to the capital, it was better that she do all the searching.

Takayev paused, started to object, but relented. A minute later, he was on the living room sofa, a glass of water in one hand, a box of crackers in the other. He flipped through a day-old newspaper. "Look." He waved the paper in the air. "My funeral is at four o'clock this afternoon at the Sioni cathedral." He read on. "They used my real name—Ashkhanadze. Says here I was a bystander killed by a bomb targeting an American diplomat."

A now-familiar weakness permeated Maggie's body. She inhaled deeply and took a quick look at the funeral notice written in both Georgian and Russian. "I should probably be the one to tell Tamaz you're still alive."

He laid the paper on his lap and nibbled on a cracker. "Good idea. I don't want to give him a heart attack by showing up at my own funeral."

She studied him for a minute. He seemed to be relaxing, perhaps more than the circumstances warranted. He'd almost been killed just last week, then was held prisoner with no idea whether he'd live or die. Under her jacket, she felt the weight of the Makarov against her lower back. "Did you know Zara was the bomber?"

"Zara?" A cracker fell from his hand. "Was I the target?"

"I don't think she knew you'd be at the café. And I'm not even sure if she realized who Steve was. She was hired to do a job, and she did it."

His eyes widened.

"Afterward, someone must've told her about your relationship with Steve. Once she found out you'd survived, she began searching for you."

"She can't find me. If she does—"

"Don't worry, she's dead." Her thoughts flashed back to the farmhouse, to the person she thought she'd seen fleeing. A woman?

In all the chaos, she couldn't be sure. Peter's assurances were all she had, and they weren't worth anything anymore.

Water spilled on his jacket as he raised the glass with a trembling hand. "Maggie . . ."

She rifled through the final desk drawer and turned to face him.

"Steve wasn't selling intelligence to the Russians. He never would. You know that, right?"

She absorbed the truth in waves of relief. "I know." The entire trip, the kidnapping, torture, fear, was all worth it now. Steve was innocent. She had proof in Takayev. She'd be able to clear his name. "And now I have proof—you."

Takayev smiled. "I'll tell everyone who needs to know the story. The CIA. The FBI. Hell, even your president."

Maggie took a cracker from the box. She was suddenly famished. "Why did Peter want me to think Steve was betraying the CIA?"

"Not sure. I suspect he's trying to cover up for something else."

But what? She glanced at the kitchen clock. They'd been here for fifteen minutes. If Peter was on his way, or if he'd been able to contact anyone involved in this mess, they could be on their way to the apartment. She really didn't need more evidence. Takayev was enough.

He interrupted her thoughts. "Steve and I were working together to find out if the rumors were true. Was an American selling intelligence to the Russian mafia?"

Maggie's breath caught in her throat. "Did you find out?"

"No, but I overheard Zara referencing someone called 'the congressman' a few times."

"The congressman," she repeated. "A nickname?"

Takayev shrugged.

If this person was an actual member of congress, the list of suspects was huge—435 people to be exact. Well, minus about five dozen female representatives. But she knew of only one who'd shown interest in Chechnya. "Did Steve know about this congressman?"

"Yes, of course. I told him. And Steve shared my intelligence with others in the Station." Takayev paused. "At least for a time he did. Until a couple of months ago, when he caught a colleague rifling through his notes. And one morning, he found his computer logged on when he knew he'd logged off the night before."

"Did he mention the name of the colleague?"

"No."

Only a couple of other people had access to the CIA Station which was tucked away in the embassy's attic. Among them—Peter. "Have you ever heard the name Carvelli?"

"No."

She frowned. Maybe she was completely off track. There was no evidence that Richard Carvelli had sold secrets to Russia. Sure, he seemed to have an unusual interest in all things Russian and Chechen. And yes, she'd seen him talking to Peter at the wake, but that didn't prove anything either. Her frustration was coalescing into a pounding headache.

"We should get out of here, but I need to warn Washington about the attack first."

She dashed over to Peter's telephone and dialed Langley, managing to connect with Priscilla on the second try.

"Priscilla, I have to talk to Warner."

"Maggie? Where are you? This is a terrible connection."

"Is he there? It's important."

"No, I'm afraid not."

Her shoulders tensed.

"I left my cell phone at a friend's house. Could you give me his mobile number?"

"I could leave him a message for you, dear."

"No need. I'll call him directly."

Priscilla sighed. "If you insist."

She scribbled down the number. What if Warner was working with Peter? He was his boss, after all. And he'd sent Peter back to Tbilisi abruptly after the wake. What if Warner was the one Peter had referred to in his note. *They're not telling you the whole story.* Her hand hovered over the phone. She dialed. Voicemail. *Dammit.*

"Warner, it's me."

A loud noise—*the elevator door?*—emanated from the hallway. She lowered the receiver. "Takayev, we have to go."

He stood, the newspaper clutched in one hand. Eyes wide with fear, he asked, "What is it?"

Maggie put a finger to her lips and cracked open the apartment door. The hallway was clear to both the right and the left. She motioned for him to follow her to the elevator. As they neared, the dented metal door creaked open.

"Get back," Takayev shouted as he caught sight of a haggard Peter standing behind the irritated old babushka, who was clutching a chain loaded with keys.

Peter and Maggie locked eyes just as she latched on to Takayev's arm. "The stairs!" she shouted, tugging him toward the exit sign at the other end of the hallway.

Takayev stumbled and dropped the newspaper but quickly righted himself. "Don't wait for me," he huffed. "Go!"

In an instant, Peter emerged and tackled Takayev from behind. "Run, Maggie!" Takayev yelled as he struggled to free his battered body from under the much younger, stronger man.

No. She needed Takayev. He was her proof. Slipping a hand under her jacket, she wrapped her palm around the pistol grip. Peter rolled off Takayev and hopped to his feet in one deft move. Before Maggie could react, he had a gun leveled at her chest. Takayev let out a primal yell and swatted at Peter's ankles. It wasn't much of a move, but it was enough to startle Peter.

"Run!" Takayev shouted.

Maggie turned heel, pausing only long enough at the stairway door to catch sight of Peter, gun leveled at Takayev, who was stumbling backwards in a desperate attempt to escape. He crashed into the old woman just as Peter fired a shot. A deafening boom reverberated down the dingy, narrow hall. Takayev dropped to the floor, motionless. Peter turned his attention back to Maggie. There was no way she could land a shot from this distance.

The door slammed shut behind her as she scampered down the metal stairs two at a time. Four flights down, Peter yelled from somewhere above. "He's dead, Maggie! It'll be your word against mine."

She hugged the walls as she flew down to the ground floor. Peter's footsteps echoed behind her but sounded no closer. At the bottom, she burst through the door into the lobby. Accelerating toward the street exit, she shouted at a woman shuffling through her mail. "*Politsiya!* Call the police!"

Outside, she sprinted, pushing herself until she saw a yellow city bus idling at the sidewalk across the street. Without a glance behind, she dashed across the road, dodging a honking car and startling passengers waiting to board the bus. Maggie slipped to the front of the line and banged on the door. The driver, who was reading the newspaper behind the closed door, studiously ignored her.

"Dammit!" Frantic, she scanned the road. Behind her, about 50 yards back, a taxi pulled up to the sidewalk. Another sprint, and she was in the cab.

CHAPTER THIRTY-THREE

"English?" Maggie blurted.

"Yes," the taxi driver smiled. "Where are you going?"

Away, she scanned the area for any sight of Peter. Should she go to the embassy? No, that was probably the first place he would look.

"Miss?"

There was only one person in this country she knew she could trust.

"The Sioni Cathedral."

"Beautiful church."

"My tour book says I can't leave Tbilisi without seeing it."

"A tourist?" The driver, eyebrows raised, scrutinized her disheveled state in the rearview mirror. "Indeed."

Maggie ran fingers through her unkempt hair in a fruitless attempt to tame it. Police cars and an ambulance, sirens wailing, flew by in the opposite direction. She hoped it wasn't too late for Takayev.

After a harrowing drive along the Mtkvari River and down side streets so narrow that a head-on collision with oncoming cars seemed inevitable, the driver slowed. "We are here." As the cab pulled to a stop, he glanced back. "It looks like a funeral is about to begin. Maybe not the best time to visit?"

Outside, elderly women in worn black shawls shuffled toward the ancient stone church. "I'll just take a quick peek inside." She paid the fare and hurried across the courtyard.

Sioni Cathedral's façade showed its centuries-old age. Large, porous-looking, rectangular stones of assorted tan and yellow hues stacked to a peak above an arched entryway. A massive, rounded spire topped with an Orthodox cross rose from the center of the building. Inside the entry, Maggie's eyes struggled for a moment to adjust to the dimness. The hushed ancient walls, which bore bejeweled icons of Christ and innumerable saints, enveloped the mourners in solemn grief. Maggie felt suddenly out of place, an intruder disturbing the grace of a moment. She slid into a pew near the back of the church to avoid drawing any attention to herself. There were only two dozen people present, most of them elderly; Tamaz was not among them.

A slight commotion behind her caught her attention. Standing in the entrance to the church was a small entourage of solemn-faced men in dark suits. Takayev worked for Georgian intelligence. No doubt these men were co-workers doubling as funeral security.

Maggie caught sight of Tamaz as he emerged from the back of the group. His tired face looked even more drawn than it had that day in her townhouse. Just an hour ago, she could have told him there was no need for a funeral because his brother was alive. But now? His brother may have bled out in the hallway of a dilapidated Soviet-era apartment building.

As horrific as Takayev's situation was, she needed Tamaz to hide her from Peter long enough for her to warn the CIA about him and the looming terrorist attack. If only she knew whether she could trust Warner. One call to him might save her—or seal her death. She shook her head, unable to believe a thought like that had entered her mind.

An organ began the soulful wail of a funeral dirge as people took their seats. The whispered hush of ancient, unanswered prayers weighed down on her from every corner of the church. The Orthodox priest, an image in black save for his long gray beard, began to chant, his deep, melodious voice echoing from the marbled floors to the soaring frescoed ceilings. The mourners and officials fell into silent prayer.

She watched as one of the security men walked toward the front of the church and then back again, apparently scanning the pews for any potential threat to Tamaz or his family. The man stopped halfway down the left aisle and pushed open a door almost entirely concealed behind an enormous icon depicting the Madonna and Child. He disappeared for a minute, then returned and walked back to his post, leaving the door slightly ajar. Maggie surveyed the rest of the Church. Two security men in back were talking quietly to each other. The men at the right entrance, who had their eyes trained on the altar, did not notice the tall, blond American man enter the church through the door behind them.

Maggie's gasp was drowned out by the organ. She raised an oversized hymnal in front of her face, slunk down, and began a silent slide to the end of the pew. She glanced back. Peter was walking up and down the far aisle. Maggie slipped down onto the cool marble floor then shifted to her hands and knees and crawled ten feet up the side aisle to the opening in the wall.

She pushed the door in a few inches and waited. The mourners sang a sorrowful hymn together, just loud enough to muffle the sound of her movements.

She inhaled and crawled through the door, pushing it open only wide enough for her body to fit through sideways. She eased it shut slowly, cringing at the creak of the ancient hinges, then stood and felt around in vain for a light switch on the wall. Nothing but clammy darkness lay ahead. Given her predicament, it was worth exploring further.

Her right hand led the way along the dewy stone wall. She chased away thoughts of rats and spiders and continued until her foot missed the floor and fell onto a step. She shuffled her other foot until it found the next step, then gingerly led herself down a flight of curving stairs. As she rounded the final bend, a dim light illuminated the walls ahead. She picked up the pace, hurrying closer to the light.

Maggie turned a corner and froze. Flickering sconces cast a shadowy pall over a stone-covered mound in the center of the room. On the wall was an inscription in unfamiliar script and an icon depicting angels watching over a great, ancient battle. Whatever saint or hero lay before her probably deserved respect. She blessed herself and fled the room and the spirits that infused it. In the murky lighting, she missed the turn for the stairs and crashed straight into an oversized statue of Joseph Stalin.

"Ouch!" she muttered as she rubbed the shoulder that had driven into the dictator's midriff. She looked up at the statue. "I thought you were in hell." Stalin stared back. A Georgian himself, he had studied at a seminary before succumbing to his totalitarian impulses. Few would admit it publicly, but Stalin still had admirers in certain segments of Georgian society. Behind him stood four statues of other stern-looking Soviets. The entire scene was incongruous. Saints to the right, murdering communists to the left.

If she hid long enough, maybe Peter would give up and search for her somewhere else. But the only way to know for certain was if she saw him leave.

"Later," she said to the statues as she brushed dust from her coat sleeves. She found her way back into the corridor, but a noise stopped her in her tracks. Footsteps? Then she saw it, a beam of light bouncing off the walls. She sprinted back down the hall and hid behind Stalin, where she ordered herself to breathe.

She couldn't see the light from there but could hear the echo of footsteps nearby. She moved away from Stalin, down to a statue at the far corner of the room. On tiptoes, she pursed her lips and blew out the lantern over his head. She pushed against the marble body and felt it tip slightly.

Steadying the long forgotten communist, she squatted down in the shadow behind him. Maggie heard nothing but silence and her own breathing. The room suddenly grew brighter. *Please don't let him see me*, she begged.

"Maggie!"

She squeezed her eyes shut. The air in front of her stirred. She held her breath and dug her fingernails into her palms.

She opened one eye. The light was sweeping around the room from statute to statue.

Somewhere nearby, a critter squealed and scurried away. Peter dropped the flashlight and muttered, "Anyone in this hellhole ever hear of an exterminator?"

Maggie peered out from behind the statue as he disappeared around a corner. She slipped into the open, still safely shrouded in the darkness. Slowly, she made her way around the statues and toward the stairs. When the toe of her shoe met the bottom stair, she slid her hand along the wall, using it for support and as a guide. One step at a time, she made the painstaking ascent, pausing every few seconds to listen for Peter.

Up ahead was a sliver of brightness. The doorway to the main church. Just behind her, in a bend in the stairway, she thought she saw a flash of light. Moving at a faster pace, she tripped on a step and fell forward onto her hands.

"Maggie?" Light bounced off the stone walls.

Righting herself, she dashed for the doorway and squeezed through. The church was almost empty, with only a cluster of people milling about near the back.

"Maggie!"

His voice was growing closer.

There wasn't enough time to escape, so she ran toward the apse at the front of the church, searching for a place to take refuge. Just as Peter emerged through the concealed door, she ducked under the altar, careful to pull the delicate lace cover over the edge. After waiting as long as she could bear, she peered out from under the altar cloth and caught sight of Tamaz approaching. He stepped up to the pulpit, shuffled through several sheets of paper, and stuffed one in his suitcoat pocket.

"Tamaz," she whispered, lifting the lace to reveal herself.

His eyes darted around, searching.

"Tamaz, here."

His eyes met hers. They grew wide.

She put a finger to her lips. "Help me," she mouthed.

He knelt down as if tying his shoe. "Maggie, what on earth are you doing here?" he whispered.

"Is there a tall, blond man in the church?"

Tamaz scanned the church. "I don't see anyone."

"You sure?"

He checked again and nodded.

Maggie crawled out from under the altar. "I'm in danger. And you might be, too." She pointed at the casket. "Because the body in that casket is not your brother."

CHAPTER THIRTY-FOUR

As instructed, Warner took the intelligence documents he'd forged, went for a casual walk in the dark, and deposited the large manila envelope in the designated neighbor's mailbox. He saw no eyes peering out house windows and no strange cars driving through the quiet neighborhood. His imagination told him there were FBI agents watching from gated driveways, snapping photographs of him committing treason. It had taken every ounce of self-control he had not to run home.

Back inside the house, he poured himself a shot of gin with shaking hands and tried Peter's office number again. No answer. He checked his watch. *Of course!* It was the middle of the night in Tbilisi. He reached into his briefcase feeling around for the scrap of paper with Peter's home number on it. The line rang and rang. "Dammit, Peter!" There had been no update on Maggie. If anything happened to her, he'd have Peter's head on a platter.

Next, he flipped through his Rolodex, nearly ripping out a few contacts with the force of his hand. He slowed at "Y" and scanned through to a card with no name, only a number, whose digits he'd scrambled to prevent anyone from discovering that he was in touch with his old nemesis. He scribbled the correct number on a slip of paper, hit the light switch, and hurried out to his car. He drove to the nearby convenience store, where he paid cash for a soda and a prepaid calling card.

He left the store, crossed the parking lot on foot, and stopped outside a grocery store in the center of a strip mall. The calling card was good for thirty minutes, more than enough time. Warner stepped into the shadow of a vending machine and dialed the payphone.

"Hello?"

"Who is this?" The former KGB man sounded groggy.

"I wanted to thank you for lunch the other day. We must get together more often."

Yuri responded with a low chuckle. "Perhaps we should, my friend. What do you want at this hour?"

Warner appreciated that a consummate intelligence professional like Yuri wouldn't utter his name over the phone. "Did I say I wanted anything?"

"No, but you've contacted me two times in as many days."

"I need to ask you something, but I think I should do it in person."

"That would be fine, but I'm afraid it'll have to wait for a week. I'm leaving tomorrow for an overseas business trip."

Warner clenched his teeth. Waiting a week was out of the question. Given the choice between tonight and too late, he decided the risk of talking over the telephone was worth it. "I hope you have a pleasant and safe trip. I'll check back with you in a week or so."

"I'm looking forward to it."

"Just one quick thing before you go. Do you know a Nikolai Sergeyevich Petrov?" The young Russian man with mafia ties. The one the CIA tried to recruit. *WATCHMAN.* The one who might be able to point Warner to Steve's murderer. Or to the blackmailer.

Yuri exhaled with a raspy hack. "Nikolai, you say. How did you figure out he was the young man I mentioned to you the other day?"

Warner began to answer, but Yuri continued. "You figured it out because you're that good, aren't you? Anyway, young Nikolai feeds me information every now and then on his boss, who is a real mafia thug, unlike me, you know." He chuckled to himself. "Nikolai will give anyone information if they wave enough money in front of his face."

Warner would cash in half his retirement if that's what it took to get WATCHMAN to reveal what, if anything, he knew about Steve's murder and his blackmailers. "I need to track him down as soon as possible and can't go through regular channels. Any idea where I could find him?"

"This have anything to do with our discussion about a corrupt American official?"

"Perhaps," Warner replied tersely.

"Petrov has been spending time in D.C." Yuri paused. "Suppose I know where he is. Why would I tell you?"

"You know I'll return the favor." *And you've already spilled a lot about him, so he can't be too valuable to you. But I'll play along.*

"Well, if you give me your word, I'd be delighted to hear more about the 'relatives' as soon as I get back."

"Absolutely," Warner lied. There was no way he was going to give Yuri information on the FBI. Besides, if he hadn't destroyed his blackmailers by then, he'd be ruined. Out of the intelligence business. Out of his daughters' lives. "Whatever you need."

"Then I think we have a deal. Call me back in ten minutes." *Click.*

Warner shivered. The first drops of a late autumn rain bounced off car roofs and slapped against the pavement. He leaned against the building's rough brick. It had come to this—standing in the rain, bargaining with a former KGB rival-turned-mafia boss on a supermarket payphone.

If only he could set everything right, he'd make up for it. He'd be sure his last years at the CIA were his finest. But first, he had to survive the next few days.

Warner checked his watch. Eight minutes had gone by. He dialed anyway.

"We've got to stop meeting like this," Yuri laughed from deep in his chest.

Warner pictured clouds of smoke pouring from the Russian's mouth and nose as he exhaled. "Well?"

"You are familiar with a favorite spot of mine from the old days, yes?"

Warner searched his memory. It'd been the FBI's job to keep track of Yuri's movements back then when he was in the U.S. on "diplomatic" business. But Warner had heard rumors about the Russian's favorite nightspot, a small pub on the outskirts of Georgetown. "Of course. You were a regular there, if I'm not mistaken." In case the FBI happened to be listening, which Warner doubted but couldn't guarantee, he didn't want to say the name of the bar.

"Yes, I must get myself back down there. Of course, all the faces have changed, I'm sure. And I'd probably be offered a senior citizen discount." Yuri laughed again.

Stop being so damned jolly and get to the point!

"Ah," Yuri sighed, seeming to fully enjoy himself. "Can you be there in a half hour? Our young friend will be waiting."

"You found him?"

"Of course. Needless to say, he has no idea he's going to be meeting you. I told him I had a lucrative business deal that might interest him. Money makes this boy's world go around. Doesn't seem to matter who's paying. Sometimes I wonder, don't you, what ever happened to principles?"

"I know what you mean. I appreciate your assistance. And believe me, I'll make sure your efforts are worth the trouble." *Don't count on it.*

"One more thing . . ." The Russian hesitated.

"What is it?"

"I prefer to talk in person, but I don't think this can wait."

Cold rain trickled down Warner's cheek. "Go on."

"You know the people I've had such difficulties with? My southern neighbors?"

Chechnya. "Yes."

"There is a group of them, well trained by a common enemy."

Al-Qaeda?

"They've obtained some dangerous material."

"Material?"

"I'm told they will bring it here through your southern neighbor, but that's all I can say over the phone."

The chill Warner felt wasn't from the weather. "You can't just drop something like this on me. I need more information. What do they have?"

"Nikolai will tell you more."

"How the hell does he know about this when I know nothing?"

Yuri sighed. "Like I told you, he plays all sides. I don't know his sources, but I believe him. You should, too."

Warner hung up after Yuri conveyed a few additional details of the meeting with Nikolai. Then he sprinted across the parking lot, getting soaked in the process. He brushed beaded water from his overcoat, ducked into the car, and straightened his hair.

The drive took him past the CIA, onto the George Washington Parkway, and across the Key Bridge.

Warner drove three times around the block, then parked two streets down. He exited the car, sheltering himself under an umbrella. All was relatively quiet in this neighborhood tonight. A woman walking her miserably wet dog didn't bother to make eye contact when they passed.

There was little cover for anyone seeking to hide from Warner—high iron gates surrounding the homes here blocked access to most hedges and trees. From what he'd read in the New York office's files, Nikolai was relatively green in the world of espionage, so Warner didn't expect much in the way of defense from him. But he was careful, nonetheless, because too much was at stake and too many people were not at all what they seemed.

He crossed the street when he reached the bar and stopped behind a parked SUV. It was too dark to see through the car's tinted rear window, so he edged closer to the clear-paned front windshield. The vantage point was not optimal, but it gave him cover. He checked up and down the street again then strained to see inside the bar. He could make out a few men sitting on stools, but none appeared to be the young Russian.

Warner muttered to himself as the umbrella blew inside out in an unexpected wind gust. He righted it and stepped out from behind the SUV. Looking directly through the window of the bar, he spotted him, sitting at a table just to the right of the door, exactly where he was supposed to be. Warner squinted, straining his eyes. And yes, the man was reading a book and drinking a glass of wine. Yuri had set everything up perfectly. The only problem was that Nikolai—better known to the CIA as WATCHMAN—was none other than Ed. The man he'd been photographed with lying naked in bed. A stab of agony went through his gut. He'd been compromised by a son of the Russian mob.

CHAPTER THIRTY-FIVE

Tamaz stood across the altar from Maggie. He brushed his fingertips along the edge of the casket. "You saw Josef? Alive? Then who is inside—"

"I don't know. One of the other people killed in the explosion, I suspect. But it's not your brother." Maggie smoothed the intricate lace altar cloth. "Peter, the man I'm hiding from paid off the coroner to identify these remains as Josef's."

Tamaz stepped back from the casket. He straightened and his eyes widened. "I don't understand. This isn't a joke? He's really alive?"

"He was." Maggie looked away. "But then he got shot. By the man I am running from. I had to leave Josef behind, but he might be okay," she offered. "There were witnesses. Someone called the police, and I saw an ambulance . . ."

Tamaz backed himself in a velvet cushioned chair on the other side of the altar. "My God, my poor mother is outside waiting for us to go to the burial." He shook his head in disbelief. "What do I tell her?"

Maggie hurried to his side and lowered herself to her knees. "Tamaz, Peter is trying to find me." She took his large hand in hers. "I don't think you're safe, either. As soon as Peter figures out that the man he knew as Takayev was really Georgian intelligence, and your brother, he might come for you. He might think that Josef shared information with you. Information that could incriminate Peter."

"What kind of information?" He squinted at her in complete bewilderment. "Who is this Peter?"

Maggie stood and tugged on Tamaz's hand. "I can explain, but we need to get out of here first." Peter could return at any moment. For all she knew, he might be waiting outside for the procession to the cemetery.

Tamaz snatched his hand away from hers. "I'm not leaving my poor mother alone. Not today."

Maggie scanned the entrances to the church. "Peter is a CIA officer. He set up Steve and Josef at the café last Monday morning."

"CIA?" The Georgian's gravelly voice fell to a harsh whisper. "Did he set off the bomb?"

She shook her head. "That was a terrorist. A Chechen woman."

Tamaz paled. "Dear, God."

"There's so much more. Nuclear smuggling and—"

"Maggie!"

Shit! Peter was at the back of the church. "It's him!"

Tamaz sprung from the chair. "Follow me."

He led her to the back of the sanctuary, where he pushed open a door to the right of the altar. Inside was a small, dimly-lit room. Full-length cassocks in various colors for every liturgical season hung on a clothing rack. To the left stood a cabinet replete with gold chalices, white pillar candles embossed with the orthodox cross, and a multitude of votive glasses.

Not more than twenty feet ahead was the rear wall. "Tamaz, we're trapped."

He ignored her and opened what looked like a closet door that led them to a short, dark corridor ending at yet another door. Tamaz pushed it open and stepped into daylight. "Come on," he urged. "My car's right up this alley."

Maggie sprinted ahead of the older man. "The silver car?"

"Yes," he huffed.

She tugged on the passenger door handle. Locked. "Hurry!"

As Tamaz unlocked the doors and fell into the driver's seat, Peter burst out into the alley. Maggie slammed her door. Peter ran full-speed, gun leveled at her. He fired wildly, the shot ricocheting off the stone façade of a neighboring building.

Maggie pounded the dashboard. "Go, go, go!"

Tamaz floored the gas on his Lada 110. The car fishtailed onto the adjacent road. Behind them, Peter threw his hands up in despair. Maggie's head fell back against the headrest. She fought to control her breathing. "You did it, Tamaz."

He nodded, still too winded to speak.

Tamaz eased the car into traffic, then turned down one side street after another, doubling back on roads several times as he monitored the rearview mirror. "I'll take you to the American Embassy."

Maggie rejected that idea. Peter could be lying in wait for her there. No one at the embassy suspected a thing about him.

"What about a police station or your intelligence headquarters?"

Tamaz wrinkled his brow. "Not the police. They're not the most capable people."

"Georgian intelligence, then. I can tell them everything. Maybe they can find Peter. And I'll call Washington and warn them about the attack."

"I can do all that. You need to get out of here—" Tamaz rubbed furiously at his chin. "Out of the country before anyone knows you're gone. Let me take you to the airport. I can call headquarters while I'm there. They'll start searching for Peter. And you can phone Washington while you wait for your flight."

"Okay," she relented, closing her eyes. Days of accumulated exhaustion suddenly weighed down on her. "I hope that Josef is okay."

Tamaz cleared his throat. "If Josef doesn't make it, at least there will be justice." Tamaz pointed at the glove compartment. "Open it."

Maggie did as she was told.

"Do you see the notebook in there?"

She fished around inside for a moment, then pulled out a small notebook with Dilbert on the cover. Steve loved Dilbert comic strips.

Her voice caught in her throat. "What . . . this was Steve's?" It looked just like the one she'd given him last Christmas.

"It was found with my brother's wallet at the café. It's not his."

Fingers trembling, she flipped through it. Steve's familiar handwriting jumped from the pages.

"I don't know if it's important, but I thought you should have it."

The entries didn't stop on the day he died. In the bottom right corner of every date was a number, circled. A countdown. Until he'd come back home. It was day 79. A couple of weeks ahead, on the 27th—Thanksgiving—he'd written NYC in red ink. Was he planning to surprise her with a Thanksgiving trip home?

"The airport is just ahead."

Maggie ran a finger across the words Steve had written and closed the notebook. "No sign of a tail?"

"No. I took a circuitous route to be sure we weren't being followed."

Tamaz pulled into the main carpark lot, the one closest to the terminal. A quick check of the area confirmed no headlights trailing behind them in the fading daylight.

It was quiet inside Novo Alexeyevka airport for a Friday evening. The terminal appeared much brighter than it had the night she'd arrived. The woman at the ticket counter refused to exchange her return flight ticket until Maggie slipped her forty U.S. dollars.

The flight to Geneva was due to depart in an hour and forty-five minutes. Plenty of time to phone Warner. If his reaction to her call was at all odd, she'd hang up and call her boss on the intelligence committee. She had to warn someone she could trust about Peter's role in the bombing and what she believed was a looming terrorist attack.

Maggie scanned the terminal for Tamaz. He was on a payphone closer to the airport entrance. She'd wait until he was done before calling Washington.

Three minutes later, Tamaz ambled over. "They're notifying all security services to be on the lookout for Peter. And they'll escort my mother to the hospital. Josef is critical, but he's still alive." A smile spread across his face and he pulled Maggie into a bear hug.

"That is the best news I've heard in a long time." Wonderful for Tamaz' family. And for her. Josef would corroborate everything she'd discovered about Peter. And he would clear Steve's name. "You should go. Be with your family." Maggie stepped back and bit down on her lip. "I'm so grateful, Tamaz. Without you, I wouldn't have been able to figure out anything."

"I owe all my thanks to you." He made a slight bow. "Please let me know when you are home and safe."

"I will." Maggie watched him leave the terminal. She jogged over to a nearby phone and pulled Peter's credit card from his wallet. But before she could dial, someone tapped her arm. "Tamaz, did you forget—"

"I figured you'd end up here." A disheveled Peter Belekov loomed over her.

Maggie gasped and dropped the receiver. She searched the terminal for help. A couple with two toddlers in tow passed, and a few people milled about outside. The people at the ticket counter and security line were too far away to notice her. "You're not going to get away with this, Peter. All of Georgia is looking for you."

"Steve was a dirty spy, Maggie."

"No, you set him up." She seethed. "And then you accused him of spying for the Russians." It dawned on her. "It was you, wasn't it?"

He tilted his head. "What?"

"You called me the night of the wake pretending to be Ivan . . . Ivan Nik-somebody. From Russian intelligence. That was your first move. To try to make me doubt Steve, wasn't it?"

He laughed. "Prove it."

Her face grew hot. She advanced on him, fists balled. "You're the one selling intelligence. And then you framed Steve to cover it up."

"Why on earth would I do that?"

"Because the NSA was on to you and you needed a patsy. You're the U.S. official mentioned in the cable."

He screwed up his face, then smiled. "Oh . . . that cable. I heard about that. From Warner."

"Warner?" She reeled, as if from a gut punch.

"You got it all wrong, Maggie. I'm not the person in the cable."

Even in her darkest moments, she hadn't dared to ask herself this question. "Is it Warner?"

"Oh please, Maggie," he scoffed. "He's too clever to let himself be spied on by an NSA satellite."

Maggie's thoughts swirled in a tangled mess. How could she trust Warner if he was sharing critical information with Peter, of all people? Did he know Peter had set up the meeting at the café? Had he been a part this? What else could explain his evasiveness, his anger, his deflections?

"You already know who the U.S. official is." Peter interrupted her frantic thoughts.

"I do?"

"Yup." He paused dramatically.

"If it wasn't you or Warner then . . ." Her thoughts flashed back again to Steve's wake. Her mouth went dry. The heated exchange she'd witnessed. "Carvelli?"

"Bingo."

It all made sense—Carvelli's visits to the Intelligence Committee every weekend provided the perfect opportunity for him to pilfer through highly classified documents.

"Wait a minute. You do know the congressman. He was in Tbilisi in January. You would've briefed him, maybe even shown him around the city."

Peter rolled his eyes. "Fine, yeah, I met him then, but so what? He just another congressman wasting taxpayer dollars on an overseas junket."

"No." She shook her head violently.

"You were in on it. You helped Carvelli, didn't you? And when you found out that Steve was onto you, you set him up at the café."

Peter's voice rose an octave. "You have it all wrong. Yes, I was told to set up a meeting between Steve and Takayev. But I had no idea why."

"Bullshit. You knew exactly what was going to happen at Dima's."

"No," he protested.

"Who ordered the hit? It was Carvelli, wasn't it?"

"No!"

"Then who?"

He ignored the question. "Once I figured out what was really going on, I tried to save them. I called Steve but he didn't answer, so I went to the café to warn him in person." His face crumbled. "It was too late."

"I don't believe you."

He stared back at her blankly.

"Do the right thing, Peter. Turn yourself in. It's over."

He advanced, and in one swift move, hooked his left arm around her right and pulled a pistol from his coat pocket. He tugged on her elbow. "Walk with me or I'll shoot you on the spot."

"You're a traitor, Peter. Why did you help Carvelli? Were you feeding him intelligence?" The cool metal of Peter's other gun, the one she'd taken from his car, pressed firmly against the curve of her lower back. She'd meant to leave it with Tamaz. Maggie resisted his pull, trying to buy time.

Peter's arm constricted around hers. She relented and walked with him a moment. His grip relaxed slightly.

"I'm not feeling well." She tugged him toward a trashcan to the left as she reached behind her back with her free arm. "I'm going to be sick." For a split second he loosened his arm, allowing her to pull her right arm free. A thrust kick against the trashcan sent it tumbling against Peter's leg, momentarily distracting him. She raised the Makarov and aimed dead center. "Drop the gun, Peter."

He shoved the metal can away with his foot and raised his weapon. "You first."

"Who ordered the hit on Steve?"

"It wasn't me." Peter shook his head, his eyes never leaving hers, the gun steady in his hand.

Maggie watched his finger slide to the trigger. She dove sideways to the ground in the split second before he pulled it. Shrieks erupted in the terminal. Maggie rolled to her knees and steadied her aim, but she had to wait for the woman running for the exit to get out of the way. *God forgive me.* She pulled the trigger. The gunshot thrust her hands back towards her face, loosening her grip. The gun fell between her feet. Peter rose from behind the toppled trash can. She'd missed. He raised his gun, contempt coloring every feature. Maggie snatched her gun and scrambled to her feet just as loud shouts erupted near the terminal entrance. At least a half dozen armed men were advancing, semi-automatic rifles aimed at both of them. Peter looked at the uniformed men and back at Maggie. He shrugged, put the gun in his mouth, and pulled the trigger.

Maggie stared in disbelief as Peter crumpled into himself, a trickle and then a stream of blood seeping out from under his head. All went silent until the armed men resumed shouting at her. She dropped the gun, lowered herself to the floor, and raised her hands in surrender.

CHAPTER THIRTY-SIX

Warner ducked back behind the SUV. Rain drove against his face, trickling down his neck and seeping under the collar of his overcoat. So, Ed *was* playing multiple angles—blackmailing him, working for his uncle's crime family, feeding Yuri information, and flirting with becoming a CIA asset. The file on WATCHMAN said he'd spent his childhood in Chechnya. And as Yuri said, he might know the Chechen assassin.

He straightened his shoulders and walked to the bar entrance. The quiet buzz of weeknight conversation greeted Warner as he stepped inside from the rain. Ed glanced at his watch and looked up from his book. He recoiled when their eyes met.

"Nikolai Sergeyevich Petrov, what a surprise. It's been ages." Warner walked over to the table and pulled out the empty chair, "May I?"

Ed leaned across the table. "Are you here to see me?"

"Do you think this is a coincidence?" Warner smiled, then casually wiped the sweat from his palm onto his pant leg.

"My friend said . . ." his voice trailed off.

"Yuri is my friend, too. We go way back. In fact," Warner paused for a moment to hail a waiter, "you might say he's working with me to clean up Russian organized crime." As the waiter approached the table, he glanced up. "A glass of Merlot, please. No, actually, a bottle if you don't mind. Top shelf."

Ed paused until the waiter left. "I'm not mafia, Warner. I'm a freelancer."

"A freelancer?" He shook his head. "What you really are is a damned prostitute. You sell information from your own family's organization to a rival family. You snitch on both families to the CIA. You try to blackmail me." Warner leaned in closer. "And for that, you may spend the rest of your life in a federal prison. Blackmailing a government official is a felony, my boy."

"I'm not the one you should be worried about, Warner."

"No? Well, I'd agree. Because you should be worried about me." Warner stared at Ed until the younger man began to shift in his chair. "Nervous?"

Ed gathered himself and sat still, stone-faced.

"Why don't I remember anything from that night?"

"I put something in your drink."

"Who sent you?"

Ed shook his head, his eyes wide with fear.

"Who got you on the moving truck crew? Who knew——"

"He'll kill me, Warner."

"Listen Nikolai . . . Ed . . . what, exactly, should I call you?" He leaned across the table. "Do you think I give a damn what happens to you?"

The waiter materialized next to their table again, a bottle of red in hand. "Are you ready to place your dinner order?"

"No," Warner snapped before turning back to Ed. "I have friends in very high places at the FBI who'd love to spend some time in a windowless room with you. So, tell me, who sent you?"

Ed looked nervously around the restaurant and lowered his voice. "Richard Carvelli."

The words threw Warner back against the chair. "Carvelli?"

Ed nodded.

Warner's mind spun. How could Richard Carvelli have known that he might be open to a tryst with another man?

"What made him think that I would—" He cut himself short, unable to admit that there was a deeply buried part of him that had been intrigued by the friendly young man on the moving crew.

"Warner, it doesn't matter."

"It matters to me," he hissed. "And it will matter to you when the FBI comes after you for bribing a public official." He waved his cell phone in front of Ed. "My friends are right here on speed dial."

Ed's shoulders sagged. "I need immunity or something. And protection."

"If you tell me everything you know about Carvelli, you will be well taken care of." Warner had absolutely no legal authority to make such a promise, but Ed didn't seem to realize that.

"Carvelli told me that he always knew you had a thing for men."

"My God," he breathed. Richard knew about his sophomore year kiss with their fraternity brother?

That bastard had tucked away a piece of gossip for decades, only to play it when . . .

"Why is Carvelli coming after me now?"

"I don't know." Ed's face had grown pale.

He almost felt sorry for the kid. Almost, except for the fact that this little sonofabitch was part of a plot to destroy his life. "Not good enough, Ed."

"They're going to kill me."

Warner leaned forward. "I swear to you, you will not be prosecuted. And we can set you up with a new identity and a new life. So tell me why."

Ed clasped his hands together. "I suppose because he needed more intelligence documents for his clients."

Warner clenched his fists under the table. "He's been selling intelligence?" All along, it had been Carvelli. Not Steve. His hands fell open, his jaw relaxed. He should've trusted Maggie's instincts. "Why?"

"For the money. In exchange for the intel, my uncle donates hundreds of thousands of dollars to his campaign fund."

"Legally?"

"Yeah. They call if soft money, or something. I don't really understand it." He added, "My uncle wants Carvelli to run for the Senate."

Warner reeled. "The Russian mafia wants a Senator it can control?"

"Yes." Ed swallowed and glanced around nervously. "And they want to know what the CIA knows about them."

"So why did Carvelli turn to me for that information? There are plenty of other people in Washington with access to intelligence. People who know a lot more than I do."

Ed drew his lips into a thin line. "Not sure information was his primary motive. He needed something he could use against you, a safeguard of sorts, in case you discovered what he was doing with the intelligence. So, he sent me to you. The photos were his insurance policy."

"And after the bombing in Tbilisi—"

"He panicked," Ed explained. "He was terrified you'd uncover the truth during the course of the investigation."

"That's why he's blackmailing me now. So I can't go to the FBI without exposing . . . what happened that night?"

Ed nodded.

"He figured he could buy your silence by threatening to release the photos."

Warner swirled the wine in his glass. He had to give Carvelli credit. It had worked. He'd been unable to juggle the multiple crises swirling around his life.

Warner took a large gulp of wine and braced himself. "Did Carvelli order the hit on Steve?"

"I don't know," Ed whispered. "I swear."

"Don't lie to me!" Warner pounded the table, drawing curious stares from people sitting at the bar.

The hostess approached. "Is there a problem, gentlemen?"

"No," both men replied in unison.

Warner closed his eyes and inhaled deeply. "Has anyone else seen the photos?"

"Not that I know of."

"What, exactly, do you do for Carvelli?" Other than seducing and drugging blackmail targets.

"I'm the courier between him and my uncle."

"And your uncle does what with this intelligence?"

"He sends it to our people in Russia." He raised his palms defensively. "I don't know what they do with it."

"You ever peek inside the envelopes?"

He shook his head violently. "No, they're triple sealed with wax or something. If I opened the envelopes, they'd know."

Warner poured them both more wine. At this rate and under these circumstances, they'd need a few more bottles.

"Yuri told me that terrorists are trying to smuggle dangerous materials into this country."

Ed blinked.

"He said you'd give me the details."

Ed remained mute.

Warner pulled his phone from his pocket. "Like I said, the FBI's on speed dial. You want a deal? You talk."

The younger man swallowed. "A group of Chechens has obtained nearly a kilo of nuclear waste."

"You know any of them?"

"Of course not!" he protested.

That's a lie. Warner took a sip of wine. "Tell me about growing up in Chechnya."

"There's not much to tell. We lived in a high-rise building like most people. Lots of us stuffed into small apartments. Shared kitchens and bathrooms with other families."

"Muslim families?"

Ed frowned. "Well, yes. Russians and Chechens didn't hate each other then. And the Muslims weren't exactly free to practice their religion, so it wasn't like they were that different from the rest of us. We were all Soviets."

"You know the woman."

The Russian lifted the wine glass to his lips and gulped.

"Could you be more specific?"

"The assassin. I hear she's pretty."

Ed blanched.

"How do you know her?"

"I . . ." Ed downed the rest of his wine. "I grew up with Zara."

Now he had a name. But he needed more. "Go on."

"Her family lived in the apartment next to ours." The words began to tumble out. "We played together as kids. We'd sneak out to smoke cigarettes when we were twelve, thirteen. She was the first girl I ever kissed." He stopped, seemingly lost in his memories.

"You love her."

"We were sixteen when the first Russian-Chechen war broke out. Her brothers wanted to wage jihad against the Russians. They forbade her from seeing me. We'd sneak out as often as we could, but then my family moved, and we could only write. A few phone calls here and there . . ."

"Heartbreaking," Warner snapped. "When's the last time you talked to Zara?"

"How do I know you won't use this information against me?"

"Because I'm not after you."

"A couple of weeks ago."

Warner nodded. "And what did you discuss?"

Ed set his glass down with a trembling hand. "Carvelli had heard that the CIA knew the Chechens were working with al-Qaeda. Selling them weapons. I . . . I don't know if she's involved, but I wanted to warn her to be careful."

The waiter approached again. "Sir, are you ready—"

"We'll start with the stuffed mushrooms," he snapped.

When the man backed off, Warner changed tacks. "About this nuclear waste. Where'd that come from?"

"The Soviets buried nuclear waste in multiple 'closed cities' in the 1980s and 90s. Yuri thinks they got this material from City 40."

"In Chelyabinsk?" He knew it well. Radioactive waste littered the landscape in that godforsaken place.

Ed nodded.

Warner exhaled. A kilo was more than enough to make multiple dirty bombs. They wouldn't kill millions like a conventional nuclear weapon. But they'd kill hundreds, maybe thousands, and paralyze the country. "And al-Qaeda will smuggle radioactive bombs across the border from Mexico?"

"Smuggled."

Warner's throat constricted. He put down the wine glass. "The bombs are already here?" Warner flashed back to the morning of September 11th. *Not again. Not on my watch.*

Ed paused to gulp down some ice water. "Not the bombs. Just the nuclear material."

"Good Lord." Warner dabbed at his forehead with a linen napkin. "Who's making the devices? When is this going down? Where?"

"I . . . I don't know."

He leaned over the table and dropped his voice. "Are you protecting Carvelli?"

"No!"

"Does he know about the nuclear waste, the bombs? Is he behind it?"

"I . . . I swear, I don't know."

"Dammit, Ed! Go find out!" His tone drew more curious looks.

At that, Ed bolted from the table and out the door.

The hostess returned. "Sir? Can I help you with anything?"

Warner balled up the napkin and tossed it at the empty chair. "I'm afraid my problems are above your pay grade." With that, he dropped a hundred-dollar bill on the table, stood, and stormed out to his car. As he reached into his pocket for the keys, his phone rang. "Thompson, here," he answered.

"Sir, this is the Operations Center. I'm sorry to bother you at this hour, but we've received an urgent message for you from the Georgian Ministry of State Security."

Warner felt as if a cannonball had been heaved into his midsection.

"The message reads, 'Urgent. Problem with Maggie Jenkins.'"

CHAPTER THIRTY-SEVEN

Once the plane was airborne and she was two vodka tonics in, Maggie tried to relax, but every time she closed her eyes, she saw herself firing into the farmhouse at Zara. And then at Peter in the terminal. The images were like movie clips playing on a continuous reel, sometimes repeating in slow-motion, other times in a rapid blur. It was impossible to reconcile her starring role in these scenes with the person she'd been not even two weeks ago. Would people—family, friends, maybe even strangers—sense the change? Would they know that she was capable of killing?

With sleep out of the question, Maggie tried to focus. Safe as she was now that Peter was gone, this was in no way over. Richard

Carvelli was a traitor. Warner's role was murky at best. And she still didn't know for certain who had ordered the hit on Steve.

Or why.

She ached for him. For his hand in hers. To wake up next to him. Steve would know what to do, who to trust. She pulled the Dilbert day planner from the seat back pocket and ran her fingertips across the cover before flipping it open to November. Below the "New York" entry on the 27th, Steve had scribbled "Macy's." *Macy's on Thanksgiving? The parade?* He'd never talked about going to the parade. Beneath that was more, something she'd overlooked earlier. There, in red ink, he'd written *D.C./LA*. It made no sense. *What does this mean, Steve?*

She closed her eyes for a moment. Even before his murder, she hadn't planned on celebrating Thanksgiving. Not without him. Now the thought of turkey and all the trimmings gave her heartburn. How could she ever celebrate another holiday?

Holiday? Her breath quickened. On the phone with a man named Ahmed, Zara had said something about a holiday. And materials already in place.

And the Chechens at the farmhouse, they'd laughed about turkey and the trimmings. What if Steve's notes meant that New York City, D.C., and LA were the targets of a Thanksgiving terrorist attack? She gripped the armrests. Thanksgiving was in less than two weeks.

She slowed her breathing and tried to see through the fog. The Chechens were dead. Even if Zara were still alive, how could she pull off an attack alone? Her mind raced. What if Zara was just the middleman? Between? *Think, think.*

Between the Russian mafia and . . . she sucked in her breath. Ahmed. The man on the phone with Zara.

Was he al-Qaeda? Did he already have sleeper cells in place? Like bin Laden on 9/11?

She needed another drink.

Maggie stood, bleary-eyed, in the arrival terminal at Dulles International Airport. She owed one to Tamaz, whose intervention had gotten her the clearance to fly and, miraculously, her luggage from the hotel. After an insomniac first flight, exhaustion took over. She'd slept some on the first marathon layover, and napped during the second, only to find out that her flight from Munich had been canceled. Instead it was on to London for another layover before the final flight home.

She'd paid a small fortune to shower at Heathrow, but with days of grime washed off and a fresh change of clothes, she'd been able to sleep most of that flight. Still, it felt as if she'd been run over by a truck.

She weaved through the crowd around the luggage carousel, found her suitcase and made a beeline for the taxi stand. Even in late afternoon rush hour traffic, she made it to her Vienna, Virginia townhouse in twenty minutes.

She walked to the hedges along the right side of the front steps and lifted the third rock from the end. She pressed the button on the bottom of the false stone and pulled out the spare house key. The rock had been Steve's idea. *I don't want to be worrying about you locking yourself out when I'm three thousand miles away.* She had laughed and reminded him that she rarely locked her door, something that Steve had worried about too, but she'd been touched by his desire to take care for her from afar.

The soft mass in her core threatened to melt. Maggie bit down hard on her lip, marched up the steps, exhaled, and let herself in. The house looked exactly the same as it had when she'd left it a lifetime of four days ago. In the kitchen, she switched on the coffee pot and called Langley.

"DDO Thompson's office."

"Priscilla? It's Maggie."

"Are you okay, dear? I had no idea you were overseas. Warner didn't say a word, but now I know why he's been so on edge."

"How did he know where I was?"

"Georgian security called to let us know about the . . . the incident at the airport. We got your itinerary so Warner would know when you were home."

Maggie swallowed. "Is he around?" She had no idea what she was going to say to him. Outright accusing him of being a traitor and a murderer might not get her very far.

"I'm afraid not. As I speak, he's headed to the Hill for an urgent briefing. Something big is brewing, real big from what I understand."

Her muscles tensed. "Do you know how long he'll be there?"

"Wish I did. I was supposed to go to my niece's house tonight for dinner, but who knows when I'll get out of here."

Her mind was already racing ahead of Priscilla's chatter. "I have to run."

Maggie grabbed a screwdriver from the junk drawer. She took the stairs two at a time to the guest bathroom. Did Warner know about the terrorist plot? Is that why he was going to the Intelligence Committee?

Whatever was happening on the Hill, she needed to be there. Up in the guest bathroom, she threw back the shower curtain, pried loose the nozzle cover, removed the baggie containing the NSA cable and shoved it in her pocket, not bothering to reassemble the nozzle contraption. Back in her room, she traded her travel attire for the only clean clothes she could find—cropped tan cargo pants, a black tank top, and a pair of black flats. She pinched her cheeks and tousled her hair. "Fabulous," she lied to her reflection.

She scurried down the stairs and went into the kitchen to grab some coffee. A sudden rattling at the front door sent the drink dribbling down her chin. "Who is it?" she called out, annoyed that some salesman or neighbor had already discovered she was home. In the living room, she pushed aside the curtain behind the loveseat. A man was crossing the street away from her house, his pace unnaturally hurried.

She watched him jump into an older model sedan, start the engine, and drive out of the development. "What the hell was that?" she whispered breaking the hush of the house. She opened the front door and saw nothing on the porch—no fliers, no delivery, no mail. She glanced out to the main road, which was easily visible through the bare autumn trees. The sedan, it appeared, had pulled over on the road abutting her street. "Now what?" Maybe it was nothing, but she wasn't going to stick around to see who he was or what he'd do next.

Back in the kitchen, she pulled a chair over to the refrigerator and shoved aside a few dust-covered bills piled on top. She grabbed the keys and dropped to the floor. Everything else she needed was in the garage. Down in the recreation room, she drew back the curtain on the sliding glass door, letting in what remained of the day's light. Upstairs she heard the phone ring. She ignored it until she heard Warner's voice echoing above.

"Maggie, I just talked to Priscilla."

She bolted for the stairs.

"I can't talk right now. Something's come up. I'm heading into a classified briefing. No phones allowed. I'll call back the first break I get."

"Hello? Warner?" He'd hung up. "Dammit," she muttered. No matter, they'd speak in person soon enough.

She tromped back to the basement and into the garage, pulled the leather jacket off the hook and slipped it on, depositing her government ID and the NSA cable in the pocket. Its oversized comfort swaddled her in Steve's musky scent. She stuffed his day planner into the inside breast pocket, walked to the left side of the motorcycle, and let her fingers encircle the handlebars, picturing Steve's strong hands covering hers. He'd traded in his old motorcycle for the Kawasaki six months after his father was killed in the World Trade Center, his way, she knew, of escaping the loss. The outrageous speed and power of the brushed silver bike took him far from the pain and back to freedom.

Swinging a leg over the ZZR600, Maggie pushed up the kickstand and forced the motorcycle forward with her feet, tilting it left and right with every step. Her thigh muscles strained against hundreds of pounds of steel and chrome as she guided it through the doorway into the recreation room. She lowered the kickstand onto the beige berber carpet, put the key in the ignition, and went back to the garage for the helmet, which slid easily over her curls. She lifted the tinted visor and studied herself in a mirror hanging near the stairs. Green eyes peered out from behind an aerodynamic mask of silver and metallic blue.

Maggie tugged open the sliding glass door and peeked out at the townhouses on either side. The rear windows of both were dark. She traversed the tiny back yard and opened the fence gate.

She checked the walking path that ran behind the house; the coast was clear as far as she could tell in the falling dusk. She ran back inside and pushed the motorcycle out, struggling against its weight to keep it from tipping over.

Out on the path, the slider and gate shut behind her, she stared at the bike. It hadn't been that long since she'd last ridden, but she was nervous, nonetheless. She swung her right leg over the bike and scooted herself forward. Steve's voice was clear in her head, repeating the instructions he'd given her before her first ride. *Pull the choke all the way out. Good. Now turn the key to the on position.*

"Got it," she answered to the still fall air.

See that switch there? It's called the kill switch. Maggie flinched. Kill switch. *Make sure it's set on run. The gear shifter should be in neutral. Yup. Now squeeze the clutch, on the left handle there. If you squeeze the right, you're screwed—that's the front brake.* She remembered his teasing laugh. *You're almost ready to go. Press the start button until the engine fires. Good.*

Maggie closed her eyes and let the motor's purr penetrate her tension. She gave it a minute to fully warm up, then felt around with her left foot for the gear shifter. A slight turn of the throttle made the engine hum louder. Her fingers eased off the clutch and the motorcycle inched ahead. She smiled under the helmet, then twisted the throttle too far, sending the bike lurching forward and her neck snapping back.

"Damn," she muttered, straightening the handlebars and kicking the engine back into neutral. She hit the ignition switch again and eased out, more cautious this time. When Maggie looked up from the instrument panel, she saw a slender, blond man, just ten feet away. His eyes widened and locked into hers before flashing over to the townhouse.

Something wasn't right.

She pulled the visor down and shifted into second, skirting past the stranger. With a quick glance back, she saw him talking into a cell phone, his free hand gesturing at the fence encircling her yard. *What the hell?* She slowed to a stop a hundred yards up where the path met the road and looked to her right. The sedan was merging onto the same road. *There have to be at least two of them.* She revved the engine and pulled onto the street with a defiant roar.

In the sideview mirror, Maggie saw the sedan get stuck at the light, but her lead didn't last long in the heavy afternoon traffic; he was only three cars behind her in stop-and-go congestion. *Who the hell are these guys?* She merged onto the Capital Beltway and dared herself to widen the gap. The bike fit beneath her, hugging her curves as well as the road's, but the sedan was still within striking distance. The next exit was Route 123, perhaps her chance to lose him. She swerved from the center to the far-right lane, taking the off-ramp so fast she could feel the rough pavement reaching up for her skin.

Maggie weaved around cars when her courage and oncoming traffic permitted, but the sedan kept pace. If she could make it the next mile without getting shot or run down, she just might escape. "Come on, come on!" she urged the red light ahead. "Change!" It was so close, she could see it, the next glorious set of lights. She accelerated past a dump truck and managed to make a left turn just as the arrow turned from yellow to red. She slowed for a moment. The sedan was stuck in the turn lane behind another car. Not that it mattered. Unless the man had a CIA badge, he would not get into the compound.

Ahead at the guard shack, officially called the "Visitor's Center," Maggie pulled the helmet from her head and tugged the brown badge from the jacket. The ID, which lacked a name or any other identifying information, was CIA-issued to staff members of the Intelligence Committee. And, it gave her relatively free access to the Agency's Langley campus. The guard waved her through without a second glance.

Maggie slid the helmet back on and drove slowly along the wooded road circling the CIA headquarters building. She wasn't surprised to feel her leg muscles aching and tense, but was amazed that despite the wild chase, her breathing was regular, and she didn't feel panicky. *Must be his jacket,* she thought. *Or Steve watching, guiding me.* At the next guard shack ahead on the right, she waved to the guard who opened the gate for her.

She wound her way through the Agency's campus to the CIA's private on-ramp onto the George Washington Parkway. She wasn't supposed to use the Agency compound as a short cut, but this was an emergency. The car giving chase would be stuck in traffic at the public on-ramp a mile back. Her grip on the throttle relaxed when she failed to find any sign of the sedan behind her. She drove as fast as she dared, but not so fast as to draw unwelcome attention. Fifteen minutes later, she passed Arlington National Cemetery and the Pentagon. Traffic eased as she crossed the Potomac on the 14th Street Bridge. Five minutes later, she turned off Independence Avenue, flashed her House ID to a police officer, and parked in a reserved curbside spot. She rested the helmet on the seat, not sure what else to do with it, and broke into a trot toward the Capitol building. Inside, she passed through all the checkpoints, garnering raised eyebrows from familiar faces. The polished Maggie was missing in action. In her place was a disheveled, exhausted, adrenalin-driven survivor.

Upstairs, she breezed into the office to find herself alone. "Hello?" she called out. The hearing room door was shut, but surely there'd be some staff around. "Wendy?" She, at least, should be there to answer the phones. No reply. She tossed Steve's leather jacket onto her desk and hurried down the hall to check the bathroom. Inside, she heard what sounded like a muffled sob coming from the first stall. She bent over and saw black, strappy pumps, one of her friend's signature accessories.

"Wendy?"

"Maggie?" came a sniffling voice from behind the gray metal door.

"You all right?"

Wendy emerged from the stall. Her eyes were red, her lids puffy. "Yeah." She dabbed at her face with a clutch of crumpled toilet paper.

"Is Warner Thompson here?"

Wendy nodded and sniffled. "If I tell you something, will you promise to keep it a secret?"

"Can it wait? I have to—"

"I'm pregnant." Wendy closed her eyes. "And he wants nothing to do with me now."

"So he's not 'the one' after all?" Maggie regretted her snappy remark the moment it escaped her mouth. "I'm so sorry, Wendy."

"Maybe he's just shocked by the news. I know he cares for me. We used to meet in here on weekends, all in secret. It was so romantic." She sniffled.

Weekends? "Who's the bastard?"

"You know who it is. I pointed out his house to you when we went for a walk last month."

"Carvelli?"

Wendy nodded, wiping her eyes with a tissue. "I'm such an idiot!"

Maggie's mind flashed back several weeks to when she'd seen Wendy and Carvelli alone in the conference room engaged in what appeared to be intimate conversation. At the time, she'd dismissed it as Carvelli hitting on yet another attractive staffer. Now it made sense. And it explained who was letting Carvelli into the office every weekend.

Wendy blew her nose. "He even gave me his house key. A guy like him doesn't give his house key to just anyone, right?"

"Right." Time was short. The conversation had to end here. "We'll figure this out. But right now, you have to get back to work. I'll run and get your purse so you can get cleaned up."

Maggie hurried back past the conference room to Wendy's desk. She found her purse and rifled through it for the keys. She peered down the hall to make sure no one was coming. "Bingo," she whispered. It had to be the one on the small Mercedes key ring. She shoved it in her pocket and dashed back to the bathroom. "Here you go. By the way, any idea how late everyone will be here?"

"I'm not sure," Wendy replied as she smoothed concealer under her eyes. "But I'm supposed to order pizzas for everyone at six."

Maggie looked at her watch. That gave her a half-hour—at least—before she could make her move.

CHAPTER THIRTY-EIGHT

Maggie slipped into the hearing room through the rear door. As she sat in her usual spot behind the chairman, heads turned and mouths dropped at the sight of her. The top half of her hair was flattened from the motorcycle helmet. The bottom half was frizzed wildly from the wind. Her skin was pale and rumpled clothes hung like deflated sails on her thin frame.

Chairman Nelson swiveled around in his chair. "Maggie, are you okay?"

She looked at Warner, who sat subdued at the witness table. "I really need to talk to Warner. I apologize, but it can't wait."

Warner stood. "Maggie, not now," he said tersely.

"I'd rather not discuss this in front of everyone, but if you insist—"

Warner raised his eyebrows to Chairman Nelson.

"Maggie," Nelson said, rising from his seat.

"Mr. Chairman," Carvelli interjected. "I suggest we call a brief recess while we get Miss Jenkins settled down. She's obviously been through hell." He looked at her as if she were a ghost. "I'd be glad to drive her home."

Why did he look so surprised to see her? "I'll pass, congressman."

Carvelli scowled at her. "Mr. Chairman?"

Warner approached the dais where Nelson sat. "If you'll excuse me for a few minutes, I'm sure I can get this straightened out."

The chairman nodded. "The Committee will adjourn for a five-minute recess." He banged the gavel with a quick thud.

"Maggie," Warner snapped and nodded to the adjacent conference room.

She followed, closing the door behind them.

"What the hell were you thinking, running off to Georgia like that?"

"What the hell were you thinking sharing information with Peter?"

His jaw fell open. "I had no idea he was dirty. I spoke to Steve's asset a few hours ago—"

"Takayev."

"I thought he was dead."

"Everyone did," Maggie conceded.

"Had I known about Peter, I would've recalled him, had him arrested." His face sagged under the weight of failure. "You never would've had to endure any of this. Maybe Steve would still be here."

Maggie stared at the floor. As much as she wanted to blame Warner, to lash out at him for not knowing about Peter . . . or Zara . . . or whoever ordered the bombing, there was no time to waste. "Warner, there's going to be an attack."

"I know. That's why I'm in there." He gestured to the hearing room. "But I don't know where or when."

"Thanksgiving Day."

Warner steadied himself against the conference table. "Thanksgiving is in ten days." He turned toward the hearing room and shook his head. "We've been devoting a lot of intelligence collection to tracking weapons of mass destruction."

Maggie's eyes widened. "You really think they'll use WMDs?"

He ignored her, continuing apace. "We would've heard about the sale or theft of them. We would've heard *something*. Even if we didn't know exactly what was going on, we'd be seeing an uptick in terrorist chatter."

"Possibly, but what if the smugglers know exactly when the CIA is listening? Wouldn't they figure out a new way to operate, one we're blind and deaf to?"

Warner's eyes bore through her. "Carvelli has been selling intelligence to the Russian mafia."

"I know!" she rejoindered.

"How did you find out?"

"Peter. He helped Carvelli."

Warner blanched. "I never trusted him. One of my worst-performing officers." He ran a hand through his hair.

"Don't you see, Warner? Based on the intelligence Carvelli sold them, the mafia could figure out when and how we are spying on them. They could get away with anything by changing how they communicated, where and how they operated . . ."

"When the cat's looking away . . ."

"The mouse will play."

Warner squeezed his eyes shut. "Let's say you're correct and there's an attack planned for Thanksgiving. We have no idea where they'll strike."

She slid Steve's day planner across the table. "Check out the 27th."

Warner picked up the notebook, brow furrowed. He leafed through it. "I don't understand."

"It's Steve's. He wrote Macy's, D.C. and LA right there on the 27th."

"Thanksgiving," Warner conceded. "But how do you know that these notes have anything to do with terrorist attacks?"

"I heard the Chechens talking about turkey and trimmings. Sounds like Thanksgiving to me. And they mentioned the axis of evil. That could be New York City, Los Angeles, and Washington, D.C. Oh, and then there was a Russian mafia guy—"

Warner squinted at her. "What? What Chechens? What mafia—"

"I'll explain it all later. And I overheard Zara speaking to a man named Ahmed."

"You know Zara?"

"Intimately." She grimaced. "Zara told this Ahmed guy that a delivery had been made to Mexico in time for the holiday."

"Mexico?" He sucked in his breath. "Maggie, I have a source that says nuclear waste recently has been smuggled in over the southern border."

Her mouth went dry. "For dirty bombs?"

"Yeah." His complexion looked positively gray. "And Yuri said several small nuclear weapons have gone missing over the past few months."

A cold sweat broke out over Maggie's body. "Who's Yuri?"

"Long story. Listen, Maggie, give me your bottom-line assessment. Quickly. I've got to get back in the hearing room and warn the committee members."

"Okay," she began, giving herself a moment to pull together all of the pieces. "A Chechen terror cell has been buying weapons from the Russian mafia. The Chechens have been selling these weapons to al-Qaeda. Al-Qaeda is planning a Thanksgiving Day attack against three of our cities."

He nodded slowly.

"Steve made notes confirming the date and location in his notebook. And we didn't have any warning because Richard Carvelli passed intelligence to the Russian mafia that helped them evade our surveillance. Someone—Carvelli, Peter, Zara—found out that Steve was onto the attack. So they sent him to the café and set off the bomb to keep the plot secret."

Warner was shaking his head. "Richard Carvelli may be many things, including a traitor, but I can't believe he would facilitate a nuclear attack on his own country."

"Maybe he doesn't know about the attack. Maybe his intelligence selling scheme spun out of control and—"

"And here we are." Warner's stare moved from the notebook to her face. "What if the terrorists and the bombs are already in place? What if it's too late to find them?"

"It can't be." A fear deeper than any she'd ever felt—even during her recent scrapes with death—seized every inch of her aching body. "It can't be too late. All we need is hard proof that Carvelli stole intelligence documents."

"That won't stop the terrorists," he objected.

"No, but if Carvelli realizes he's facing decades in jail, maybe he'll cooperate."

Warner frowned. "But if he doesn't know about the attacks—"

"He will still have names, contact information, paper trails, electronic breadcrumbs. We have ten days to track down every lead." She squeezed the sides of her head with her hands. "I just need evidence."

"How are you going to find it?" His voice was laced with alarm.

"I know exactly where to look. Your job is to keep Carvelli occupied."

"Maggie—"

Chairman Nelson opened the door to the hearing room. "You said the matter at hand is urgent, Mr. Thompson. Let's resume."

She peered in at the assembled congressmen and looked back at Warner. "He's gone."

"That sonofabitch."

"Mr. Thompson, are we ready?" Chairman Nelson intoned.

"Absolutely. I appreciate your indulgence." Warner turned on his smile as easily as Maggie flipped on a light switch.

She lowered her voice. "I'll be back in a few minutes."

"Don't, Maggie."

She smiled and shook her head. After everything she'd gone through in Georgia, she wasn't about to ignore her instincts. There was too much at stake now. With a few final pieces of evidence, she could prove that Carvelli was selling intelligence to the Russians. That would clear Steve's name.

And it would give them ammunition to pressure Carvelli into cooperating in the hunt for the dirty bombs. Carvelli was a self-righteous, power-hungry traitor, but Maggie agreed with Warner. He wouldn't allow another massive terrorist attack against the United States. Once he understood what havoc he'd unleashed, he'd cooperate.

Warner mouthed "no" to her as she shut the door between the conference and hearing rooms. She snatched a piece of scrap paper off the credenza and scribbled a note. She scurried to her office, grabbed Steve's jacket and an envelope. She stuffed the note inside the envelope and handed it to Wendy.

"What's this?" She looked up from her desk.

"This is going to sound crazy, but if I'm not back by quarter to seven, give this envelope to Warner Thompson." That would give her an hour.

"If I ask you why, you're not going to tell me, right?"

"Right."

CHAPTER THIRTY-NINE

Maggie hurried from the Committee office down to the Crypt where she saw her boss, Frank, phone to his ear, head down, coming her way. There would be a lot of explaining to do, but now wasn't the time. She ducked behind a large column. As soon as she heard the elevator doors slide open and shut, she scrambled out the east side of the Capitol. It was only three blocks from there. She weaved through pedestrians, took a right, then another right off Pennsylvania onto his street. On that day when she and Wendy had taken a long walk at lunch, she'd thought nothing of it when Wendy had pointed out Carvelli's brownstone. Up ahead, someone was walking down the front steps of his house. It was Carvelli. *Dammit.* What if he'd beaten her to his intelligence stash already? Maggie flattened herself against an old iron gate guarding the courtyard of a neighboring brownstone.

The gate gave way under the pressure of her back, sending her sprawling onto a flagstone patio. She stood, rubbing a sore elbow and tailbone before poking her head out to see if Carvelli was gone. She ducked into the courtyard as he drove past in his red Mercedes convertible.

Maggie waited a minute before easing herself back onto the uneven brick sidewalk. The political and societal elites of this neighborhood wouldn't be home at this hour. They'd be engaged in feting others of their ilk—senators, lobbyist kingpins, and government undersecretaries, deputy secretaries and assistant deputy undersecretaries. Even if someone did notice her, they'd probably assume she was yet another girlfriend enamored of the congressman's power and ego.

Maggie strolled, as casually as she could muster, past the well-appointed attached homes of white and red brick. She climbed the stairs, careful not to act too skittish. She looked at her watch under the glow of his porch lamp—twenty minutes had passed already, giving her another twenty inside before she had to head back to the office. She didn't want Wendy to have to give that envelope to Warner.

The key was warm against her cold fingers. The lock and deadbolt turned easily with a slight twist. She entered and secured the door behind her, holding her breath for a moment as she took in Carvelli's lair. Exquisite antique furniture filled the foyer and living room in perfect formation. The décor was evidence enough of Carvelli's malfeasance. A congressman with no family money couldn't afford such accoutrements of social nobility on a government salary alone.

She proceeded to the dining room, which was adorned with a crystal chandelier so ornate it bordered on the obscene. The kitchen was a scene straight from an interior design showroom—stainless steel appliances without a scratch or smudge, an intricate tile mosaic framing the space over the gleaming sink, and fresh flowers in a delicate porcelain vase. No wonder Wendy had been sucked in so easily. The place was impressive, to say the least, but its inhabitant was another matter entirely.

Around the corner was the room she'd hoped to find—his office. The décor echoed that of the rest of the house—oversized and over budget. She went straight for a stack of papers piled neatly on the far corner of his desk. It contained press clippings about himself—*not surprising*—and a handwritten list of political contributors, which included notes about how much he expected them to donate to his next campaign.

She opened the desk drawers; each was organized to perfection. Pens here, paper clips there. No mingling or meshing of chaos that was a hallmark trait of her desk. Maggie exhaled. There had to be something here, evidence she could hand over to someone empowered to make Carvelli confess. That Sunday in the office, she'd overheard him on the phone saying something about documents at his house. If they weren't here, she was screwed. There was no Plan B. She opened the closet door. Before her stood a large gray file cabinet. She pulled on the top drawer. Locked. "Damn." As were the two below it.

Her eyes scouted the room for a tool. A thin, gold-plated letter opener caught her eye. *Miss Jenkins did it in the office with the letter opener.* She was starting to understand why Steve had loved being a spy. The adrenaline rush alone was addictive. She set to work on the file cabinet, poking the tip of the makeshift tool into the small keyhole then jiggling it until she felt it engage. She turned it to the right, where it jammed. Turning it the other way, however, resulted in a triumphant *click.*

Maggie tucked the letter opener behind her ear and pulled open the drawer. "Richard Carvelli, your days of power and corruption are numbered."

The top drawer was full of legal documents and bills. She yanked open the second drawer, flipping frantically through the hanging file folders. No intelligence documents. Then she saw it. The paper shredder in the corner, its power light a steady, bright green.

She yanked the cover off, unveiling a full bin of shredded paper, and sank to her knees. The CIA could reconstruct the shredded pieces into full pages, but it would take weeks. Minutes had made the difference between life and death for Steve. And now they might make the same difference for millions of Americans. If only she'd come straight here instead of talking to Warner, maybe she could've secured the documents before Carvelli panicked and destroyed them.

With one hand on the shredder bin and the other on the adjacent trashcan, she pushed herself to a stand. Inside the trashcan she noticed a large manila envelope with "2002" written across it in black marker. Maggie turned back to the file cabinet and began removing the hanging folders, which she stacked on the floor. Inside the drawer, peeking out from under the sixth olive green folder, was another manila envelope. Maggie slid it forward—"2003" was scrawled along the long edge.

"Bingo," she whispered. Perhaps Carvelli thought he'd shredded all the incriminating documents he'd stolen from the Intelligence Committee. Or perhaps he'd just been sloppy and hadn't finished the job.

She pinched together the brass clasp that secured the envelope and pulled out a handwritten, three-page list of intelligence document titles, presumably ones he'd stolen from the Committee: "Russian Organized Crime: Infiltration of the Russian Military-Industrial Complex" (January 2003, Top Secret), "Insurgency in Chechnya: Easing the Way for Terrorist Activity" (February 2003, Top Secret), "Chemical and Biological Agent Stockpiles in the Former Soviet Union: An Ongoing Concern" (September 2003, Top Secret).

She stopped reading the list after the fourth item: "Russian Control over Tactical Nuclear Weapons." These highly classified documents revealed not only how, but when, the CIA was collecting intelligence about Russia. Human sources who risked their lives to get this information might be caught and executed if the documents fell into the wrong hands. The capabilities of American spy satellites and other eavesdropping technology were likely exposed. Years, decades of technological advances and spy tradecraft had been compromised because of Richard Carvelli.

And worst of all, the Russian mafia could continue to traffic weapons because they'd be able to figure out how to evade American spies and satellites.

"You bastard," she seethed. His pursuit of ever more power, which required ever more money, had led him down this path—selling U.S. intelligence to the highest bidder, regardless of the consequences. In the dark recesses of his arrogant mind, he probably excused his actions as necessary for the greater good of America—his advancement into higher office. And worse still, he was so arrogant, he never thought he'd be caught. Otherwise, he wouldn't have locked evidence of his treachery away in a flimsy file cabinet in his own home.

She folded the list of pilfered intelligence documents and slid it into her jacket's inner pocket. Could this evidence, obtained without a warrant, be used in court? If not, she'd take it directly to the press. They'd handle Carvelli's trial in the court of public opinion.

At the back of the drawer was a bulkier envelope. She pried open the tab with a fingernail to find a smaller envelope, a minicassette recorder, and three tiny audio cassette tapes inside. She shoved two of the tapes into her jacket pocket, inserted the other one into the recorder, then froze. That sound was unmistakable. A faint click of metal, a pause, then a closing door.

CHAPTER FORTY

Maggie shoved the hanging folders into the drawer, lunged across the Oriental rug and swatted at the light switch. Someone was moving around in the front part of the house. When the footsteps grew louder, she ducked behind the office door, then noticed the closet was still open. Clutching the envelope in her right hand, she closed the closet with her left, and returned to her hiding place, not daring to breathe. A minute went by, then the office light came on. She shrank as far behind the door as she could. There was a quick shuffle of paper from the vicinity of the fax machine, then darkness again. Maggie let the air trapped in her lungs escape.

She was safe, but still stuck until he left again or went to bed.

Carvelli's voice echoed from somewhere down the hall. "Where the hell have you been? I left a message a half hour ago." There was a pause, then, "Don't give me that bull. You screwed up royally . . . No, I'm not interested in your excuses. The last time I heard from you, you had eyes on her from outside her house. How the hell did she get past you?"

A chill coursed all the way down to her fingertips.

"She escaped on what? A motorcycle? You've got to be kidding me. Fix this, now! Do you understand?" Carvelli let out a roar of frustration punctuated by a string of choice words. It hadn't been paranoia; those men outside her house really had been after her.

She strained to look at her watch but couldn't make out the time. The phone rang, a call Maggie prayed would take Carvelli out of the house. She had what she needed. Now she had to escape.

"Yes, of course I will be there. I wouldn't dream of missing your annual banquet, Charles. You've been a very generous supporter . . . Yup, okay then, I'll see you at seven."

So, he had no intention of going back to the hearing on the Hill? Political fundraising obviously trumped national security. Maggie leaned against the wall. As soon as he left the house, she'd do another quick sweep for more documents and get out. The next step? To get Carvelli hauled away in handcuffs, preferably live on the evening news. He'd finally have the type of national attention he'd always craved. She smiled at the delicious image of the congressman in an orange jumpsuit.

Her vision was interrupted by the sound of him approaching. She slid a little further behind the door and waited. Was he heading upstairs? A moment later, she was sure of it—there were footsteps overhead and two minutes later, the sound of surging water. *He's taking a shower!* She wouldn't have to wait until he left, she could make a break for it now. She slipped out of the office, pausing for a moment to listen. Blessed silence greeted her. She stole back through the kitchen and was in the hall on her way toward the living room when the doorbell chimed.

Maggie turned to run back to the office, but the sudden thuds of footsteps and Carvelli's voice calling, "I'm coming, I'm coming," sent her diving into a coat closet halfway down the hall.

Coats swished against her, and underfoot, his shoes made her stance precarious.

Maggie heard the front door open, and Carvelli saying, "What the hell are you doing here?"

"You son of a bitch," the visitor replied. "Where is she?"

The letter. An hour had passed. Wendy had done her job and given the letter to Warner, who'd come to the rescue at the most inopportune time.

"Where's who?" Carvelli spat back.

"Maggie."

What would happen if she jumped out of the closet roaring? The shock might give Carvelli a heart attack.

"She's gone missing? Maybe you should check the hospitals. I wouldn't put it past her to harm herself."

There was no mistaking Warner's anger. "If you did something to her, so help me God, I'll kill you with my bare hands."

Carvelli answered, the pace of his words slow and methodical. "What makes you think I'd know where she is?"

Don't tell him, Warner. Don't!

"Because Maggie left a note with your girlfriend telling me to come find her here if she wasn't back at the office by now."

"That little whore."

She wasn't sure if Carvelli was talking about Wendy or her.

"Tell me what you've done with her, or I'll take this note straight to my buddies at the FBI. This is your final chance. Where is she?"

Even through the door, she could hear Carvelli's dramatic sigh. "No idea. But let me tell you that she's fireball under the sheets. I should've known, what with the red hair and all." There was a sound of movement. "You're not leaving already, are you Warner?"

Maggie balled her fists and choked on the scream in her throat. She heard the front door open.

"I know the whole story, Richard. Everything. With all the dirt I have on you, I could bury you ten times over. And I have Maggie's note."

"There's no proof she was ever here, Warner."

"Doesn't matter. I have evidence that you attempted to bribe a government official."

Carvelli snorted. "Now you're making things up out of whole cloth."

"What was it about me, Richard, that you've always been so obsessed with?"

"Me, obsessed with you?"

Maggie leaned closer to the door. *Where is this going?*

"Just another poor city kid that Yale admitted out of pity. Decent grades, but nothing particularly special about you. That has always gnawed at you, hasn't it, Richard?"

"The only reason you got into Yale was because your daddy went there. Unlike you, Warner, I had to earn my way."

"Unlike you, my father actually earned his money. Legally."

Silence.

Warner continued. "I know you're the one who set me up and sent the photos."

"I wondered how long it would take you to figure it out." He laughed. "You're nothing but an arrogant sonofabitch with dark secrets."

"I wouldn't be so fast to talk about dark secrets."

"I have no secrets, Warner. Besides, no one will believe any of your so-called evidence after *The Washington Post* publishes its story about your sexcapades with a Russian spy."

Russian spy? Fear jolted her nervous system. Her hands trembled, her legs weakened, her breathing became painful. *Warner? He'd been involved after all?* She shoved her hands inside her pockets to control the shaking. The panic was coming on strong. *It's okay, it's okay,* she repeated silently over and over again until she could breathe.

Almost immediately, her panic gave way to disbelief, then anger. Warner was sleeping with a Russian spy? Had he tried to divert attention from his own treachery by hatching the rumor about Steve selling intelligence to the Russians? *Would make sense.* She began to shake again, only this time it was with rage. She clenched her fists inside her pockets, where she felt the minicassette recorder. She squatted down to catch the light filtering through the space under the door, found the record button, pushed it, and placed the device on the floor.

After a moment of silence, Warner spoke, his voice so quiet that she had to strain to hear. "Richard, I know you sold intelligence to the Russians. I have multiple sources to prove it. And an officer of mine, Peter Belekov, also told me that you orchestrated Steve Ryder's murder."

What?

The ease with which Warner wove a story was impressive. He was obviously trying to throw the congressman off balance, make him believe it was all falling apart.

"Peter Belekov?" Carvelli snorted. "Spare me, please. That dirty SOB was betraying you right under your nose. He showed me around Georgia when I was there with a congressional delegation in January. Suggested we go to a casino. It wasn't hard to figure out he was up to his eyeballs in gambling debt." He laughed. "I took care of his money problems, so he owed me. Not a big deal."

"Killing a CIA officer isn't a big deal?"

Maggie's hand flew to her mouth. Peter had denied that Carvelli ordered the bombing. Was that just another one of his lies? She bit down on her hand to keep from screaming.

"I did not kill Steve Ryder."

Warner's voice took on a steely edge. "You sent the bomber. Zara."

It took every ounce of self-control Maggie had not the hurl herself out of the closet to throttle the congressman. Carvelli sent Zara?

"Who the hell is Zara?"

"Why'd you do it, Richard?"

"Warner, Warner, Warner. After all these years in Washington, you, of all people should understand what makes the world go 'round. Money. It's money."

"So, you betrayed your country for money?" Warner sounded incredulous.

"Give me a little credit. The money isn't for me. It's for my Senate campaign. This country needs leaders like me."

Warner laughed. "Leaders who kill?"

"I've never killed anyone in my life."

"You killed Steve Ryder."

"I most certainly did not." He snorted. "You have no evidence. Maybe Steve was simply in the wrong place at the wrong time. Such a tragedy."

"You started the rumor that Steve was selling intelligence to the Russians so that no one would look at you. With the traitor dead, there'd be no need for an investigation into any other suspects." Warner paused. "Case closed, right?"

"Something like that."

The rush in Maggie's ears was like rolling thunder. Peter had known that Steve was on Carvelli's trail, which would eventually and inevitably expose both of them. They had no choice but to eliminate the threat, Peter's suicidal protestations about trying to warn Steve at the last minute aside.

"I understand that Peter's no longer with us. Seems that everyone who knew about me is either dead or incapacitated."

Maggie pictured a twisted smile crossing Carvelli's mouth.

"But there's still me."

She closed her eyes and breathed out some tension. *And me.*

"Except for you, Warner. That's right."

Maggie heard a rattle and slam.

"Put the gun down, Richard."

"Shut up."

"You can't kill me here. I'll leave unpleasant little pieces of my brain and DNA all over this beautiful furniture."

Her eyes widened at Warner's brazen tone. He didn't sound the least bit frightened.

"Not here. I have friends who handle these sorts of things."

"Oh, I see. You're going to have your thugs kill me somewhere else. Clever. But what about Maggie? And Wendy? If I disappear, you're going to have to kill them, too." Warner yawned loudly. "I hate to sound trite Richard, but you're not going to get away with it."

She wanted to cheer.

Carvelli had the gun, but Warner was thinking clearly, casting doubts on Carvelli's plan, playing with his mind, delaying their departure. And even if Carvelli could force Warner into his car, she'd be on the phone with the police before they pulled away from the curb.

"Don't worry about those details, Warner. It'll all be taken care of." Carvelli paused, the brief silence broken by the dialing beeps of a telephone. "I need you over here now. A special assignment."

Who's he talking to?

Warner interrupted her racing thoughts. "Were you born without a soul?"

She held her breath, wondering where he was going with this one.

"Excuse me?"

"Because of you, terrorists have bombs that they plan to detonate right here in this country. Cities will be uninhabitable for years, lots of innocent people will die. I remember when you actually cared about those people."

"Your scaremongering is tiresome."

"It's the truth."

"For the record, Warner, I don't traffic in weapons. I simply sell documents to willing buyers. What they do with that information is none of my business."

"That information you've been selling? It has allowed the Russian mafia to remain undetected while selling weapons to al-Qaeda. Nuclear weapons went from Russia, to Chechen terrorists, and on to bin Laden's people."

Silence.

"If you'd stayed at today's briefing you would've learned that al-Qaeda plans to use dirty bombs to contaminate our cities. Then they'll unleash the nukes and wipe out millions."

If Warner was trying to alarm Carvelli, it seemed to work. The congressman's voice sounded markedly less steady. "I had nothing to do with that. Do you honestly think I would put my country in such peril?"

"It's called the law of unintended consequences, Richard. Look at all the money you've made from this deal. Great for you, but now, oops, there's a nuclear disaster looming." Warner's tone was patronizing.

"Shut the hell up. We're leaving. Let's go!"

She tensed. Seconds would count for Warner. Getting to the phone was her urgent first task. The men were moving in the living room. She bent down to pick up the minicassette recorder. A sudden clatter broke the silence of her dark hideaway.

CHAPTER FORTY-ONE

"What was that?" Carvelli snapped.

Maggie froze in a squat. The two cassette tapes in her jacket pocket had fallen to the floor. After a painfully long silence, Carvelli muttered something about mice as he passed by the closet.

Relief coursed through her. *Warner, go! This is your chance.* She heard movement in the living room. But then, Carvelli's voice boomed nearby.

"Get away from the door, Warner, or I'll shoot." He sounded panicked.

Maggie pictured Carvelli pointing the gun at Warner's chest.

Her knees couldn't take it anymore, so she stood, as quietly as she could in the cramped space.

"Is there a problem, Richard?"

"Shut up and stay put while I get the evidence from my file cabinet."

"Evidence?" Warner prompted.

"The photos. They'll prove you're a traitor."

Traitor?

"You're delusional, Richard."

Someone stomped past her hiding spot.

"Don't forget to destroy all of the documents you stole from the Intelligence Committee," Warner called. "Wouldn't want those falling into the FBI's hands."

From down the hall, Carvelli let loose a string of expletives. No doubt he'd discovered the open file cabinet and the missing documents. "Damn it all to hell!" the congressman raged, his voice growing closer.

It didn't occur to Maggie until the last split second that he was coming for the closet. As the door opened, she shrank back, trying to conceal herself behind his coats. It was too late.

CHAPTER FORTY-TWO

A fierce scowl clouded the congressman's face. He grabbed Maggie by both arms and flung her from the closet to the floor, sending the cassette recorder and the manila envelope skittering across the room.

"Maggie!" Warner jumped up from the sofa.

She scrambled to her feet but was knocked back by a kick to the ribs. She yelped and tried to slide away from Carvelli.

"You little bitch. Sticking your nose where it doesn't belong." He cornered her next to a massive, antique grandfather clock.

She caught her breath and took a chance, hoping her words would distract Carvelli long enough for Warner to get the upper hand. "You killed Steve. And you've put millions of Americans at risk. I hope you rot in hell."

A primal yell burst from Carvelli as he lunged for her. She dove out of his direct path but lost her footing on the polished floor. He righted himself and came at her with the Glock drawn. For the second time in as many days, Maggie's eyes met the barrel of a gun. She didn't blink. She just waited.

From the corner of her eye, she saw Warner hurdle a glass-top coffee table and propel himself toward Carvelli. The resulting crash sent a crystal vase shattering to the floor. Maggie watched, too stunned to react. Warner had the advantage in strength, but Carvelli had the gun. He tried to pin Carvelli down while reaching for the weapon but was thwarted by the smaller man's flailing limbs.

The cassette recorder—her proof of Carvelli's deeds—was lying on the floor behind the men. She dashed over and shoved it back into her jacket pocket. Next to it was the gold letter opener, the one she'd tucked behind her ear and forgotten. It must have fallen when Carvelli flung her across the room. She grabbed the cold, slim handle and without hesitation, slashed at Carvelli's arm.

"Maggie, get out," Warner ordered between heaving breaths.

A shot rang out, the bullet whizzing past her head.

She lunged again, this time striking blood near Carvelli's wrist. The gun fell to the floor. Warner grabbed it.

"Get the phone. Call 911." He pointed the gun at Carvelli's forehead. "Don't move." He pulled back the slide on top of the barrel.

Carvelli's eyes darted back and forth between the two of them. "You can both go to hell," he said, a sudden calm permeating his voice. The congressman sat up and wiped a trickle of blood from the puncture wound in his arm.

In a move faster than Maggie thought him capable of, Carvelli hurled himself at Warner's legs, which buckled under the assault. As they both tumbled to the floor, the congressman clawed at Warner's right hand, seeking possession of the gun. A sudden, explosive shot threw Maggie back against the wall. She reached for her left shoulder as she slid to the floor, and felt sticky warmth. "I'm bleeding," her voice quavered. She watched the blood ooze out of a perfect circle in Steve's jacket, then felt the room begin to swim around her.

"Maggie," Warner shouted, "No!" He scrambled to his feet and ran to her. "Go to a neighbor, get help. You can do it." He grabbed her by her good shoulder, helping her to stand on shaky legs. "It's not a bad wound. You can do this." His words came out fast in between labored grunts.

"Okay." She blinked hard, several times, to bring the room back into focus. The pain was like nothing she'd ever experienced. "Warner!" Behind him stood Carvelli, weapon raised.

"Nice shot. A little lower and to the right would've helped." He wore the smile of a man whose delusions of grandeur were fighting for their survival.

"The great Richard Carvelli," she said, "reduced to murder. I wish I could be around to see you try to spin your way out of this one."

"Maggie, don't," Warner warned as he slid in front of her, a shield to take the next bullet.

She shifted to the side next to him, leaning against the wall for strength. "No. If I'm going to die, I'm not going quietly."

"You will die tonight, Maggie. So just shut up. Running your mouth off won't change a thing." Carvelli traced a finger along the receding line of his hair then looked at his watch. "It looks like I'm going to have to do this myself."

"You poor thing. You'll have to do your own dirty work for once."

Warner cast her a glare more powerful than words. She averted her eyes.

Carvelli backed slowly toward the cordless phone, which sat on a table near the clock. He hit the redial button. "Where the hell are you?" He listened. "Just park the car and get in here, now, damn it."

"Reinforcements," she muttered to Warner.

"You okay?" He eyed her shoulder.

She winced. "You got a plan?"

"This is my party," Carvelli rejoined the conversation. "My plans are the only ones that matter."

Moments later, there was a knock at the door.

"Come in!" Carvelli barked. The door opened. "Ed, don't ever make me wait like that again."

"I," he began before catching sight of Carvelli's houseguests.

Maggie's mouth dropped open at the sight of the blond man. The one who'd been lurking behind her house just hours before.

"Evening, Ed," Warner said without emotion.

Ed? How did Warner know this man?

His gaze flitted between Warner and Maggie, shock registering in all his features.

"Special assignment tonight. There'll be a big bonus involved." Carvelli nodded toward his captives. "And if you want to have your fun first with either or both of them, feel free. Just make sure they're dead and dumped somewhere far away before morning."

"You're not really going to kill us, Ed, are you?"

Maggie looked at Warner then Ed, bewildered. Ed nodded his head ever so slightly before he addressed Carvelli. "I didn't know this kind of job was in my contract, but if you make it worth my while, I'll do it." He unzipped his jacket and pulled out a gleaming

Magnum revolver. "Before I leave with them, Richard, I want to make one thing clear. You never told me who the targets were."

"That's enough," Carvelli growled.

"I only told Zara where to be and when." He locked eyes with Maggie. "I didn't know anything else. I didn't know about the bomb. I am so sorry."

Maggie turned to Warner, confusion written all over her face. How did this man know Zara?

Warner raised a hand as if to calm her.

She was so busy staring at him that she missed Ed tackling the congressman.

Carvelli's head hit the floor with a heavy thud, which stilled him for a moment, but his grip remained tight around the Glock. He kicked at Ed, landing a foot square in the man's gut, then rose to a seated position and fired a shot that whizzed by Warner's neck and lodged in the front wall.

"The gun, Ed!" Warner shouted.

Still doubled over, Ed sucked in some air and tossed the gun, which landed behind Warner.

Maggie inched back along the wall hoping to reach the front door before she was shot again. Another gunshot echoed from mirrored walls to the ceiling and back down to the floor. Maggie shrieked as Ed dropped into a lifeless heap.

Carvelli stood, rising from the edge once more. "This will be headlines for weeks. Rogue CIA officer and his homosexual KGB lover attempt to kill congressman and his girlfriend. Congressman survives. Girlfriend dies." He sneered at Maggie.

Warner . . . homosexual?

Carvelli turned his attention back to Warner, staring him down with the Glock aimed dead center. Maggie spotted Ed's gun not three feet from where she stood. She fell away from the wall and slumped to the floor in a false faint, placing herself almost entirely in front of the love seat.

She heard Carvelli snicker. "That'll make it easier."

She cracked an eyelid. Carvelli appeared to be relishing the final moments. "I think my story will sell. After all, there will be no one else around to dispute it. Your prints are on my gun, Warner, proof that you tried to kill me. Or so it will seem in the court of public opinion."

Maggie took advantage of the congressman's redemption fantasy to inch her way toward Ed's gun. She reached out, her hand exposed past the end of the love seat. With adrenaline-fueled strength, she rose to her knees, supported her right arm the best she could with her injured left, and stood. Her eyes locked with Carvelli's. He swung suddenly towards her, in the process firing a shot that dropped Warner to the floor.

Maggie focused on her target and squeezed the trigger. Carvelli staggered, hands to his chest, his brow furrowed in disbelief. In slow motion, he fell to the floor, moaning, mumbling.

"Give me the gun, Maggie." Warner's eyes were wild and unfocused. Blood seeped through his pantleg.

She stepped closer and unloaded two more shots into the congressman from New York.

He responded with a gurgle.

The final shot silenced him.

CHAPTER FORTY-THREE

"Miss Jenkins?" Maggie heard a distant, unfamiliar voice. Then pressure on her arm. "I'm taking your vitals. It's okay."

Maggie pushed against the great weight bearing down on her eyelids. She blinked up at an older woman with a soft, round face. A nurse was taking her blood pressure.

"How did I get here?" Her voice was little more than a croak above the rhythmic *beep, beep, beep* of the ECG monitor.

"You were shot, dear."

She cleared her throat and spoke more strongly.

"I know. But—"

She raised her right hand, the one that had pulled the trigger. "Is he dead?"

"Mr. Thompson? No, he's very much alive."

She tried to sit up. "I meant Car—"

The nurse placed a firm hand on her good shoulder. "Shhhh . . . you've been through a lot. Lie back down."

"But, I . . ." The acrid smell of gunpowder suddenly overwhelmed her. And the gurgling sound of Carvelli's dying breath filled her ears. "I shot—"

The nurse glanced up from a clipboard attached to the foot of the bed. "The bullet lodged nicely just under your clavicle. A clean wound. You'll be okay."

Okay? She'd just killed a man. A United States congressman. "I need to talk to Warner Thompson."

The nurse glanced into the hallway. "I'm afraid that's not possible. Some government men are in the room with him. Looks serious." She lowered her voice. "I probably shouldn't say anything, but they asked when they could speak to you."

· ★ ★ ★ ·

The heart monitor began to beep more insistently. The nurse frowned and took note. "I didn't mean to agitate you. Settle down now and get some rest."

The men must be CIA. She needed to tell them everything she knew about the impending attack. And give them the evidence from Carvelli's house. "One more thing," she called to the departing nurse. "My jacket. Where's all my stuff?"

"In a bag under the bed. I'm surprised the police didn't take it last night. They must've forgotten in all the commotion." She tsked in disapproval. "Some congressman or senator somebody-or-other got shot dead."

"Could I have the bag, please?"

"'Course, sweetie. And I'll make sure they bring you some breakfast."

Maggie elevated the head of the bed and took the bag from the nurse. "Thanks." Once alone, she pulled out the leather jacket and searched the pockets. The cassette recorder was still there, as was the list of stolen files.

She glanced inside the small envelope. Photos of two men. Naked. *Warner?* She slipped the envelope under the blankets. Whatever that was about, it was his business and his business alone. Everything else would go straight to the CIA.

She snatched the remote and clicked on the TV. The lead news story featured a video of men in blue windbreakers with "FBI" emblazoned across the back of them.

Federal authorities in Washington, D.C., reportedly are on the hunt for a suspected MS-13 gang leader. An anonymous FBI source says a massive sweep against the notorious crime gang has begun in major urban areas around the country, including the nation's capital, New York City, and Los Angeles.

That's the lead? The FBI should be hunting down terrorists. And nuclear weapons. Not gang members. She squinted at the TV as two people in full hazmat gear passed behind the men in the FBI windbreakers.

A hazmat team for a gang investigation? Was this a cover story to keep people from speculating about why the FBI was crawling all over D.C.? They must be searching for the terrorists and the bombs. They had to be. It was the only explanation that made sense.

"Miss Jenkins?" Two men in dark suits entered the room. "Special Agents Jackson and Crowell. FBI," said the taller of the two.

"We'd like to ask you a few questions about the murder of Congressman Carvelli."

She snapped her head in their direction. "Murder?" Her voice cracked. "He wasn't murdered."

"Miss Jenkins—"

"Didn't Warner Thompson tell you what happened last night?"

"Why don't you tell us your version, Miss Jenkins?"

"My version?" Maggie shrank back against the bed. "I went to his house to collect evidence of his involvement with—"

"We'll get to that," said the taller agent. "Right now, we need to know who shot the congressman."

"I don't understand. What did Warner Thompson say?"

"Miss Jenkins, if you don't cooperate, we will detain you here in the hospital if necessary."

"Detain me?" Maggie's mouth went dry. "For what?"

The shorter man exchanged a look with his partner.

"Look, Warner was with me at the brownstone. He can confirm that Carvelli's the one who planned . . ." The news anchor's urgent tone grabbed her attention.

In other breaking news, New York Congressman Richard Carvelli, widely considered a rising political star, is dead at the age of forty-nine.

His official photo shared the screen with a live feed from outside his house, which was roped off with yellow crime scene tape.

Police in Washington, D.C. have confirmed that Carvelli and an unidentified man were shot to death inside his Capitol Hill brownstone last night. A high-ranking CIA official and a Hill staff member are under investigation for their alleged involvement in the shooting.

Under investigation? Her shoulder throbbed. It became difficult to swallow.

The live feed switched to the photo Maggie kept on her office desk. The one of Steve and her sitting on an oceanfront jetty. The radiant face that filled the screen was nothing more than a ghostly apparition of her former carefree, innocent self. As for Steve, the world couldn't see his smile, or his eyes, or his spirit on the television. They'd cropped him from view. All that remained was the image of his arm draped across her shoulder.

ACKNOWLEDGMENTS

Writing *The Wayward Spy* has been a long journey, one I might have abandoned were it not for the steady support of many people along the way. Words are not sufficient to express my gratitude, but I will try.

To the team at CamCat Books, I am thrilled to be counted among your authors. Thank you to CamCat's founder and CEO, Sue Arroyo, for believing that readers will want to "live in" this book. And to Helga Schier, editorial director extraordinaire, your insight and direction have elevated this story beyond my greatest expectations. And to the entire production and marketing team who have worked tirelessly to get this book ready for its readers.

To my wonderful agent, Steve Hutson, at WordWise Media Services, I am grateful for your persistence in finding a home for this novel. And many thanks to Ruth Hutson for your keen eye and guidance along the way.

For my husband, Dan—all my love and gratitude for supporting my writing dreams, and especially for keeping the boys occupied when I needed to escape into my fictional world. And speaking of the boys—Andrew, Shawn and Bryan, thank you for giving me the space (and quiet) to write. Sometimes, your simple question, "How's the book?" was all it took to keep me going. As you chase your own dreams, remember the words of St. John Paul II: "Never, ever give up on hope, never doubt, never tire, and never become discouraged. Be not afraid."

Many thanks to my beta readers, especially Brian Drake, a prolific thriller author himself and an honest critic and cheerleader. I also am indebted to Dr. Mark Lowenthal for hiring me to work for the House Permanent Select Committee on Intelligence. It was there, tucked away in the attic of the U.S. Capitol Building, that I first conceived of Maggie and the threads of this plot.

And finally, for Sara. You taught me more than you'll ever know about kindness, optimism, courage and love. I wish you were still here.

ABOUT THE AUTHOR

 Susan Ouellette was born and raised in the suburbs of Boston, where she studied international relations and Russian language and culture at both Harvard University and Boston University. As the Soviet Union teetered on the edge of collapse, she worked as an intelligence analyst at the CIA, where she earned a commendation for her work done during the failed 1991 Soviet coup. Subsequently, Susan worked on Capitol Hill as a professional staff member for the House Permanent Select Committee on Intelligence (HPSCI). She participated in several overseas staff and congressional delegations focused on intelligence cooperation with allies and classified operations against adversaries. She also played an integral role in a study about the future of the post-Cold War intelligence community.

Susan lives on a farm outside of Washington, D.C., with her husband, three boys, cats, chickens, turkeys, and too many honeybees to count. She loves to read, root for Boston sports teams, and spend time staring out at the ocean on the North Carolina coast.

AUTHOR'S NOTE

Popular culture depicts the CIA as an independent agency that operates in the shadows and, sometimes, outside of the law. While the Agency has had its share of scandals, it isn't the rogue agency portrayed in the movies. Not only does the U.S. Congress approve the CIA's budget, several congressional committees have oversight of the Agency's activities. In Maggie's capacity as a staff member for the House Permanent Select Committee on Intelligence (HPSCI), she analyzed intelligence budgets and investigated operational failures and other items of interest to congressmen on the committee. Everything Maggie did as a HPSCI staffer, including her missteps, is fictionalized, but based in reality. As a HPSCI staffer myself, I walked the same storied halls, unlocked the same vaults and safes, and had access to the same highly-classified information as Maggie. In fact, it was there, tucked away in the hidden attic of the Capitol Building, that I first conceived of a courageous female character thrust into a dangerous situation borne of tragedy. Next came the threads of a plot, and from that blossomed *The Wayward Spy*.

FOR FURTHER DISCUSSION

1. What is Maggie's greatest character flaw? Her greatest strength?
2. What character or moment prompted the strongest emotional reaction in you? Why?
3. If you had to trade places with one character, who would it be? Why?
4. Which character would you want to meet in real life? Why?
5. What part of the story left you on the edge of your seat? Why?
6. Which plot twist surprised you most? Why?
7. Did you guess the ending? If so, at what point?
8. If you could write a different ending, what would it be?
9. Did *The Wayward Spy* make you think differently about the political conflicts that provide the historical background to the novel? How?
10. What do you think will happen next to Maggie? Warner? Other characters?
11. If *The Wayward Spy* were made into a movie, who would play each of the lead characters?
12. If you could ask the author anything, what would it be?

AUTHOR Q&A

Q: *How did you get the idea for this book?*

A: When I worked for the House Intelligence Committee on Capitol Hill, the mundane part of my job involved reviewing portions of the intelligence community's budget. It was then, when I was tucked away in my office in the Capitol Building's attic, buried in spreadsheets, that my mind would wander. I began to imagine a young, female Intelligence Committee staffer who uncovered a scandal that sent her on a perilous quest. Eventually, that seed of an idea blossomed into a character who persevered through personal tragedy, battling threats on multiple fronts in order to uncover the truth.

Q: *You have two very strong female characters in this book. What made you write them? And what do you perceive as their strengths and weaknesses?*

A: *The Wayward Spy* originally featured only one strong female character—Maggie Jenkins, my protagonist. With a career path and a personality much like mine, she was a natural choice for me to write. I knew what she'd think, say and do in every circumstance—including tragedy—I threw at her. Maggie is persistent, loyal, and highly analytical. Her instincts almost never fail her because they are based not on emotion but on her innate ability to analyze situations from every angle. Maggie's greatest weaknesses are fear (of failing, of being wrong, of angering others) and a lack of confidence in herself. I love that her weaknesses diminish and her strengths grow as the story progresses.

When I first began writing *The Wayward Spy* many years ago, the antagonist was Osama bin Laden, someone few had heard of outside of national security circles. But after the attacks of September 11th, I decided he should have no role in the story. I started playing around with the idea of a female antagonist, a character Maggie could relate to despite vast cultural and geopolitical differences. Zara Barayeva was just that woman. A young Chechen who also had endured great tragedy, Zara is on her own quest for justice. Only for her, justice doesn't necessarily mean finding the truth. It means vengeance. Like Maggie, Zara is persistent, intelligent, and loyal. Zara's greatest weakness is her hubris. Convinced of the justness of her cause, she harbors no self-doubt. Maggie is both appalled by and sympathetic toward Zara. I'm convinced that under different circumstances, they'd be friends.

Q: *What was the most difficult thing about writing this story? And what was your favorite aspect of writing it?*

A: My favorite aspect of writing *The Wayward Spy* is also what made it so difficult to write—weaving together the various plot threads into a cohesive story. I love puzzles of all sorts, of making sense out of a jumble of unknowns. It took several rewrites to ensure that the various threads fit together seamlessly. I couldn't have done it without some great readers along the way, including, of course, my fabulous editor. It was incredibly satisfying to see all the puzzle pieces come together at the end of the process.

Q: *How did you research the locations for this book?*

A: I did a lot of research for *The Wayward Spy*, particularly for locations in the Republic of Georgia, where much of the story takes place. I already knew a fair amount about Georgia from my days as an intelligence analyst, but since I've never visited the country, I needed to supplement what I knew with online images, articles, and maps. The Washington, D.C. scenes were easy to write since I live in the area and have walked the halls of the CIA and Capitol Hill.

Q: *What are some common misconceptions about CIA work? Did you find yourself seeking to address any of those in* **The Wayward Spy?**

A: Common misconceptions about the CIA tend to focus on negative characterizations. To some, the Agency is an overly powerful, world-manipulating, evil organization. To others, it's an incompetent, bloated bureaucracy that can't predict, much less stop, devastating events. Neither is entirely true. The CIA has done some incredibly bold things throughout its history that have ensured our national security. It also has been accused of failing to predict major world events and of engaging in illegal acts. I don't address misunderstandings about the CIA directly in *The Wayward Spy*. Rather, I show that CIA is comprised of every kind of human, including the heroic, the cowardly, the conniving, and the honest. It is a complicated organization filled with complicated people.

The Wayward Spy addresses a lesser-known dynamic in the intelligence community—the place where politics and intelligence collide. That's where Maggie comes in. She is one of the individuals tasked with keeping Congress informed of CIA activities. In this role, she sees both politicians and the CIA use intelligence to advance their own agendas. Somewhere in that murky mix lies the truth. It's up to Maggie to find it.

If you've enjoyed Susan Ouellette's
The Wayward Spy,
you'll enjoy Michael Bradley's
Dead Air.

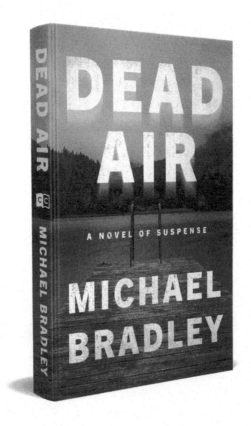

CHAPTER ONE

S he'd been found out. There was no other explanation.

On any other night, Kaitlyn Ashe would relish the breathtaking view of the Philadelphia cityscape. The twinkle of white streetlights, red, yellow, and green traffic lights, and the white and red hues from car lights on the streets below looked like a swirling star field, constantly changing as if at the whim of a fickle god. From the twentieth-floor broadcast studio, she could look down upon Center City, could see as far east as the Walt Whitman Bridge and across the Delaware River to the distant lights of Camden, New Jersey.

Yes, every other night, this view was mesmerizing. But not tonight. Tonight, Kaitlyn Ashe trembled at the thought that someone out there knew her, knew her secret, and was making damn sure she didn't forget it.

The past had come a step closer each time another letter arrived. Her fingers tightened their grasp on the latest, a crumpled paper creased with crisscrossed lines and folds. It was a cliché. The mysterious correspondences consisted of letters and phrases torn from newspapers and magazines, crudely pasted onto plain paper. Always the same message, always the same signature.

Behind her, music played softly. She turned away from the window and moved around the L-shaped counter in the middle of the room to slide onto the tall stool behind the control console. Kaitlyn leaned forward, glancing at the needles on the VU meters that jumped and pulsed to the music's beat. She touched one of the ten slider controls and adjusted the volume to remove some mild distortion.

Kaitlyn watched the onscreen clock count down to the end of the current song. Fifteen seconds to go. She slid the headphones over her ears and drew the broadcast microphone to her mouth. She tapped the green button on the console and pushed the leftmost slider upward.

Kaitlyn leaned into the microphone. "Taking things back to 2005 with Lifehouse on WPLX. That was 'You and Me,' going out to Jamie from Kristin, Tiffany from Steve, and to Tommy—Jackie still loves you." She glanced again at the clock in the upper corner of the computer screen. "It's ten past ten. I'm Kaitlyn Ashe with Love Songs at Ten. 888-555-WPLX is the number to get your dedication in tonight. I've got Adele lined up, as well as John Legend on the way next."

Her fingers darted over the control console, tapping buttons and moving sliders. Kaitlyn took the headphones off. As a commercial for Ambrosia—her favorite seafood restaurant in downtown Philadelphia—played, she stared at the crinkled letter that rested beside the console. She read it once again beneath the dim studio lights. Her eyes focused on the name at the bottom.

The Shallows. She shivered. Who knew? And how much did they know?

Kaitlyn slipped a green Bic lighter from her pocket, lit the edge of the letter, and pinched the corner as the flames swept up the paper. She'd stolen the lighter from Kevin O'Neill's desk. She knew the midday DJ would never miss it. He had half a dozen more where that one came from.

She dropped the paper into the empty wastebasket, and watched the fire dwindle into nothingness, leaving behind blackened flakes. A faint trace of smoke hung in the air, then dissipated quickly. She wrung her hands and sighed. There'd be another waiting in her station mailbox tomorrow, just like the four others that she'd received, one each day this week. She was certain of it.

The flash of green lights caught her eye, and she looked down at the studio telephone. All four lines were lit up. She hesitated for a moment, then tapped the first line. "WPLX, do you have a dedication?"

"Yeah, I'd like to dedicate my weekend to kissing your body from head to toe." The smoky voice echoed through the darkened studio.

Kaitlyn laughed, and felt her face become warm with embarrassment. "Brad!"

"How goes it, babe? Having a good night?"

She forced a smile, trying to sound upbeat, just as she'd learned in her voice-over classes. "It's not too bad."

"What's wrong?"

She cursed under her breath. She never could hide things from Brad. "I got another letter today."

The line was silent for a moment. "Same message?"

She glanced at the computer, then back at the phone. "Yeah. Exactly the same."

"You should call the police."

It was the same suggestion he had made a month ago, when the letters started arriving on a weekly basis. With this week's sudden volley of letters, he had taken to repeating his advice nightly. Kaitlyn had shrugged it off as just some crank. "You get those in this business," she'd told him.

"Still no idea who sends these letters? Or what they are about?"

She hesitated for a second before replying. "No idea," she lied.

"You need to tell someone. If not the police, at least tell Scott."

Kaitlyn frowned at his remark. The last thing she wanted to do was tell her program director Scott Mackay about the letters. His overly protective nature would mean police involvement for certain. "I can't tell Scott. He'd place an armed guard on the studio door."

Brad laughed. "Would that be so bad?"

"There's no point. It's probably some infatuated teenager." She knew how ridiculous the words sounded even as they escaped her lips. No teenage listener would know about *The Shallows*.

"Do me a favor—watch yourself tonight when you go home." The concern in his voice was evident. If she asked, he'd be there in a moment to escort her home. But she couldn't do that to him. Not without revealing something she'd worked so hard to bury in her own past.

Kaitlyn said, "I will. Promise."

"How's the rest of the night going?"

"It's been crazy. Lots of lovers out there tonight. I can't even get them all in. Just not enough time."

"I wouldn't expect any less from the most listened-to night show in Philly."

With a glance at the computer screen, Kaitlyn noted where she was in the commercial break, and then turned back toward the phone. "What are you up to, sweetie?"

"Working my way through a couple briefs. I've got to have these ready for review by tomorrow."

"Sounds like a late night."

He sighed. "Probably."

Kaitlyn sensed fatigue and frustration in his voice. She knew nothing about corporate law other than what Brad had told her. The reams of paperwork and bewildering legalese seemed boring and unappealing. She knew he had a lot on his plate and hated to see him work as hard as he did. A mischievous smile crossed her lips. "If you want, I could slip over later tonight, and help you with your briefs."

Brad's chuckle echoed through the studio. "That'd be nice, really nice."

She leaned closer to the speaker phone and spoke almost in a whisper. "You know you want to." She added a sensual emphasis to each word. "It'll make you feel good."

"That's not fair." He paused, then asked, "Can I take a raincheck? I need to get these done."

Kaitlyn glanced again at the computer and reached for her headphones. "Hang on."

Her fingers clicked on the microphone, and, out of the commercial break, she gave a quick weather forecast before starting the next song. Then she turned off the microphone and turned back to the phone. "Are we still on for lunch tomorrow?"

"Absolutely. Just you and me in a dark corner at Toscana's."

Looking down at the phone, she noticed that the other three lines were still flashing. "I've got to go, sweetie. Love you."

"Love you too. Talk to you later."

When he'd hung up, Kaitlyn turned to face the window and gazed out across the cityscape. The lights below seemed brighter somehow, a little more stunning than before. She sighed with deep satisfaction. There was something about Brad's voice that always relaxed her and quelled her fears. He was trusting, gentle, and loving. She was lucky to have him. For four weeks, he had accepted her word that she knew nothing about *The Shallows*, or why anyone would send her these letters. Brad may have suspected that she was lying, but he never pushed her. It would all come out eventually. She couldn't go on being dishonest indefinitely. She just needed time. Time to figure out how to explain that she wasn't who she pretended to be.

Kaitlyn turned back to the computer to check the playlist. Her gaze froze, and she frowned. REO Speedwagon was coming up on the list. Her shoulders gave a momentary shudder.

She'd loved the band for as long as she could remember. While her high school friends were listening to likes of Justin Timberlake and Christina Aguilera, Kaitlyn had dug back a couple decades and discovered REO Speedwagon. She loved their songs, but this particular one held a spell over her. Its impact had diminished over the years. She'd almost reached the point of being able to play it as opposed to deleting it from the playlist whenever it showed up. Until recently, it only invoked the briefest of memories. She would twinge at the brief reminder and use the song's deletion as a way to purge herself of her past.

That, however, was then. The arrival of the letters had changed everything. Now, the sheer appearance of the song frightened Kaitlyn, reminded her that her past was catching up. Some secrets couldn't stay hidden forever. She'd hoped the anniversary would pass unnoticed again this year. But with only three weeks to go until that date, someone was making sure that she remembered every detail.

She jabbed the delete key and a sense of relief washed over her as the song vanished from the screen. Breathing slow and deep, she allowed her uneasiness to subside. Then, she leaned toward the phone and clicked the next blinking line. "WPLX, do you have a dedication?"

When the elevator doors opened, Kaitlyn stepped out into the building's attached parking garage. An hour's worth of commercial voice-over work had been waiting for her when she went off the air at midnight. It took longer than usual for her to plow through it. She was too distracted, making too many mistakes, leading to far more retakes than was her norm. On her way out, she'd stopped by the studio to tell Justin Kace, the overnight personality, that she was leaving. They talked for another hour. Between station IDs and weather forecasts, Justin showed her pictures of his latest girlfriend—his third this year—and explained how they met. Kaitlyn suggested a couple places he could take her. Longwood Gardens. The Art Museum. Justin shrugged them off, saying the girl "was more into the unusual and bizarre."

Kaitlyn rolled her eyes and laughed. "Then try the Mütter Museum. That should be bizarre enough for her." Then she said her farewells and left, imagining Justin and his new girl finding romance amidst anatomically correct wax figures, glass cases full of pathology specimens, and ancient medical equipment fit for a steampunk horror movie.

Pausing by the elevator doors for a moment, she scanned the empty parking garage, just as she'd done every other night for the past four weeks. The night air was crisp on her face and she caught the faint whiff of the city. It was a mix of odors almost unique to

Philadelphia. Bitter and often pungent. She shivered in the chilled air and an unwanted memory flashed through her mind. Back then, on that fateful night, the air had been brisk as well.

She didn't see anyone around but couldn't shake the sense that she was being watched. For a while, she had chalked it up to paranoia induced by the letters, but their increased recurrence left her more anxious every day. Her fingers gripped a little more tightly on the pepper spray canister on her keychain.

Kaitlyn gave the parking garage one more inspection. No one was in sight and no sound came other than the hum of a nearby flickering fluorescent light. She strode toward her motorcycle. Her boot heels echoed throughout the empty garage. The chrome of the handlebars and exhaust pipes on the Harley-Davidson shone in the overhead lights. She smiled as her eyes glanced over the motorcycle's candy apple red fuel tank and fenders.

She'd always wanted a Harley, even as a child. But a bike was a luxury that had eluded her until last year. When she topped the Arbitron ratings as the highest-rated nighttime on-air personality in Philadelphia, Kaitlyn had celebrated by fulfilling her childhood dream.

The promise of more spring-like temperatures for April was the catalyst she'd been waiting for to bring the motorcycle out of winter storage. Kaitlyn had changed the oil and washed and waxed it the previous weekend. Three days into the new week, she was re-experiencing the joy of riding she had longed for throughout the winter.

She straddled the black leather seat and zipped up her tan leather jacket. As the motorcycle rumbled to life, Kaitlyn raced the throttle a few times just to hear the engine's roar echo through the deserted parking garage.

She got a rush every time from the engine vibrations racing from the handlebars up through her arms. She smiled, and for a moment, forgot about the letters. Then, she slid a black helmet over her head and drew the visor down over her eyes. Her foot pulled the kickstand up, and, revving the engine one more time, Kaitlyn sped down the ramp of the garage and onto the dark Philadelphia streets.